6/25/21

Ghost of a Chance,
or Old Tom and Harry

Carol —
thank you for my new
LIBRARY!
warm regards,

Charles Brandt

GHOST
OF A
CHANCE

or, Old Tom and Harry

Charles Francis
Gould

JAMES A. ROCK & COMPANY, PUBLISHERS
FLORENCE • SOUTH CAROLINA

Ghost of a Chance, or Old Tom and Harry by Charles Francis Gould

JAMES A. ROCK & COMPANY, PUBLISHERS

Cover illustration by Craig Howarth
http://home.wol.za/~20291447/

Address comments and inquiries to:

James A. Rock & Company, Publishers
900 South Irby Street, #508
Florence, South Carolina 29501

E-mail:
jrock@rockpublishing.com   lrock@rockpublishing.com
Internet URL: www.rockpublishing.com

Trade Hardcover ISBN: 978-1-59663-798-6

Library of Congress Control Number: 2007928323

Printed in the United States of America

First Edition: 2009

To Jeanne

ACKNOWLEDGMENTS

The author wishes to give special thanks to John Cutts, Don Gronquist and Hildegard Weiss and to acknowledge the following list of sources.

"From scenes like these …" from "The Cotter's Saturday Night" by Robert Burns.

"Come Under My Plaidie," by Robert Burns. Charles Mackay, ed. *The Songs of Scotland*. London: Boosey & Co., 1877.

"Oh! sure the world is all run mad …" from "Julien's Grand Polka" by Louis Antoine Jullien. *Modern Street Ballads*. John Ashton, ed. London: Chatto & Windus, 1888.

"Ah! Sweet Mystery of Life," Rida Johnson Young and Victor Herbert. NY: M. Witmark & Sons, 1910.

"Let warlocks grim …" from "Address to the Deil" by Robert Burns.

"It's good lofting balls …" with apologies to Robert Burns' "Here's a Health to Them that's Awa'."

"So long sweet golfer of the year …" with apologies to Robert Burns' "Address to the Shade of Thomson."

Perhaps it may turn out a sang,
Perhaps turn out a sermon.
—Robert Burns

Some books are lies frae end to end.
—Robert Burns

Is my friend in the bunker or
Is the bastard on the green?
—Anon.

CHAPTER 1

Permit me an introduction: my name is Ernest Spectre, and I'm the oldest member here in St. Andrews. There is little else you need know of me other than I relish a good story, find delight in an estimable claret with mutton, and always savor an exquisite brandy with my late night cigar. I also maintain a modest golf handicap and, though I abominate neeps and haggis, I unhesitatingly elected to spend eternity, for the most part, here in St. Andrews where I am free to enjoy the local amenities with like-minded souls.

Whilst idling on the terrace of Club Elysium overlooking the 1st and 18th fairways of the Old Course, St. Andrews, I reflected between thoughtful sips of a seltzer and lemon on the fact that of all the remarkable golf stories that I have narrated to entertain and instruct beseeching club members over the past century, none has affected my auditors with greater sympathy and gratification than the illuminating adventures of Harrison Golub.

Undoubtedly the name Harrison Golub and his singular links exploits once so prominently headlined in the international press are known to you; yet, there are many facts concerning this man's history to which the general public has not been privy, nor, for that matter, has the golfing fraternity for whom Harrison Golub has ever been a puzzlement.

Any lingering questions you may have concerning Golub following his abrupt disappearance from public scrutiny, I'm sure I can lay to rest. But first you must disregard all checkout stand tabloids that still persist in unearthing "new" sensational Golub fictions to titillate their scandal-loving subscribers. Sadly, there are no effective means of stifling the damage wrought by smut-slut-and-gut journalism. On this point let me assure you, Harrison Golub has been and continues to be a gentleman entirely inno-cent of the unseemly charges and innuendoes depicted in those shameless rags.

The crucial facts and affairs surrounding this extraordinary amateur golfer are known to but a few of his confidants. My honor compels me to admit that though I am not one of Harrison Golub's inner circle of friends, I have nonetheless followed with keen in-terest his career from the very moment he first entered the con-fines of the Royal Burgh of St. Andrews, Fife, Scotland until three months later when his meteoric ride foozled and crashed. It will give me immense pleasure to enlighten you with an unembellished narrative of our hero's rise from workaday obscurity to fairway greatness.

We all dread rhetoricians who wander aimlessly from the stick-ing place. I assure you I am not of that species, one who absently relapses into ellipses and then scrambles about circumlocutions; nor am I in the habit of convoluting syntax; nor have I developed the guile of asides whispered out of one corner, then out of the other corner of my mouth. And heaven forbid that I should weary you with cataloging piddling matters or of particularizing each leaf on my family tree.

The subject of trees does however bring to mind a curious episode concerning my lamented friend Wycliffe Windhover, who, fancying himself a raconteur, began to bore his guests, as we sat to dine, with a tedious accounting of his recent bit of fox hunting. An unsavory topic under any circumstance. For some unaccount-able cranial short circuit, Windy, about to cry the "View Halloa," instead interjected rubbish about his childhood remembrance of a particular Christmas tree. "Oh, Cwithmath twee, Oh,

Cwithmath twee," he lisped with an air of lost innocence. His mind had gotten jumbled into such a state of untidiness that he felt urged to subject us to finite descriptions of each and every recollected bauble dangling from old tannenbaum's stout limbs. It was, as I recall, a rather largish tree. Mind you, it was midsummer! Windy hadn't slipped back onto the fox hunting track until sometime after the gooseberry fool had been served. But I have long forgiven the pointless ramblings of Wycliffe Windhover because of the memorable claret and Stilton he graciously served to us, aged to perfection and as companionable as a boy and his dog, a girl and her looking glass, stout and oysters.

As I was saying, Mr. Golub's story is a crackerjack tale engaging the vital elements that interest intelligent humankind: intrigue, avarice, vengeance, lust, and golf. My own mounting excitement begs me to get on with it, so without further preamble I shall begin.

A few years past, on a balmy spring afternoon in which an uttered cautionary "Fore" would safely carry 300 yards, Hamish Macpherson, a middle-aged Scots travel agent, was chauffeuring a passenger van from Carnoustie to St. Andrews. Macpherson, an obliging chap, was speeding along, not because he was late for tea or a tee time, but because he was eager to discharge his disagreeable cargo of vacationing golfers from America. The roster contained professional golfer Brewster "Brew" Payne, his agent and friend, Malcolm "Mal" Baldwin, and their companions Phil, Tony, and Gunther, all of whom basked in an aura of self-importance. They were tall, trim and good-looking, and they exhibited upperclass breeding, including all of its prejudices. They were in their early thirties and on the whole cast from the same imperfect mold. All in all they stood out as grievous insults to goodness and compassion, these five rude, snobbish, quibbling asses from southwestern Connecticut. Thomas Hobbes must surely have had a similar baleful pack irritating his thought processes which caused him to declare that life is indeed "nasty" and "brutish." Our 17th century philosopher also mentioned that life is "short," which no longer applies owing to the longevity of present day Homo sapiens including myself who fell a smidgen shy of the century mark.

Still, "short" does apply in another sense to the sixth passenger in the van rushing along quaint byways of rural Scotland. Harrison "Harry" Golub is unquestionably short—squat, to be precise, rather like a roma tomato. By any stretch of the imagination, Harry was not an heroic figure. And yet our tale's protagonist is that very roma tomato.

Harry brought to mind St. Sebastian as he sat in the front passenger seat benignly disregarding a hail of barbs propelled from the sneering lips of the aforementioned querulous quintet. Their unwarranted disdain for Harry was not due entirely to his stunted stature, nor to his ethnic background, his New York accent, his zest for life, nor for his unabashed enthusiasm for all things Scottish; no, it was primarily due to his inability to strike a golf ball squarely! Otherwise they may have deigned to overlook one or two of Harry's "regrettable peculiarities," but they could never excuse his woeful ineptitude at playing the royal and ancient game.

Alas, truth to tell, poor Harry was the furthest removed from an athlete and was therefore doomed to remain a hacker of the extremist sort. No matter how earnestly he endeavored to improve, no matter how many golf books he studiously read, no matter how much instruction he painfully underwent, he would never break a hundred—for nine holes. The sad reality—as his fellow travelers discovered to their mortification—was that it almost always took Harry a minimum of ten strokes to reach a par four green, and then four or more putts to hole out. The snobs on the other hand were each capable of breaking par, except when partnered with Harry, for then they were completely put off their game by vexation.

Oh, how Harry loved golf. The game held him more firmly than he held his niblick. And though his ball was rarely in the right spot, his heart was. He was at all times a good sport and exhibited numerous worthy qualities that the quibbling five disregarded out of hand.

Harry's continuing presence filled his traveling companions with such an overpowering resentment that it blinded them to the scenic splendor through which they motored. The rain had passed, continuing its northerly path toward Aberdeen, leaving behind a glorious, glossy mid-day in spring—azure sky, puffy white clouds, lush verdure everywhere, and lurking worm casts on the greens. In the approaching distance the gleaming spires and rooftops of ancient St. Andrews lifted themselves above irregularly positioned medieval rock walls and hedgerows. The road glistened in the sun, leading them on into the town that rightfully claims possession of the most famous golf course in the universe. The lark's on the wing, the snail's on the thorn.

"Great country, this Scotland," said Harry, taking in the retreating scenery. He was highly animated and heartily informal. "Beautiful, extraordinary, clean … oh, look, guys, there's a bunch of sheep!"

"It's not a bunch, you dodo, it's a flock," Phil bleated.

The Brew crew elbowed one another and snickered at Harry.

Accustomed now to these frequent jibes, Harry ignored this latest with equanimity. He was determined to make the most of his holiday from start to finish. He would allow no one or no thing to spoil it.

"That was the longest drive you ever saw," boasted Brew to Phil, reliving their morning round.

"Hell, I can launch one farther with a two iron," responded Phil with bravado.

"In your dreams," said Brew.

"I don't even carry a two," said Harry attempting to join in on the conversation.

"Harry," scoffed Tony, "you should toss all your clubs in the North Sea for all the good you get out of them."

"Right on," agreed Phil. "Your game—if you can call it that—sucks big time. Give it up."

"Just started playing," said Harry. "Gimme a break. Bound to get better."

"Not in a hundred years," said Brew with an undisguised sneer.

Unshakable optimism, one faculty Harry had to a rare degree, caused him to blurt, "Just you guys wait and see. I'll be as good as you."

"Can you believe this guy?" asked Phil.

"Never happen," said Gunther.

"No way," said Tony.

"Pipe dream," said Mal.

Brew rolled his eyes.

The driver, Macpherson, smiled and nodded his endorsement of Harry's prognostication.

"In a minute we'll be entering the mecca of golf—imagine," Harry beamed. "St. Andrews. Think of it, guys ... the Old Course ... the Royal and Ancient Clubhouse ... the home town of Tom and Tommy Morris. Man, it's like entering heaven."

"More like hell," murmured Phil to Gunther, "with that idiot along."

About eight blocks from the golf course the van pulled up in front of the Bishop Seaton Hotel. Macpherson hopped out and quickly began unloading luggage and golf bags. The passengers emerged and stretched. Harry looked around in a state of rapture. His attention was soon drawn to a shop window displaying traditional Scottish men's-wear—tams, sweaters, tweeds, kilts, and a wide assortment of clan neckties. He entered the shop. The others entered the hotel leaving the baggage in the care of Macpherson. Brew reminded everyone to meet at the Cleek and Thistle at one o'clock.

CHAPTER 2

The venerable Cleek and Thistle pub occupied the ground floor of an early Victorian three-story limestone building facing the Old Course and commanded an unobstructed view of the 18th and 1st fairways. Almost directly in front of the pub the Swilcan Burn bridge arched out of the 18th fairway. Down to the right, just beyond the finishing hole's Valley of Sin, stood the Royal and Ancient Clubhouse with its suggestion of grandeur and inhospitality.

Before and after a round of golf the Cleek and Thistle was the perfect gathering spot for the golfing fraternity. To my mind, nothing more commends itself to a man's ease of body and spirit than muted amber light, polished brass, glossy mahogany, and honey-hued liquid refreshment shared with kindred souls. And in no place in the United Kingdom was this more evident than inside this time-honored pub with its decor of antique golf prints and posters, paintings and photographs of Open champions, and its unique collection of ancient hickory-shafted golf clubs fastened to the walls. Truly a gentlemen's chamber where handicaps and wagers were established; and later where all debts were surrendered and received under the rule of sportsmanship. Sadly, that venerated refuge from the petty annoyances of the workaday world was being defiled by the rendezvousing presence of the Brew crew.

Mal, Phil, Tony, and Gunther were sharing a pitcher of beer in a window snug and were attempting to beguile each other with fables of their "admirable" qualities which they expressed in the sincerest, most flattering tones, when in truth their prattlings proved nothing less than exercises in deception, distortion, song-and-dance, cock-and-bull, and taradiddle.

Brew, meanwhile, leaning on the far end of the bar conversed with barmaid Fiona Huntly. At the opposite end of the bar sat Cameron Flett smoking a pipe and nursing a teacup half-full of whiskey. The tweedy, sixtyish Flett was eavesdropping.

Fiona cast a cold eye on Brew as she wiped the bar with a towel and worked her way toward him. She was a shapely highland lass in her earliest thirties with hair the color of butterscotch and a face, though pretty, fixed in a scowl.

"Why did you not telephone," scolded Fiona, "or write to me, or E-mail? Is Connecticut such a wilderness that it is impossible to connect with the world outside?"

Brew reached for her mopping hand. She pulled away.

"It's been over six months, Brewster Payne, and now you would start where you left off. You must take me for a fool."

"I'll explain it all to you ... tonight," he said, trying to make light of her displeasure.

"I do not think so," was her icy reply.

Hamish Macpherson, mildly disturbed, entered the pub and located the majority of his charges.

"You don't look happy, Macpherson," observed Gunther expecting a major glitch in their itinerary.

"Yes ... well ... I regret to say that your tomorrow morning tee time has been rescheduled for half-six in the evening."

Phil angrily, "That's a whole day shot. How'n the hell did you screw up?"

"Entirely out of my hands," answered Macpherson with restrained animosity. "The Old Course has been shut down this morning. It will reopen at 2 o'clock. All tee times have been pushed back. The starter is at his wits end trying to accommodate those golfers on a tight schedule—particularly foreigners with planes to catch. I did the best I could. It was either half-six tomorrow evening or not at all. I hope I did the right thing."

"What went wrong?" asked Mal.

"One of the local caddies was threatened with bodily harm as he was crossing the Old Course last night. He was chased by a man wielding a cudgel of some sort."

"Is this some kind of a joke?" demanded Phil.

"No joke, sir. A serious matter indeed."

Macpherson hesitated before proceeding with his report. In a small way he enjoyed their bafflement. A deserved comeuppance ... well deserved.

"Well, go on, get on with it," commanded Phil.

"Yes. The caddie in question, Mackegan by name, swears to the authorities that a large man, bearded and arrayed in nineteenth-century attire, threatened to bludgeon him if he did not exit the golf course posthaste."

"Where we're from," Tony pooh-poohed, "that sort of thing happens all the time. No big deal."

"I'm sure you are correct in that, sir, however, this sort of thing rarely occurs in St. Andrews—so it is a big deal, as you might say." Macpherson paused again before delivering his next tidbit for he knew it would be received with victimized incredulity and he wanted to relish the response. "It must be admitted that Mackegan is perceived hereabout as an imbiber and is capable when so stimulated to utter the most outlandish yarns." As he expected, this last bit of information caused them to collapse in their seats with an irritation bordering on fury.

Mal spoke quietly, "We're being held up by a local drunken lunatic." Then to Macpherson, "Is that what you're telling us?"

"Quite so."

"I don't believe this," bawled Phil in a tone of high exasperation.

"Because Mackegan was discovered in a very nervous state of anxiety," continued Macpherson, "and because he would not retract nor alter his story, the local constabulary are compelled to investigate fully."

"Have they found the old man with the club?" asked Gunther.

"Of course not, Gunther," interjected Phil. "There was no old man. Was there?" he challenged Macpherson.

The tourist agent ignored the question and addressed the assembled at large, "So, gentlemen, do I confirm your tee time for half-six tomorrow evening?"

"Yeah, do that," grumbled Mal by way of dismissal.

"Very good, sir."

"Thanks," said Gunther.

The men shared a quiet moment stewing. Their best laid plans in bonnie Scotland gang agley, and they had no recourse but to abide.

"Playing that late we'll never be in before dark," Tony snorted.

"I think we'll be just fine," explained Gunther. "This far north, this time of year, it stays light late. By the way," looking around, "where's Harry?"

"Who cares," said Tony.

"I hate to bring this up," said Mal, "but whose turn is it to partner Harry tomorrow night?"

"Not me," answered Phil hastily.

"Me neither," added Tony.

"One of us has got to," said Mal.

"Why?" they all asked.

"Because," Mal explained, "as you all quite well know the golf club manufacturer sponsoring this trip of ours wants his grand-prize contest winner to have a good time."

"Then you show him a good time," said Phil.

"Let's talk this over," said Mal glumly shoving aside his mug as though making room for a war map to plan his strategy as director of Operation Golub. They had heard it all before. They were adamant. None would volunteer. At this point Operation Golub was little more than paper coasters and spilled suds.

Brew, meanwhile, was trying various ingratiate maneuvers on Fiona. His efforts were proving fruitless. Still, he pressed on. All the while Cameron Flett quietly studied the goings on around him. His eyes were filled with amusement as he quietly sucked his pipe.

"Fiona, I can't believe you would cut me out of your life forever," pined Brew in mock despair.

"I'm leaning that way, surely."

"Lean this way," Brew posed with open arms inviting a hug.

She withdrew in a huff to the sink to wash glasses.

CHAPTER 3

Back in the war room the belligerents stood their ground. "I was stuck with that cretin this morning at Carnoustie! Never again, never!" said Tony through clenched teeth.

"And I had the misery of his company at Royal Aberdeen," complained Gunther.

Phil, as though about to relive a torturous episode in a lower circle of hell, blurted, "He absolutely ruined Gleneagles for me. He lost eleven balls! Six in the same patch of tall grass! It took him twelve strokes to get out of a bunker! When the ball finally popped out, he yelled, 'Hey, Phil, did you catch that great shot?' Can you believe such an idiot exists?"

Cam could hardly wait to meet the instigator of so much animosity and discomfort.

Gunther called out to Brewster Payne, "Brew, Brew! We're trying to find Harry a partner for tomorrow. Want to volunteer?"

"I wouldn't play golf with that twit for all the world's wealth." He turned to Fiona and said softly, "But I'd walk through fire to have the pleasure of spending another night with you."

Cam spluttered a trifle as he sipped his whiskey. Incensed by Brew's indiscretion, Fiona's face reddened, and the mug in her quivering hand appeared to Brew threatening. "I think you have gone too far this time. You'd best be joining your friends and be leaving me to myself. Go!"

Brew threw up his hands. "Okay, Fiona, okay. We'll talk later." He backed away sheepishly.

Had anyone at that moment bothered to look out the window he'd have noticed a taxi pull up below and would have seen Harry's bobbing head sporting a new tam as he paid the cabbie. Also observable in the distance were pairs of policemen crisscrossing the fairways and scanning the ground.

Brew forced himself into the crowded booth.

Phil, tauntingly, "Struck out, huh?"

With an attempt to save face, Brew responded offhandedly, "Ahh, who cares. There's lots around. Barmaids are a cheap commodity."

On his way to the loo, Cam overhearing Brew's remark, stopped at his booth and casually tapped the dottle from his pipe onto the floor. As he patted the ash underfoot he addressed Brew matter-of-factly. "Nae, sir, the 'cheapest commodity' hereabout is the rude, pestilent, bloody vulgarian I'm peering at."

At this, Brew's bruised vanity smarted sorely. He glowered, and was on the point of suggesting to this aboriginal Caledonian where exactly to insert his pipe when into the pub burst a highland whirlwind.

"Ta Da!" was how Harry heralded his entrance. And there he proudly stood for all to see, in full Scottish regalia vigorously pumping a blackthorn walking stick as if he were the piper major of the Gordon Highlanders. He was full of himself as he spun around, strutted, minced and reeled to his own tunes. One could almost hear skirling pipes charging the air. A spirited performance it was, and executed with Chaplinesque flair.

All present were startled by the loud splendor of Harry's appearance. Because of his stature—his roma tomatoisness—the heavily-pleated kilt he was wearing, stopping just short of the knee as is traditional in Scotland, looked at first glance like a tartan tutu. And just beneath the chubby knees were argyle stockings with an ornate dirk thrust into the right sock. A fur-covered sporran hung loosely from a wide waistband. And topping off the vision was a jaunty bonnet garnished with a sprig of purple heather.

Harry's joy in his new trappings was warmly received by Fiona and Cam, for locals always appreciate a foreigner's regard for their culture. The Brew crew were aghast. One could instantly sense that their antipathy toward Harry grew beyond endurance. Some ancient sage, Horace, perhaps, said that it is delightful to be silly at the right moment. Harry's moment was decidedly ill-chosen.

"Well, guys, whaddya think?" pirouetted Harry in front of their booth.

Not a hair of good-natured humanity stirred. Like so many punctured tires the Brew crew hissed in unison. Slowly, by degrees, they buried their perfectly groomed heads in their perfectly groomed hands while muttering a lamentation of "Noes."

Resembling an innocent defendant in the dock who had been adjudged guilty of an heinous offense, Harry stood stunned.

"You are an utter idiot," Brew, without looking up, addressed Harry.

Mal, without looking up, "Go away, pleeease."

Tony maintained the see-no-evil position and shook his head, "That's the ugliest woman I ever saw."

Phil and Gunther were struck dumb.

Cruelly dashed was the favorable reception Harry had planned. When no convenient path to honorable withdrawal materialized, he improvised a swaggering image of camaraderie: "Drinks for everybody!"

It was at this juncture that I realized Harry Golub would never assume the posture of a disputant. I suspected that throughout his life he had met each personal affront with smiling compromise or victimized capitulation. Furthermore, I doubted that the hallowed walls of the Cleek and Thistle had ever witnessed such a barbarous response to an innocent attempt at jollity and affability.

Having just stabbed Harry to the quick with his show of callous disdain, Brew now felt inspired to attack Harry's purse and called out for a double shot of one of the dearer scotches. Mal, Tony, and Phil followed suit with gleeful alacrity. Gunther ordered black coffee.

Harry moved glumly to the end of the bar and abstractedly watched Fiona expertly pouring drinks. She turned and smiled. He dropped his eyes as though he had been caught with his hands in the till.

Cam held up his teacup and addressed Harry

From scenes like these, old Scotia's grandeur springs,
That make her loved at home, revered abroad.
Princes and lords are but the breath of kings,
An honest man's the noblest work of God.

"To your good health, sir."

"Robert Burns?"

"Aye, lad."

Coming from behind the bar with a tray of drinks, Fiona paused by Harry, "Don't you mind those heathens. We," nodding at Cam, "think you look quite grand, indeed."

She slid her tray onto the booth table and served drinks around while avoiding eye contact. She spun away quickly when Brew reached for her hand. She returned to Harry to take his order.

"Nothing for me, miss."

"Fiona, please call me Fiona."

Craving acceptance from any quarter Harry grabbed her hand and shook it vigorously, "Harry ... Harry Golub, from New York. I'm awfully glad you met me ... no ... I mean, glad to see you." He then dropped her hand like a hot potato. Close association with an attractive woman was evidently something with which Harry lacked experience, even casually. To regain his bearings he caught Cam's attention and smiled into his receptive countenance.

Fiona tapped Harry on the shoulder, "Won't you be having something for yourself, Harry Golub from New York?"

"Nothing, thank you."

"Even if it's my treat?"

Tony called out, "Give the wee lassie a Shirley MacTemple!"

Harry, visibly demoralized, "All right you guys, you've had your fun." To Fiona, "What do I owe you, Miss?"

She told him and he began to fumble with his sporran.

Phil pointed at Harry, "Hey, fellas, check out Harry playing with himself."

"What's the matter, Harry, you been shortchanged?" snickered Tony. Derisive laughter followed.

Fiona cast a Medusa scowl at the needlers. Their faces froze with contrition for a scant second, then settled back into their customary, deep-rooted arrogance.

The necessary funds plus generous gratuity were extracted from the cumbersome sporran and deposited on the bar. Eyes welling with tears, Harry turned to leave.

"Where are you lodging, Harry?" asked Fiona.

"The Bishop Seaton."

"A fine old place. I live near to there. I'm done here for the day, would you mind terribly if we walked along together?" she offered.

Harry jumped at the offer, "Be my pleasure." An honorable withdrawl had after all materialized.

Undoing her apron, "Cam, I know it's a wee early ... do you mind?"

"Always at yer disposal, m' love."

Harry, ever the gentleman, gallantly opened the door for his lady and at the same moment caught Brew's baleful, shudder-inducing stare before exiting the Cleek and Thistle into warm St. Andrews North Sea air.

Cam moved to the authoritative side of the bar and there willed himself to personify the dour, imperious magistrate. Between sips from his teacup and pulls on his briar he directed towards the heartless hecklers a fuss-with-me-and-I'll-toss-you-all-out-on-your-ear-for-the-remainder-of-your-natural-lives countenance. I'm very well acquainted with Mr. Cameron Flett and can assure you that at his advanced years he possessed little more strength than a weary golden plover. Still, his ruse succeeded. The duped yielded him his ground as if there just might be hidden beneath his quiet reserve a barbarous, rock-hurling, blue-breasted Pict.

As gentlemen more elevated among the golfing fraternity arrived within for refreshment and diversion, tensions dissipated. While Cam was busy drawing beer for a German foursome the Brew crew talked among themselves in a quieter manner so as not to annoy the keeper of the premises.

"We all agree Harry is a complete wash as a golfer," said Gunther gathering everyone's attention, "but you must admit, gentlemen, the nitwit scored better than Brew with the barmaid."

"She'll come around. They always do," assured Brew.

"Gunther," whispered Tony, "were you referring to *the* Harrison Golub, prize-winning sporting goods salesman from Manhattan, and sometimes Chief of the Highland Clan Golub?"

"Golub, Golub, Golub," intoned Phil mimicking America's holiday fowl.

"Must belong to the turkey clan," said Tony.

"Okay, since we're on the topic of our feathered friend, let's get serious for a minute," said Gunther. "We've still got a major problem unresolved—who gets Harry tomorrow? The only fair way to determine it is for us to draw straws."

"You can count me out," said Brew.

"Hey, you're in this the same as the rest of us," said Phil.

"No way."

"Gentlemen, gentlemen, be reasonable," interposed Mal. "Our good friend Brew is the only professional among us. He needs players of your calibre to challenge him, to keep him on his game. What he doesn't need is irritations and distractions."

They acquiesced on this one point grudgingly.

Mal snapped bar straws and handed them to Brew. "And to show how a true sportsman handles himself, I'll pick first."

Brew adjusted the straws in his fist and held them up to Mal. They made eye contact and Brew glanced left. Mal picked a long straw.

"Lucky me, lucky me," he shammed a sigh of relief.

Impatiently, Phil grabbed a straw ahead of the others and got the short end. Wide-eyed disbelief froze his face. He brought the bit of straw quizzically up to his nose and slowly, like passing ships, his eyes crossed. Guffaws and titters compounded his mental torment. "Oh, Gawd," he groaned. "No. No. No." He addressed his untouched double shot of 20-year-old single malt whiskey, "I gotta play 18 holes of golf on the most famous course in the world with … Help me, help me." The 20-year old was unmoved.

Sniggers accompanied these mournful utterances.

I am not ashamed to admit that I, too, took no small delight in the warranted pain and misfortune of this foul Phil fellow. But it soon followed that I became aggrieved to think that his accumulating bile would later be turned against Harry Golub.

CHAPTER 4

Wending their way to their respective abodes we find Harry and Fiona on busy North Street. Still smarting over the jeers he received in the Cleek and Thistle, Harry felt self-conscious about his apparel, so much so that he rarely raised his eyes from the sidewalk for fear he would see someone laughing at him. Had he dared to face passing pedestrians—mostly university students— he would have observed that none took notice of his being out of the ordinary whereas Fiona turned a great many heads with nods of admiration, and a few with longing. Harry, shyly, was also aware of her allure.

I myself can attest to the inalterable fact that Miss Fiona Huntly is a most lithesome lass. Her butterscotch hair, radiant in the sun, was styled in imitation of a startled chrysanthemum and caused her to look somewhat surprised at anything her lovely green eyes lit upon. Her complexion seemed to be of a tannish hue but on closer inspection proved to be mottled with myriad freckles. And her shapeliness showed to its fullest advantage against the roma tomatoishness of Harry, who, at five-feet-three, was four inches shorter. Fiona would not admit to it, but she was at that time 32. Harry I would have guessed to be two or three years older.

Harry looked up at her and said with sincerity, "Walking along with you may turn out to be the highlight of my trip here."

"Go on with you, Harry."

"No. I really mean it. Because of the knuckleheads I'm with I'm rarely out of earshot of smart-assed wisecracks thrown at me. And now, on this first sunny day I've had here in Scotland, this gorgeous, brilliant, remarkable day, a bonny lassie has offered to walk with me through this charming old town. And she's too nice to tell me I look like an idiot or an imposter."

"Oh, Harry, you look a wonder now. Nobody excepting those rotters that pestered you would deny you the privilege of honoring us by donning our traditional costume. I'll prove to you that your misgivings are totally indefensible."

Two elderly women, deep in conversation, toting shopping bags, approached them.

"May I trouble you ladies for an opinion?"

They perceived no mischief in Fiona's request and agreed with nods.

"What do you make of Harry here?" She pointed to a man who had removed himself a dozen paces away and appeared to be searching far above his head for a rope to climb or use to hang himself.

The women examined with a practiced eye the finer details of a proper Gordon Clan tartan and its attendant accessories. They adjudged him sound on all points.

"Aye, Miss, he looks a braw lad," approved one.

"Aye, indeed, ye mak a bonnie couple," pronounced the second.

"You are both very kind. Thank you."

"Ta."

"Ta."

The women continued on their way and chuckled good-naturedly. They glanced back once with amusement and approval.

"There now, I rest my case."

"What did they say?"

"They said we make a lovely couple."

"Half a lovely couple."

The university bells tolled two o'clock. Somewhat attuned to Pavlov's salivating dog, Harry's stomach growled.

"I'm hungry."

"Me, too. Shall we grab a wee bite?"

"Anywhere you like. I'll treat you to the finest meal in St. Andrews. You lead the way."

"You're on, Harry Golub. Come along." She took hold of his arm and hurried him across the street to a nearby establishment named Dunbar the Makar—known locally as the Poet's Pub.

As should be expected of a university town the pub had a fair-sized gathering of animated young scholars befogged in tobacco smoke. Between cigarette puffs and mouthfuls of fish, chips, and bangers, and quaffs of light and black ales, they debated their grasps of the morning's lectures.

Some tackled the phlogistic theory and believed they had discovered the answer to end the world's dependence on fossil fuels; a pair playing darts grappled whether a posteriori meant a person's bum or a position unwisely held by Duns Scotus. Throughout a game of draughts one fond biology couple compared and contrasted their own exploratory sex-capades with that of a gribble. And in a remote snug there convened a murmuring foursome of spiritualists in a seance mode attempting to fathom the mystery of the most recent ghost sighting on the Old Course. In lieu of a crystal ball in the middle of the table they instead gazed expectantly into a lap-top computer. Judging from the vapid expressions on their transfixed faces, no explanation was immediately forthcoming. Their trusted medium had failed them for the present. But one could tell that their determination to get at the bottom of this phenomenom was whetted for the long run, especially when they ordered another pitcher of Tennants.

Ah, the evolution of groping young minds is a wonder to behold. I see a day when intolerance, the root of all misunderstanding, will be harmoniously adjusted by this new educated generation in which a large part will be played by their skillful use of computers and dietary supplements. In the meantime humanity continues to be ensconced in a pulsing age of snits, snarls, sneers, and snubs; offenses which have formed the basis for many of my most harrowing tales— rather like this one. Let us return to the moment.

Conversations in the Poet's Pub, though loud and intense, were altogether congenial. Harry had difficulty understanding the overheard voices in the smoke-filled room.

"Feel like I'm in a foreign country."

"You are, Harry. Remember … Scotland?"

"Oh, yeah."

A college-age waitress placed plates of hot food on the table. "There you are. Will there be anything else?"

"This will do nicely, thank you," said Fiona reaching for the malt vinegar.

"Right you are," and off she went.

"I think the gal goofed," said Harry looking at his food.

"How so."

"We ordered fish and chips, right?"

"Quite."

"Look what we got."

"Fish and chips."

"Nope."

"Nope?"

Harry held up a forked piece of fish. "This, I would guess—" he popped it in his mouth—Wha whawhawa.. is a damn hot piece of fish." He gulped water. "Whew."

"Poor Harry, are you okay?"

"Yep. Anyway, it is fish and it is very tasty. But this … is a french fry," he pronounced pointedly, poking at one with his finger.

"Well Mr. Smarty Pants New Yorker, in Britain this is fish, truly," She said and popped a morsel from her plate in her mouth. "But these are chips. Chips of potato … potato chips. Get it?"

"You are, I see, unacquainted with potato nomenclature," said Harry, assuming the air of a stuffed-shirt professor. "In the realm of po-ta-to gastronomy, chips, my dear, are paper thin slices of the noble spud that are fried to a crisp ... ."

"Ah ha, you perjured yourself, professor Know-_t-all; I have you now. Fried to a crisp, you say. What you recognize as chips, we refer to as "crisps" because they are crisp. Crisp, crisp, crisp."

"I get your point," acquiesced the professor. "_f profound thinkers like ourselves fail to agree on acceptable definitions for specific cuts of commonus spuddus, why should we expect diplomats to see eyeball to eyeball over arms control."

"Or finger food."

"Or nose jobs."

"Or footwear."

"Or lip service."

"Or ears pierced."

"Or body searches."

"Or body bags."

"Or bawdy houses."

"Really, Harry. Bawdy houses does not qualify. It's body parts we are after."

"There are no body parts in bawdy houses?"

For the duration of their mid-day repast they diverted themselves in this frivolous fashion. By the time they departed Dunbar the Makar to continue homeward they had become warmly acquainted.

Harry's attraction for Fiona was inevitable. Besides her obvious charms, she possessed Harry's childlike flair for nonsensical indulgence. Levity became a mutual touchstone which they alternately rubbed to a polish. No serious note intruded until they turned down the quiet street whereon Fiona resided.

"Harry, is Brewster Payne a friend of yours?"

"Not a chance. You should have seen the evil eye he gave me when we left the Cleek and Thistle. Man, if looks could kill I'd have a hole the size of the Lincoln Tunnel right here," he pointed between his eyes.

"Then why are you with him?'

"Fate. I won a golf manufacture's sales prize. The prize?—an all-expenses-paid trip to famous Scottish golf courses with golf pro Brewster Payne who, by the way, endorses the manufacture's golf equipment. He fixed it with the company so that his friends could tag along, too."

"You're not getting on, are you?"

"Tried every way I know to be friendly with him and his friends but nothing so far has worked. Those bozos hate me because I'm a lousy golfer, and because of that, they say, it prevents them from enjoying their rounds. The golf package we're on is set up so that they have to play with me. You'd think that that would be such a little thing to abide by. After all it's because of me that they are here in the first place. A group of ingrates is the way I see it."

"You must be miserable, surely?"

"I'm probably the worst golfer that ev … ."

"No, no, Harry. I was referring to your feelings," she grabbed his arm and patted his hand as they proceeded along.

"My feelings? Don't worry about my feelings, Fiona. I'm not gonna let those mugs get me down. Gonna enjoy myself in spite of them."

"Bravo, Harry."

"Love golf," he said. "Been watching this sport on TV ever since I was a teenager. When you live and work in New York in winter and it's freezing, grey, and miserable outside, it's nice to stretch out in a comfortable chair on Sundays and watch golfers enjoying themselves in sunny Florida, California, and Hawaii. There's flowers in bloom, birds chirruping, and well-behaved people in shorts and short-sleeved shirts walking leisurely on green grass. And not one of them is coughing or sniffling or blowing their shnozzes. So if you love golf as I do it should be the treat of a lifetime to visit the home of golf. Look at me, I'm possessed. I wanted so much to fit in here I bought this crazy outfit." He pirouetted, his kilt fanned out displaying more of himself than anybody had a right to witness. His embarrassment caused his face to instantly flare like a struck match.

"And happily you are here," said Fiona muffling a chuckle. "You do fit in, Harry. A huge lot more than those Brewster Paynes in the arses."

"Well put."

She halted. "I live just two blocks from here, Harry. If you turn up that way you'll go steady on back to North Street, and your hotel will be there on your left."

"If you don't mind I'd like to walk you to your door."

"Good of you, Harry"

"You know, Fiona, the very first round of golf I ever played was a few days ago. Gleneagles! Wow! what a thrill. Ben Hogan won the British Open there. Of course Ben did a little better than me. But I did break 200. Got a 198," he announced with more pride than his score deserved.

"198?"

"Terrible, huh?" realizing finally that his inflated score was not an accomplishment by any standard for a first timer; especially one who admits to a rare fondness for the game.

"Harry, you don't perhaps mean ... 98?"

"Don't I wish. Phil says I hold the record score for the worst round played by anyone over three-years old. He may be right."

"Poor Harry. I've never heard the like."

He felt considerably diminished in her regard and wished he had not revealed to her this unmanly inadequacy. "Guess I'm a complete flop."

"Poor Harry," she repeated. She could think of no proper condolence for his ineptitude. How could one hope to go through life burdened with such an elevated score? 198! Who ever heard the like? It must be a wicked curse or an error in accounting.

"The game has got me completely mystified," he kicked at an imaginary Phil. "It shouldn't when you think of it. Good grief, the ball doesn't move, it just sits there like a mushroom. And you whack at it. What could be simpler? It's not a baseball coming at you a hundred miles an hour. Only when I whack at the mushroom it doesn't go straight … or far. Sometimes it just stays rooted to the spot."

"Poor Harry."

"When I do hit the ball its generally a hop, skip, and a jump away."

"Poor, poor Harry."

"Sydney will be awfully disappointed."

"Sydney?"

"Sydney Levinson. My boss. My friend. Nicest guy in the world. You'd love him. While I'm over here he's installing an indoor practice range in the store, and he's counting on me to demonstrate our various lines of clubs. Stupidly, we both thought that by the time I got back from playing golf in Scotland I'd be proficient enough to at least swing a club with a little skill. Dumb, dumb, dumb," he pounded his forehead with his palm. "I wish I could play better."

As Harry spoke, Fiona seemed to be grappling with an idea. "And so you shall, Harry my lad."

"Wha … ?"

"I'll wager I can teach even Harry Golub from New York how to play well enough to break 100."

Harry, dumfounded, "You play golf?"

"Certainly, Harry. After all, I live in St. Andrews, do I not? But I'm no expert, mind you. Still, I know the fundamentals inside out. That's almost all one hears at work—slice, hook, push, fade, inside/outside swing, stance, follow-through, Vardon grip. I'm sure I can help you. Yes, I'm quite sure," she said with a degree of uncertainty.

Harry's depressed countenance dramatically metamorphosed to a height that was close to below average.

He was aglow over his good fortune as they came upon two carpenters who paused in their trade on the sidewalk cluttered with tools and boards to better ogle Fiona as she detoured around their work area. Harry noted their unabashed admiration for his companion which he felt dignified his presence as her escort. As a boon to his new-found dignity, our kilted Manhattanite added another scant millimeter to his growing stature in Scotland.

"Bet you're a terrific golfer."

"Adequate, Harry, merely adequate. Shall we give it a go?"

"I'm all for it a hundred per cent."

"This is home, Harry." She halted before a typical attached Scottish flat. "Thank you ever so much for accompanying me here."

"My great pleasure."

"Suppose we meet tomorrow. Ten sharp, say ... at the Jubilee?"

"Great. I'll be there with bells on."

"Who is Belle Zohn?" was her quick retort.

"Zimmer's bat boy."

"Zenobia's brother."

"Zivic's cut man."

"Xerxes' general."

"Babe's Zaharias."

"Xanthippe's ne'er-do-well."

"Ziggy's tailor."

"Zola's Nana."

"Umm ... Zorba the Greek."

"Zeus the god."

"Zasu the pits."

"Zasu the pits? Uh uh, Harry. You lose. A pit is not an occupation, nor a calling, nor a position in life which I believe were the categories we were following. However Britain did have two former statesmen named Pitt, though neither was a Zasu. Both were William. Still, it was a brave effort on your part.'

"You're good at this, but I'll be ready for you next time."

"We'll see. We agree on tomorrow? Ten o'clock?"

"You bet."

"We'll spend the better part of an hour together before I'm off to work."

"Wouldn't miss it for the world." He grabbed her hand and shook it vigorously, "Thanks for everything."

"Oh, tut, Harry. Thank you for the jolly companionship and the splendid dinner." She mounted the stairs, hesitated, "Oh … and, Harry … tomorrow … you might wear something more … you know."

"Gotcha," he said looking down at his attire. He offered up to her a silly smile and curtsied.

She entered her house laughing at his unaffected tomfoolery.

Harry clapped his hands and rubbed them together as though complimenting himself on a successful enterprise. His outlook on life, primarily with regard to golf, showed promise. And his friendship with Fiona, though incomprehensible to himself, was greatly to be cherished. It was the nearest he had ever come to having a real date with a woman. And what a woman! He pinched himself. He developed an unaccustomed pluckiness and self-assurance as he manfully marched down the center of the sidewalk and nonchalantly hurdled the stunned carpenters's tools, boards and sawdust while modestly holding down his kilt.

"What a glorious day," he sang to himself. "Magnificent. Splendid. Great. Great? No, no, positively greater than great. Even greater than great big."

CHAPTER 5

The Bishop Seaton Hotel's granite and limestone facade confronted the late afternoon sun's rays with stately aplomb which seemed at the moment the proper attitude to adopt for receiving the dignified, fully-caparisoned clansman from New York City.

In the lobby Harry's progress was diverted by a group of onlookers encircling a TV crew focusing on an interview. The subject was Brewster Payne. The interviewer was the ubiquitous sports commentator, Ward Diggs. Permit me an interjection here. I do not like Diggs in the least. The fellow is like the grub in the salad, like rain during a tournament, like chewing gum that quickly loses its flavor. He sours every event that he is assigned to analyze. And the devil somehow manages to pop up here in St. Andrews for the Open and the Dunhill speaking gravely of the events as though they were memorials to golfdoms dearly departed. And he loves to show off how many eminent names he can dig out of the past. And not once has he mentioned my name. Not once.

And who cares a fig about Diggs' personal bias on this and that which he conveys in a most unctuous baritone. He enunciates each measured word as if he were instructing debutantes elocution; perfectly nice young ladies whom he knew could never attain his own meliflorous prolixity. Why he is able to continue in his profession is beyond understanding. It only proves that one can fool some of the people all of the time.

Harry, too, did not esteem Diggs, and we are fully aware of his feelings toward Payne, so he unhesitatingly wended his way through the crowd toward the elevator.

Diggs to Payne: "Are you gainfully sojourning in soberly friendly St. Andrews, Mr. Payne?"

Payne to Diggs: "Yes, I'm … .?"

Diggs to his cameraman: "Quickly, there." He pointed to Harry. The camera followed him onto the elevator as Diggs provided a running commentary: "Hail to the Chief who in triumph advances. There, ladies and gentlemen, is the strikingly real heart and heather of Scotland. Sterling, simply sterling."

Brew sees it is Harry and turns to reappraise Ward Diggs who he now sees as a knucklehead of the first order.

Diggs: "By his proud bearing—sterlingly composed, as we all bear witness—that grand fellow is assuredly a mighty and honorable chief, a noble representative of an indigenous clan. How fortunate that I was here and able to espy in the periphery this rare incident for you, our world-wide viewers." This was all said with an unhurried roundness of tone. The instant the elevator doors closed Diggs resumed his inquiry of Brewster Payne.

"Mr. Payne, what brings you to Scotland?"

"Ward, one of my sponsors arranged a small tour of this fine country for myself and a few of my associates to test a new line of golf clubs that I designed."

"I should think traveling entirely unnecessary to test clubs. Couldn't that more readily be accomplished stateside?"

"Good question, Ward," he answered, toadying up to Diggs and his vast audience. "You see, British links courses play differently than the courses back home. Here you'll find different grasses, less elevated greens, more wind … ."

"Thicker fog."

"I hadn't thought of that."

"Fewer trees."

"That, too. My sponsor wants to be able to assure all those

thousands of serious golfers who'll be purchasing sets of Brewster Payne signature irons that they will produce the best results under any condition, on golf courses anywhere in the world."

"Jolly good, I'm sure. Have you an upcoming tournament?"

"Good of you to ask. A week from Thursday—the Poor Richard's Almanac Classic in Harrisburg. Maybe we'll see you there?"

"Oh, but indubitably. I rarely miss an opportunity to behold the menacingly capable Tiger Woods run roughshod over the commonality," he pronounced with a calculated stab and twist that he had hoped would elicit a pained response. It didn't.

There followed an uneasy lull as they matched supercilious grins. Then, "Thank you, Brewster Payne for taking leave of your busman's holiday to enlighten us with your astute insight into the benign treachery of Britannia's links courses." He then added by way of dismissal, "And I do sincerely hope that your new self-designed clubs improve your presently considerable aptitude for this game we all love so dearly."

"Always a pleasure, Ward," said Brew attempting a cordial smile that too easily slid into frozen scorn.

With a confidence borne from his imagined cerebral celebrity, Ward Diggs addressed the camera: "This is Ward Diggs from St. Andrews, Scotland, saying, catch you up next time … from somewhere … in our world." He held a controlled look of superiority for a full five seconds before the cameraman called it a "wrap." The moment Diggs and crew began gathering their equipment, onlookers departed.

Brew entered the elevator with Mal and in an aside murmured, "That nitwit is an arrogant ass."

Diggs spoke to his cameraman, "That ass is an arrogant nitwit."

CHAPTER 6

When Harry entered the room he shared with Phil, he found him primping before the dresser mirror. "Where you been, Harry?" he asked disinterestedly.

"Sightseeing."

"In that get-up?"

"Nothing wrong with my get up." He began undressing. "Scots all over town treated me like one of their own, I'll have you know."

"Speaking for all my friends, we think you look a complete fool in that kilt and we don't want you wearing it around us."

Harry tried to ignore Phil's scoffing so that he might continue reliving his cherished afternoon with Fiona, but the fellow never let pass an opportunity to plague him.

"You should have your head examined," said Phil as he attempted to flatten a few unruly hairs above a forehead showing signs of enlarging. First he tried to paste down the hairs with spit-wet fingers, to no avail. Then he ground them down with his thumb, and up they sprung like jubilant wallabies. His frustration mounted. His entire focus was bent on the maverick hairs. In a matter of seconds his peevishness expanded from brushing aside an insignificant trifle into an Herculean labor. He braced himself for one rash final foray. He attacked the hairs head-on with a full body slam using the heel of his hand. The jar knocked his head back with a forceful jolt that quite stunned him for a moment. He bristled at Harry.

"You're driving me nuts, Harry. Your silly costume ... your crummy golf ... your unnatural enthusiasm for this gloomy country," he sneered and his ears were red and glowing. "Everyone and everything in this country is not necessarily nice, terrific ... whatever. That's baloney. I got news for you—this is not paradise. Scotland is far from the perfect place you keep on describing. It's far from perfect. For instance—rain. Maybe you hadn't noticed, Harry, but it has rained four of the five days we've been here. Wake up to the real world."

Laying his sporran on his bed and patting it like a pet kitten, Harry said, "Rain is to be expected here, you know that, it's one of the features that adds to its charm ... makes it interesting, unique ..."

"There you go again with the 'interesting'." He returned to the mirror and sighed, "Everything in Scotland is interesting."

"No, Phil, not everything. I've seen a few tourists here that are horses' asses."

Unsure if the dig was directed at him, Phil peered at Harry via the mirror and watched with dismay as Harry casually slipped off his kilt. "Gawd, Harry, you're weird." He took hold of his fingernail clippers and snipped off the recalcitrant filaments, studied the result, and uttered a victorious huzzah.

"By the way, Harry, how'd you make out with Brew's old girlfriend?"

"Fiona?"

"Yah, that one."

"He just met her today."

"Wrong. Met her months ago when he flew over to work with the local pro—whatshisname—Charlie Maxwell."

"Do you believe everything Payne tells you?"

"Does insignificant little Harrison Golub mean to suggest that Brewster Payne, a man whose ancestors arrived on the Mayflower, is a liar?"

"Rats came over on the same boat."

"Ooo, an unrefined comment from the proletariat. You're treading dangerous ground. Anyway, why should you care, she's just a barmaid."

"Whaddaya mean, just a barmaid?" Harry was incensed at the coarseness and insensitivity of Phil's appraisal of Fiona. "She's a very nice person. And I'm tired of listening to your crap." He was shaking.

"Have it your way," was the indifferent response. "Think what you like, it's a free country." Phil entered a thinking pause, then, "Scotland is a free country, isn't it?"

Harry decided to ignore Phil completely as he stood in his shorts and gartered kneesocks while leaning over the bed folding his pleated kilt.

Phil, finally satisfied with his appearance, headed for the door, "Don't wait up for me. I feel tonight's my lucky night. Maybe spend it in the arms of a barmaid. Later." And in a whiff of patchouli, he was gone.

Harry grabbed a towel and headed for a soothing shower.

"Where's Brew?" asked Phil, joining his assembled clones in the hotel lounge bar.

"Dunno," answered Mal, "expect he'll be along shortly."

"What's the plan?"

"Don't have one yet."

"We're working on it," said Tony.

"We'll think of something," offered Gunther. "It's early yet."

For the present let us abandon this shepherdless flock to their wool gathering and revisit another part of the old burgh.

CHAPTER 7

The doorbell beside the name F. Huntly was pressed into service. Shortly thereafter the front door eased ajar and emitted a cheerless voice, "What do you want?"

"Only you," said Brew, proffering a long-stem rose.

"I'm not available to the likes of you." She accepted the bloom with reluctance and instinctively sniffed its heavy fragrance with restrained pleasure.

"Can we talk?"

"I've nothing to say to you, nothing whatsoever."

"I'm here to apologize for the rotten way I've treated you, Fiona."

"You have treated me more rotten ways than one, Mr. Love-'m-and-leave-'m Payne."

With a contriteness that should have melted the heart of Torquemada, "Believe me, Fiona, I'm deeply sorry for every actual and imagined indignity that I caused you."

She opened the door wider, leaned on the frame and studied him for signs of insincerity. The handsome face, petitioning for absolution, seemed angelic.

The scoundrel was an artful dissembler. Even as she peered into his eyes she saw nothing but total remorse. A more despicable manipulator of the truth would be hard to find unless one ventured into the Bishop Seaton Hotel lounge bar.

"I want to make amends, Fiona. I'm a new person altogether."

"Aye, and Loch Leven has turned to honey, altogether."

"May I come in?'

"Absolutely not." She stepped out and sat on a stoop. "I'll listen to your innumerable expressions of regret, here. You may proceed."

He sat directly behind her so better to keep his feigned expressions from giving away his true purpose, which was nothing more than seduction for a day or two, thereby winning a laurel for his bruised ego. He gingerly placed a hand on her shoulder. She tapped it with her rose and shrugged it off. With shammed innocence, while wearing a supercilious smirk, the cad simpered, "Fiona, please don't hate me."

"I do not hate you, Brew," she breathed softly, "but I have been enormously disappointed in you. I thought we were getting on famously, then … when I didn't hear from you … why?"

"It's a long story … ."

"Cut to the quick."

"When we first met it was a difficult time for me. I was trying to put an end to a long-standing relationship with someone back home. I didn't want to involve you … the press and all, you see. They can be ruthless with those of us in the public eye. Thank Gawd that's over," he said manufacturing a convincing sigh of deliverance. "Now I'm free." Sensing her indignation ebbing he again placed his hands on her shoulders. "I've finally come to my senses, Fiona. Can't we pick up where we left off? Start a new chapter?"

"No more chapters. Our story is a shut book."

"Fiona."

"All those months without a word … I wasn't sure where I stood with you until … ."

"Until?"

"When I saw you again I must admit my feelings for you returned for … ."

Brew pulled her back and hugged her with his arms across her breasts. "Then everything's okay?"

She disengaged herself and stood. "As I was about to say, my feeling for you returned for an instant—and then disappeared entirely when I witnessed how you and your barbarous friends behaved toward Harry Golub."

"Harry Golub!" The name ignited his dander. "Harry Golub is a complete idiot and an utter nuisance. What has he told you about me?"

"He didn't have to tell me anything. With my own eyes I saw how mean and contemptible you and your mates can be." Up the stairs she flew. "And I do not wish to see you or your lot again!" She pitched the rose over his head and slammed the door in his face.

Stunned, he stood with his mouth looking like the hole in a birdhouse, and not a peep came out of it. He stomped down the steps, stomped on the rose, stomped up the street, and startled the carpenters by stomping on their swept up sawdust pile. He turned into the nearest pub hoping Harry was in there.

CHAPTER 8

Harry, meanwhile, refreshed from his shower, was passing through the hotel lobby on his way out for an evening stroll.

Phil hailed him from the lounge bar, "Harry! Harry, where you headed?"

"For a walk."

"If you run into Brew tell him we're here waiting for him."

Harry waved acknowledgment and bounded out onto the sidewalk happy to be by himself. His mood was jaunty, carefree. He paused in front of the hotel and deeply inhaled while peering at the full moon sailing above whispy twilight clouds. "Hey, old moon, I see you followed me over here. Wanna join me on a walk? Come along." And the moon did indeed follow Harry along North Street passing buildings suitably pleasing to an antiquarian's eye. The formidable, substantial, enduring look of granite and limestone disposed Harry to think back in time.

His readings about Scotland—though primarily centered on golf—did now and again touch on other aspects of the country's rich and colorful history. He wondered if some of the buildings he passed in this ancient burgh had housed any of the thousands of women who James VI had condemned and burned at the stake as witches. He was appalled and fascinated that such abominable acts could be justified and carried out in a country he revered almost as much as his own. Mulling over those sad times and the desperate plight of those poor innocents, Harry awakened to the fact that he had happened upon the Royal and Ancient Clubhouse.

Leaning on the railing below the club, Harry watched the day's last golfers, a Japanese foursome, putting out on the 18th green. Their joy in the moment was ecstatic, infectious. Harry knew that they would relive this round time and time again, bore their friends with its recounting, as he knew he would after his round here tomorrow. The tired caddies proceeded to the car park toting the players' bags. The players bowed and shook hands with vigor repeatedly in an effort to prolong their pleasure and accomplishment at having played a round of golf on the most famous golf course in the world. To the smiling roundish man of fellow feeling propped against the railing they nodded a sort of half bow, pleased that they had a spectator who shared their joy. On the way to their car they chattered like happy schoolchildren. Harry could make out a few words among the Japanese: "Nickrus," "Watson," "Montgomery," "Aoki," "Grenrivet."

With the moon over his shoulder, Harry sauntered along The Links, the quiet roadway that parallels the 18th fairway. He stopped and looked back with mystical pleasure as the last rays of the fading sun quit the sky above the clubhouse and gave way to the expanding glow of the moon. He released a melancholic sigh when he realized that there was no one with whom he might share this spiritual moment. His reverie was broken by raucous voices nearby. He resumed his walk by crossing Grannie Clark's Wynd, the pedestrian pathway that bisected the 1st and 18th fairways.

Angus Mackegan, tipsy and melodramatically animated, stood holding court in front of three leaden-eyed cronies sitting on a bench just ahead of where Harry turned to cross the Old Course. All four were above threescore and had flasks in hand.

"The giant speerit o' auld Tom loomed afore me wi' an eerie aspect," intoned Mackegan. "Faster than ye ken sae—Dow Finsterwald— he bounded efter me wi' huge strides." He mimicked the strides with uncertain footing. "Whan I chanced to leuk back I saw the fearsome speerit nigh upon me and him brandisheeng a mammoth wuid-shafted club grup thusly in his massive gnarly fist. I bolted like a Grand National champeeon, running faster than mortal mon! Aye, lads, it war a nichtmair."

Exhausted from recreating the event, Mackegan joined his auditors on the bench and took a long nerve-settling pull from his flask.

"Aye, a nichtmair, indeed," agreed the first crony and likewise imbibed.

"Aye," repeated the other tipplers.

"He must o' run oot o' steam," commenced Mackegan, "for whan I reached this verra spot, he war gone. Vaneeshed. I tell ye, lads, niver agen wull I be daft enough tae be on the auld coorse efter sundoon. Nae, lads, niver." He took a drink.

"Nae, niver." They drank.

"Angus, where exactly was it the ghaist of auld Tom himself appeered?" asked the third crony.

Mackegan pointed, "Nixt that large thicket by the 5th tee."

All tried to focus on that general area. They were surprised to see a short roundish figure in the gloaming heading out toward the very spot mentioned.

Mackegan became alarmed, "Wha brazen foo wad that be trampin' there this nicht of the fu' moon?"

"Ach, the poor innocent is acteevely engaged in loonacy," said the second crony.

They looked appealingly to one another for a clue as to what course to follow in warning the unwitting pedestrian. No right-minded idea was capable of formulating under their present condition. After an extended bafflement the third crony was moved to say, "Shanna we drink to his safe return?"

"Aye, a wise suggesteeon."

"Aye."

"Aye," concurred Mackegan and offered up a prayer: "Matheoo, Mark, Leuk, and John, Bless the grun' that foo walks on."

As Harry neared the 5th tee a heavy dark cloud blocked out the moon and pitched him into darkness. He stumbled and brushed against the whin. He looked ahead and could not make out the path. The only lights in view were those back in town, hundreds of yards behind. The wind picked up and swirled around him in eddies. The path back was barely discernible. The faint sound of someone sanding and humming an unfamiliar tune reached his ear from he knew not where. It must be the wind playing tricks, he thought. Alone in the darkness, far from habitation, his surroundings had become eerily chilling. He turned about and hied back the way he came. The humming and sanding drifted in and out of the whin. When he again attained the paved path, the clubhouse stood before him bathed in moonglow. He now felt very much at ease but extremely tired. He headed back to his hotel for much needed rest after having experienced a wonder-filled day.

No sooner had Harry entered the hotel lobby before a boisterous cry from the lounge bar impeded his direct line to the elevator.

"Hey! Harry! d'ja she Brew?" It was Phil. He had become the dupe of a distilled agent with soda.

"Nope," proceeded Harry apace.

"F'ew she 'em, tell 'em we're shtill waitin' on 'em, okay?"

"Sure thing."

The only occupied table in the lounge that late in the evening featured the Brewless crew. Four or more empty glasses per person signified their idle occupation. Gunther, the lone animated member, used his swizzle stick to assist him in counting the ice cubes in his glass. Time and time again he lost count before they mysteriously disappeared. Besides the alternate gulps and the clinkings of ice against glass, the only other sound was the persistent smoking cough of the barman which increasingly sounded like taps.

"Gawd ... huk ... this is a ... huk ... nothing town," hic-cupped Tony.

"You can thank your lucky shtarsh Harry didn't join ush," said Phil, "or we'd be bored to tearsh."

Whoever suggested that drink makes people free and easy never observed this cheerless still life.

CHAPTER 9

The following morning the sidewalk below the Bishop Seaton Hotel streamed with activity. The gainfully employed were pressing along clutching their lunches and briefcases. Many among them gripped umbrellas for insurance even though the day blossomed with warming sunshine mellow as gorse bloom. Students of all ages were also afoot, or cycling; some lolled, others hied to their classes as belltowers from various precincts pealed the hour just as they had done for centuries.

Inspiriting salt and seaweed vapors from the North Sea whiffed throughout St. Andrews, yet their therapeutic benefits were of no consequence to the four chaps waiting without the hotel.

Hamish Macpherson was noticeably in harmony with this glorious morn as he cheerfully loaded golf bags into the van; however, a funereal pall had overtaken Mal, Phil, Tony, and Gunther. Hangovers had forced upon them their look of bereavement. To a man they stood erect as columns, stiff-necked caryatids supporting an entablature of excruciation. Conscious immobility prevented their brains from caroming against their fragile inner skulls. Silent they were in their misery, except Tony who unconsciously whimpered.

Harry emerged from the hotel carrying his golf bag. He looked refreshed and eager to fulfill his golf date with Fiona.

"Good morning, guys."

They were unmoved by joy.

43

"Howya doin', Hamish?"

"Very well, sir, thank you."

"All accounted for?" Harry addressed Mal.

"All but Brew," he grimaced as if an invisible strap was cinching his head. "I don't know where he is. I think we had better wait for him."

"Can't," said Harry, "got a golf lesson in a few minutes. Catch you later." He threw his clubs into a standby taxi. "The Jubilee, my good man."

"Right you are, sir, the Jubilee it is."

The ailing quartet watched Harry driven off. Ordinarily they'd have hurrahed his departure, but even this unexpected boon failed to ease their persisting indisposition.

"Macpherson," mumbled Mal, "have you seen Mr. Payne?"

"That I did, sir. Just moments ago I drove him to the Jubilee where he is to join Mr. Charlie Maxwell for an impromptu instruction with a mid-iron."

"Why didn't you tell us this earlier?"

"I was unaware of it's importance, sir. Dreadfully sorry."

"Augh!—never mind. Let's get going."

The hungover boarded the van in slow motion.

"Macpherson peered into the rearview mirror and took wicked delight in what he saw there.

"Have you properly breakfasted, gentlemen?" he inquired.

Imperceptible grunts fouled the air.

"The Bishop Seaton is celebrated for its breakfasts of smoked haddock and cream sauce—Cullen skink. Myself, I had kippers, a wee oilier than customary, but … ."

"Macpherson!" screamed a frazzled Tony. "Will you quit it with the skinks and kippers! Jeez. Just get us to the Crail course … and don't talk."

"Quite."

CHAPTER 10

The taxi dropped off Harry and drove away. He attempted a few warmups which amounted to little more than jogging in place and flapping his arms. He reminded one of a plump fledgling petitioning for a worm. His exercise lasted barely a minute. He then selected a niblick and swung it toward a distant target. Harry was surprised to note that the distant target was Fiona. She was engaged in conversation with Brewster Payne. They seemed to him to be arguing.

"You lied ... you used me," burned Fiona turning away.

"I meant what I said when I said it," Brew explained.

"What good I ever saw in you ... you are contemptible."

"Come off your high horse, Fiona, you're no innocent."

She turned about and slapped him hard, "You arrogant, self centered, bloody bastard!" She left hurriedly, weeping. "A proper fool I was ... utterly stupid to think you were serious about me. Stupid, stupid, stupid."

Rubbing his smarting cheek Brewster Payne was truly stunned, stupefied, not solely from the force of the blow—for it was considerable and well-directed—but because of the realization that he just might have deserved it. Seeing Fiona about to join up with Harrison Golub ended his feeling of self-reproach, that is to say his mean-spiritedness had fully recovered possession of his faculties—he bristled, he fumed, and then, by Jove, he cussed wickedly ... and spat. Charlie Maxwell arrived, a no nonsense man, and proceeded right away to examine Brewster Payne's swing which seemed quicker and more forceful than need be.

Harry, pretending not to have noticed the parting combatants, faced away from them. After an interval he cavalierly swung his niblick in their general direction. Pausing at the top of his backswing he responded as if he had just then noticed Fiona. She was drying her eyes with a tissue. They waved greetings.

"Good morning, Harry, " Fiona called cheerily while wiping her eyes and nose.

"Hey, Fiona, good to see you. How's it goin'?"

"You must excuse how I look. I'm having a beastly bout with allergens this morning; gorse pollens I expect. Not to worry though, we'll still go about our task."

"Task is right. Formidable task, unrewarding task, fruitless task."

Fiona seemed not to hear him. She was glancing back from whence she came and was lost in thought. Harry followed her gaze and saw Brew scrutinizing an address Maxwell mimed.

"Harry, after our lesson—but only if you are free this afternoon—would you like it if I showed you around St. Andrews?"

"Would I. Wow. Terrific. Great idea."

"I'm scheduled to work today, but I've decided to ask Cam to fill in for me. He never says no."

"The poet?"

She smiled warmly. "Cam's accomplishments are many—a poet, no. But he is quite fond of poetry, particularly old Scottish ballads, and scotch whisky. The Cleek and Thistle is his place. And in the rear of the Cleek he has a shop where he makes replicas of ancient wood-shafted golf clubs. Tourists, mostly, buy them."

"Do people actually play with them?"

"By and large they're souvenir purchases. Still, there is a local group that play the Eden course once a month with these old clubs—the Hickory Jocks. Cam is a founding member. He's not as adept with the old clubs as he once was but he believes using them preserves the purity of the game."

"Cool."

"The Hickory Jocks also insist on using sand tees. Their only concession to modernity is the golf ball—featheries and gutta perchas are no longer available outside museums and private collections. Did I mention that Cam is my uncle?"

"I like him."

"I'm glad."

"And I'm glad you're taking the day off."

"Truth to tell, Harry, I didn't want to have to deal with those horrid friends of yours."

"Hold on there. Those pea-headed, bird-brained, dim-witted lug nuts are not my friends. No way."

"Sorry, Harry. I should have said the boorish friends of the boorish Mr. Brewster Payne-in-the-arse from Connecticut, Massachusetts."

Their hearty laughter caught Brew's attention. His face tinged with animosity. For the moment he had forgotten why he was there.

"Mr. Payne," admonished Charlie Maxwell, "I dinna understand why ye wish to squander your weal and my time by gawking into space. We are, are we not, attempting to correct ye backswing?"

"What on earth does she see in that excuse for a man?"

"I'm sure I dinna know, nor is it any of my affair." Dropping a ball, "Address yersel' to the ba' and send it toward the flag, if you please, Mr. Payne."

He overswung and pulled it left.

"Shall we then?" Fiona plucked a nine iron from Harry's bag.

"Ready as I'll ever be. Hope you know what you're getting into. I'm a real bummer."

"Bosh, Harry. No negative thoughts. Understood?"

"Understood."

Forgive my reticence in recreating for you this particular episode in the affairs of Harrison Golub. For me to describe this grotesque parody of a travesty would be painful in the extreme for any lover of the game. Let me simply say—dare I ... shanks. There I've said it. The most taboo word in the English language. Harry delivered more—insert taboo word—during his lesson than there are haddocks on ice in Peterhead. By allowing myself to be mesmerized by the horrific nature of his impotence, my own game was confounded for weeks thereafter. Had not my good friend and physician, Mr. Stanley Bloodletter, counselled me back to *mens sana,* and had not another friend, Sir Harry Vardon, restored my mechanics, I fear I'd have voluntarily quit golf and Club Elysium and dashed to New York, a city that had received me warmly, regardless of my failings, mortal and otherwise.

Fiona's steadfast patience; Harry's flailings—oh, I simply cannot, for the life of me—pardon the jest—I simply cannot describe the scene. No one should be subjected to such disturbing recollections. Believe me when I tell you that Harry's vain endeavor at the noble game fell shorter than that of a beginner. His downswing had this odd halting motion that culminated in a flailing forward thrust with his whole body, forcing his extremities to end in a most unnatural arrangement. Still, bless his soul, I will voice this much in defense of Harrison Golub: he charged into the breech against odds greater than most men have dared encounter and like them failed heroically and miserably—unwept, unhonored, and unsung.

With a determination borne of a will few possess, Harry applied himself and scattered balls left and right, with many worming, dribbling, and daintily hopping their way aslant forward for negligible yardage; while on the opposite end of the practice area, Brewster Payne, under the tutelage of Charlie Maxwell, unerringly lofted golf balls 190 yards with a five iron which dropped them within a few feet of each other. Although I dislike Payne I did admire the classic beauty of his swing. We must give the devil his due.

I also marvelled at Fiona's self-possession and skill at golf as she devoted herself to the seemingly futile task of implanting golf fundamentals in our roma tomato. And so indeed did two passing members of the constabulary, tipping their caps to Fiona in admiration of her exquisite form. Without breaking step they continued their dogged pursuance of clues relative to the existence of a crazed combative ancient. Was he real, or was he a spirits-induced figment.

After an unbroken succession of mis-hits, Harry intermittently lofted a half-dozen balls a goodly distance somewhat west and east of target. Each passable shot was attended with shouts of rapturous glee by Harry, and Fiona's glowing praise. He allowed as how he was getting the hang of it, finally. As expected, Discord raised her ominous head, whereupon ball after ball hopped along like a startled toad and came to rest tauntingly in plain view a score of yards away.

"I'm hopeless."

"Nonsense. I've overworked you. You're tiring. It happens to everyone. Buck up, Harry. Near the end there you made a fine number of pitches—some really brilliant. With a bit of practice those shots will become second nature to you." As she might a puppy, she patted his head. "Practice, Harry, practice. Remember, Rome wasn't built in a day.

"No? How long did it take?"

"Eons, I expect."

"Great. Then I've got plenty of time."

"It isn't the time, Harry, it's the effort."

"Okay, I'll practice. I promise."

"That's my Harry. Are we on for our little tour later?"

"Absolutely."

"We meet in front of the golf museum; say, two o'clock?"

"It's a date, coach."

"Ta, Harry."

"And to you a toodle-loo and a ta too."

Instead of taking the direct path back to town, Fiona crossed West Sands Road and walked down to the beach. Harry guessed she chose skirting the course to avoid Brew. His eyes followed her as she strolled over the cement-hard sand with a shoe dangling from each hand. A steady breeze fluttered the hem of her light dress, exposing her shapely legs to well above the knees. She was, as poets throughout the ages have often expressed after similar sightings, a vision of loveliness.

Watching her produced in Harry the very same sensation of lightness and unclouded serenity that he experienced when he was about to consume a hot pastrami on rye, with kosher pickle on the side.

With spirit abounding he rounded up his scattered toads; ran out to the area in which he expected to retrieve the five or so with which he had connected. He could find one only; others were irrecoverable, successfully camouflaged in knee-high grasses. The lost balls did not in the least dampen the overall effect of the morning. With gear gathered, Harry shouldered his bag with military smartness and stepped off lively for his hotel and the prospect of a pleasant lunch, a refreshing shower, and another date with Fiona.

Brew was no longer with Charlie Maxwell. He had been replaced by Colin Mackay, a professional barely out of his teens. Mackay was a very attentive student. He took a few practice swings with his driver as Maxwell teed up a ball for him. Mackay addressed the ball, then with one slow motion drew back the club, and with an unhurried downswing struck the ball squarely. It soared over the range 280 plus yards.

"Yes!" called out Harry, pumping his arm.

Maxwell was not amused, but Mackay smiled to Harry and nodded an acknowledge thank you.

Harry waved and left. "Nice kid," he said to himself.

CHAPTER 11

It was the type of afternoon that challenged the unfettered to get off of their duffs and take to the out-of-doors. Golfers by the dozens were nervously swatting the air with their drivers while awaiting their tee-time on the first hole of the Old Course. How well I recollect the feeling I had when I nervously piled up a sand tee for my initial crack at this venerated shrine. Each golfer's recurrent mental image during every mile of the thousands of miles traveled to play here, had been a booming drive that parted the fairway. Picture perfect. But, the short delay before one's turn to tee off gives the dreamy mind ample time to insert previews of mis-hits of every conceivable variety. The intimidation factor is most assuredly provided by the nobility and renown of the Old Course and its unperceived hazards, and the additional panic of possibly not performing well in front of spectators, caddies, and fellow golfers standing by anticipating disaster. For the most part the better golfers are inured to these jitters. Not so the middle- and high-handicappers. Prior to inaugurating the backswing they have already lost conscious control of their minds and bodies. Yet, oddly enough, most come through with flying colors; for ofttimes, Golf, our ruling passion, conquers timidity. It can be a balm as well as a bur. Paraphrasing the old Jansenist—Golf has reasons that the mind cannot fathom.

Anxiously awaiting Fiona's arrival, Harry paced to and fro between the Royal and Ancient and the golf museum with a camera strapped around his neck. He snapped his camera at tourists entering and leaving the museum: Americans, Indians, Pakistanis, Germans, Swedes, Japanese, Italians. He guessed their nationalities by the accents overheard. After shooting a roll of film on these tourists he realized his effort lacked reflection. He had intended these snapshots to provide undisputed proof of the universality of golf when and if he should ever encounter a skeptic. But there would be no way he or anyone else could distinguish the homelands of these folk preserved in his photos because none were dressed in their native raiment. Their attire was in fact universally non-committal.

He reloaded his camera and took a picture of the Royal and Ancient clock. It was almost a minute past two. He adjusted his watch accordingly.

He counted circling seagulls: "One, two, three, four, five … ."

He looked at his watch. It was a few seconds beyond a minute after two. He looked up at the clock. Ditto.

From out of nowhere she materialized at his side, stunning in a pale green dress with matching darker green leather belt, shoulder bag, and shoes. And growing out of all that green sprouted her honey-colored hair with more chrysanthemum-like radiance than ever. Harry nearly swooned when Fiona greeted him with a light peck on the cheek.

Before he could master so much as a "hello" she grabbed his arm and whisked him into the museum.

Moments earlier in Crail, Mal, Phil, Tony, and Gunther had teed off on the short par three 18th. All landed safely on the green on a day that produced little wind on a course that usually blusters with stinging salt sea air.

"What a joy to play without Harry around," said Tony.

"I'm stuck with that hacker of hackers later today," bristled Phil. "I'll give anyone here a hundred dollars if he trades places with me tonight. Any takers?"

"Thanks, but no thanks," said Mal.

Gunther, away, was the first to putt. He stood over his ball chuckling, "I think Harry adds spice to our trip."

"If you consider hemlock spice," said Phil. "Two hundred—last offer."

Gunther, still enjoying Phil's squirming, sank his long putt.

"Gunther, want to add more spice to your humdrum life? I'll give you spicy Harry and two hundred smackers. What do you say?"

"I say he's all yours, you lost the draw."

"Gawd!" Phil then putted six feet beyond the hole, "Gawd!"

All putted out and headed for the clubhouse.

"Mal," asked Tony, "do you think Brew spent the night with that barmaid?"

"If not her then some other floozy. He seems to always find a playmate no matter where we go."

"She's a real looker."

"How does he do it?" asked Phil. "What's Brew got that I haven't got?"

"Looks," answered Gunther, "sex appeal, talent .. ."

"Up yours, Gunther. I beat you by three strokes."

CHAPTER 12

Out of consideration, dear friend, I shall not burden you with a running account of Fiona and Harry's tour of the golf museum's exhibits. I find it tedious. To be sure, it is a most worthy repository of matter and such pertinent to golf; but you must understand, I have long been acquainted with the game and its illustrious annals, its luminaries, and its ever-evolving equipment—which has of late been commanding far too much space. There is little merit to be found in a great many of the market-driven "aids" to golf betterment. A decent set of clubs and instruction from a qualified golf professional is, and always has been, the proper avenue toward achieving one's utmost ability on the course. But, back to the museum. I was pleasantly surprised to discover how fine a student of the game was Harrison Golub. His fund of trivia was encyclopedic. Before each display he overwhelmed Fiona with a flurry of relevant anecdotes, numbers, and dates. And to my astonishment, he got them right.

While holding forth before the Bobby Jones exhibit, Harry offered this quote: "'If I could choose just one golf course to play forever it would be the Old Course here in St. Andrews.' Bobby Jones said that, Fiona, in a place here called Younger Hall, when he was made an Honorary Burgess of the Borough. Up to that time he was only the second American so honored. The first was Benjamin Franklin. How about that?" Harry froze. "Whoa!—look over there."

Harry hurried to a photo display of Old Tom and Young Tom Morris. "Here they are. Gosh. Tom and Tommy—father and son."

"St. Andrews has produced a number of accomplished people," said Fiona, "but none more so in golf than the Morrises."

"For my money, Fiona, Tommy Morris and Bobby Jones were the greatest ever. They were the dominant players of their eras and had very short careers. Jones walked away from further competition at age 28, and Tommy Morris died when he was only 24."

"Nick Faldo is my choice," said Fiona, "and he's quite handsome."

"Sydney's favorite is Byron Nelson. Today most people argue the merits of Tiger Woods and Jack Nicklaus. But no matter who you choose you cannot deny the greatness of Tommy." Harry pointed to a display of clubs made by Old Tom, "Playing with those funny-looking old wood-shafted clubs Tommy kicked butt, winning four British Opens before he was 24 years old. Imagine that. He was unbeatable." Throughout his discourse Harry focused reverentially on an 1870s photograph of his idol and seemed to implore its image to resurrect itself.

Fiona took Harry's hand and pulled him out of the building. "Come, Harry, I've something to show you." After a brisk 15-minute walk they entered the Cathedral Churchyard at the east end of town. The roofless medieval ruin was surrounded by time-worn gravestones, many names and dates lost to the ages.

Some thirty yards before they reached their destination Harry recognized the statue of Tommy attached to a wall cluttered with memorial plaques to other dearly departed. He approached solemnly. There, for all time, posed Tommy with an open stance addressing a ball; mustachioed, doublebreasted jacket, Scotch bonnet with a natty tilt, eyes on the target, and holding a cleek with a baseball grip. Harry guessed he played cricket too. To be actually standing in proximity to the remains of a man who may rightly be considered the world's greatest golfer, and one of the most unfortunate of men, filled him with wonder and pity. Sensing Harry's absorption, Fiona stood apart. Harry was one degree away from weeping.

"Tommy," sighed Harry, "what a marvel you were."

A Japanese couple touring the cemetery stood nearby examining the Morris memorial. Harry ran up to them, "This man won four Opens; the first at age seventeen. He also made the Open's first hole-in-one."

The couple bowed politely.

Without asking, Harry handed the man his camera. He called to Fiona and led her in front of the statue. The kind fellow clicked their picture and returned the camera with another bow and went on his way.

"What," asked the Japanese wife, "was that silly man carrying on about?"

"How should I know, I don't speak Scottish."

An interjection here. Where I reside, all languages are known to us—even Esperanto and pig Latin. Why this is so I cannot explain. It's simply one of the perks in Elysium. Comes with the territory, you might say.

Still in the throes of strong emotion, Harry addressed Fiona, "Did you know that Tommy died of a broken heart on Christmas day?"

"Aye."

"The cause of his misery was the recent passing of his baby and wife during childbirth. Did you ever know a sadder story?"

"Never. I wonder if I'll ever find someone who'll love me half as much as young Tom loved his missus."

"I have no doubt of it; you'll have many to choose from."

"And," taking his arm, "you also, Harry Golub from New York."

Sadder, but more drawn together, they left the Cemetery. Soon after, they reached Fiona's house.

"Thank you so much for being my friend, Harry. When you come back to Scotland, please look me up. I shall always be delighted to see you. Bye." She kissed him on the cheek and hurried up stairs.

Harry mouthed the word "Bye" but emitted no sound.

Peering through the door curtain inside the hallway she watched Harry back away. He walked slowly down the street. She was unable to see that he was as downcast as she.

CHAPTER 13

Harry arrived at the Cleek an hour before the start of his antici-
pated round on the Old Course. He placed his clubs alongside those
of his fellow travelers. Full of high spirits he entered the Pub.

"Hi, guys."

Those pitiless assassins of joy stirred not, but groaned loudly.

Some astute observer said hatred is swifter than love to strike
down its victims, and that groan crushed Harry as if he'd been
felled by a piano. I remember a similar groan, but the context was
quite different. It was a groan of loss, not one of perceived eminent inconvenience. It was a concerted groan dislodged by members of my London club, the Camelopard, Chelsea, following the
unexpected announcement by our bereft provost, Blackstone
Wilburforce, regarding the retirement of our celebrated chef,
Rabindranath Bangaloree. Sri Bangaloree had dutifully provided
Camelopardians with the sub-continent's most toothsome fare for
two-score years. Who of us could forget his ambrosial Chef-
d'oeuvre, mango biryani with shredded asafoetida, cracked carda-
mom, pan-roasted dal, and the whole served in an indecorous
clay pot but brought to masterly refinement by a well-appointed
dollop of yoghurt amidst a flourish of coriander. Visually and
gustatorily smashing. Ah, Rabindranath, sainthood awaits you—
but certainly not the groaners in the Cleek.

"Greetings, Mr. Harry Golub," said Cameron Flett from behind the bar.

Brew's agitation was palpable, "Look, gentlemen, it's New York's gift to Scottish links and lasses."

Ignoring the hostiles, Harry sat at the end of the bar. Cam poured him a cup of tea.

"Your lesson went well, I take it?"

"Went better than expected, far-and-away better. It was terrific ... wonderful ... ex ... ."

"It was wonderful, terrific," mimicked Phil to his mates.

Harry addressed Cam with a touch of bravura, "Few more lessons from Fiona and I'll take on those guys even money."

"Not in your wildest dreams," scoffed Tony.

Phil, deliberately taunting and insulting, "Fiona? Fiona? Say, Brew, you gave a certain Fiona a few lessons yourself, didn't you?"

Brew smiled lewdly.

"Cool it, Phil," warned Gunther.

"Phil, lay off," demanded Mal.

Undaunted, Phil pressed on. "Tell me, did she find your lessons fantastic, wonderful, outstanding?"

"Outstanding? Oh, outstanding indeed."

Mal, Tony, and Gunther shifted uneasily in their seats. Cam's outrage caused him to gnaw the stem off his pipe. Harry quietly rose from his stool, picked up an abandoned half full glass of beer from the end of the bar, carried it to where Brew sat and turned it over onto his head. Brew leaped to his feet and drove Harry over a chair and down to the floor. Wide-eyed, he lay on his back expecting to be pummeled. Phil propelled himself toward Harry but was restrained by Gunther. Mal and Tony held Brew as he straddled Harry.

Brandishing a mashie poised for a vigorous downswing, Cam charged into the affray—left arm straight, full shoulder turn, knees slightly bent, head steady, grip firm. "Hold on, there! Nobody move an inch."

Mal, Tony, and Gunther forcefully hauled Brew outside.

Phil shadow-boxed above Harry and challenged him to get

off the floor and take him on. Cam jabbed Phil in the ribs with the blade of his club, "Begone ye bloody filthy-mouthed son of pig snot! Begone, or I'll loft yer foul head from yer pestilent carcass."

Phil strutted to the door, "As you wish old man, as you wish."

"Enough!" Cam ran at him, "Get out!"

Phil dashed for his life.

Cam snarled at the door, "And don't ye pack o' worms come back."

Harry sat up. "Boy-oh-boy."

Cam helped him to his feet, brushed him off and led him back to his bar stool. Harry shook from head to foot.

"To yersel', Harry m'lad. I toast yer chivalrous nature."

"Chivalrous? I ended up on my tokus."

"Aye, but in defense of a fair lady's honor. 'Twas a noble and braw gesture."

"You really think so?"

"That I do."

They click teacups, "Cheers."

"That was dumb," admonished Mal as he drew Brew aside from the others.

"That cretin splashed beer all over me!" he fumed while drying his head with a towel.

"And with damn good reason. You cannot talk abusively about women in public. And the guy you dropped just happens to be the person your sponsor sent over here to have a good time." Brew attempted to walk away. Mal yanked him around. "Listen to me. Your sponsor likes Harry. Harry sells hundreds of his clubs. Your sponsor has a vested interest in the guy. Lots of those clubs have your name on them, for cryin' out loud. Use your head, Brew."

"Gawd, I hate that little … it annoys the hell out of me that that twerp … what does she see in him?"

"I'm sure I don't know. Listen, you've got to put this Fiona business behind you. It's unlike you to become this attached to one of your groupies."

"She's not a groupie. She's not like the others."

"Well whatever she is she's causing you to not think straight. Wow, if the media got wind of this you'd be history. Think of that. You've got to apologize."

"No way."

"You've got no choice. Apologize now."

"Dammit, you're right. Gawd, I'd rather shoot myself in the foot" He took a deep breath. "Well, here goes nothing."

Brewster Payne re-entered the Cleek and Thistle attempting a look of total humiliation that was far from convincing. Eager to get done with his miserable task he sought out Harry straightaway. Cam grabbed his mashie; Harry raised his teacup in the launch mode.

"Harry," said Brew with gall rising in his throat, "Harry, I want to apologize for what I did."

"It's not what you did that bothers me as much as what you and Phil said."

"We were wrong on all counts. We're sorry." He reached out his hand.

Harry, relieved, accepted it. "It's all forgotten, Brew. Let me buy you a drink."

"No!" spoken more sharply than he should have. Then, with an attempt at civility, "Thanks anyway. See you on the tee." He left abruptly.

"Well, Cam, waddaya think?"

"He dinna act nor sound sincere, Harry. I'm convinced he's still the same unrepentant scoundrel." He looked out the window. "Weel noo, look ye here."

Harry joined him. Outside Brew was re-enacting for Mal his apology to Harry, and feigning a gag. They laughed heartily.

"What a dirty, rotten, two-faced, scum bag butt-pimple," said Harry.

"Aye, me very words."

They returned to the bar. "Think I'll sit here a minute to cool off," said Harry. His blood was still warm and aroused. It was the first time he had initiated a fight—and a barroom brawl, at that. Even though he came out on the short end, he felt great satisfaction. He could feel mettle straightening his backbone. Never again would he lick hands that flogged him.

Cam gave the ceiling a pensive gaze. "All lives are bound by destiny, Harry. You are a good man. Good times await you. But that lot … I feel certain that there is some discomforting circle below awaiting them; if not, they are surely creating their own torment here and now."

"Who knows. Maybe they'll wake up and join the human race."

"Not bloody likely."

CHAPTER 14

The five high-spirited young men executing deep knee-bends, leg-stretches, waist-twists, and swinging two clubs at a time beside the Old Course 1st tee impressed me with their athleticism. Their graceful actions suggested the robust figures represented pictorially around ancient Greek amphorae, with one major difference—the Brew crew were fully, though casually, clothed. Their spirits were further heightened by a warm golden evening and, for the moment, the absence of one Harrison Golub. They moved about as if stirred from within by Terpsichorean strains.

The Nordic threesome about to tee off were duly affected by the jubilant Yanks and, casting aside their deep-rooted brooding reserve, talked openly together for the first time of the unalloyed happiness August Strindberg and Ingmar Bergman had ushered into their collected psyche. Upon that note my vision suddenly metamorphosed from amphora to urn and on to Keats' depictions of Arcadian youths gamboling off to witness a pagan sacrifice. It then struck me how thrilling it would be to have the muttonheaded Brew crew similarly offered to, say, Polyphemus. Just a fleeting thought. Never, never would I subscribe to such a victimization. Nor would you. But, as Eurydice Greenways used often to say, "Ernest, sometimes an impaired speculation can charm the knickers off of one for a moment with none the wiser." She'd then scrabble my hair and hurry home to bake biscuits. When she came of age she opened a tea shop in Bath and eventually eloped with a bald Indian sitar plucker. After a spell she disappeared altogether. Eurydice was ever enchanting and mysterious, and, beyond question, bonkers. But enough of this. Let us return to Brew, Mal, Tony, Gunther, and Phil.

"Oh, oh, lookee there," pointed Tony.

Harry had just shouldered his clubs in front of the Cleek and was hurrying as fast as his short legs permitted. He held up play as the Nordics waited for him to cross Grannie Clark's Wynd.

One of the Northmen addressed the group behind, "Would anyone here join with us to make foursome?"

"Yes! Me!" whooped Phil.

"I am Jan."

"Phil."

"I am Walther."

"Phil."

"I am Karl."

"Phil." They shook hands in turn.

The second Harry cleared the fairway Walther hit a booming drive. In order, Jan, Karl, and Phil also drove the ball well.

"Later, gentlemen," Phil beamed to his friends as he marched down the fairway stride for stride with his new-found comrades from the land of pickled fish, lingonberries, and melancholy.

Harry arrived on the tee panting heavily and flushed as a vine-ripened Bonnie Best. "That Phil I saw with those guys?"

Brew ignored him completely.

"Guess he thought you weren't coming," said Mal indifferently.

"Weren't coming!" Harry was crushed. "Hell, I lived for this moment. What a rat. When ... who ... guess I'll have to play along with you guys."

"Not allowed," said Tony, "foursomes are the limit and we're maxed out. Tough break."

"Damn that Phil."

All but Gunther were delighted by Harry's blighted hope. "There is a bright side to this, Harry."

"Oh, yeah."

"Sure, you are the last scheduled golfer. No one behind rushing you along. You can play at your own pace."

"Shut up, Gunther," admonished Mal, "Brew's teeing off."

Soon, they were gone.

As if abandoned by a pirate crew, Harry stood forlorn and alone surrounded by a sea of green. The steeple clock read 6:50; daylight would begin to wane in a couple of hours. The starter was closing his booth for the day. Harry ran to him.

"I'd like to hire a caddie."

"Much too late, sir. Caddie's are either finishing up or have gone off for the day. Enjoy your game, sir. Good evening."

Walking back to the tee Harry watched two players putting out on the 18th. One player had use of a caddie. He tipped the caddie and left with his partner. The caddie was slowly walking away counting his day's earnings.

Harry called out to him, "Hey, there! Mister! Mister!"

He turned and saw Harry waiving. "Wadya be addressin' m'sel', sir?"

"Are you a caddie?"

"Aye, that I am."

"I need a caddie … now … I don't know my way around the course, and I really want to share my experience with somebody. Whaddaya say?"

"It's a wee late tae be startin' a roun'. And, m'sel'—I've had a lang day o' it."

"I'll pay you double," Harry begged.

The caddie glanced at the steeple clock, almost 7:00, and weighed Harry's offer. "Dooble, ye say?"

"Here, I'll pay you now."

He accepted the Bank of Scotland notes and counted them. "Weel, if ye are feelin' despeerit fae my assistance, sir, I dinna see hoo I cad in guid conscience leave ye stranded. Mind ye noo, I wi' no be oot on the links when the sun gae doon."

"Fair enough. My name's Harry," joyfully extending his hand.

"Mackegan, sir."

"Mackegan. You're the first Mackegan I ever met."

"Aye, there be those that fear I may be the last o' the Mackegans."

He took Harry's clubs and handed him the driver.

Harry teed up and stood behind the ball with an expression of ecstasy and reverence. By degrees he surveyed the course before him.

"Ye had better be stroking' the ba', sir, or weel ne'er feenish afore dark."

Harry addressed his ball with the utmost cordiality, then swung as if to do it permanent injury. The Top-Flite sauntered lazily off to the right and came to rest 20 paces away. The cuss or curse Mackegan expected after such a piddling performance did not follow. Instead, he watched Harry nearly leap for joy.

Mackegan frowned painfully, "I got me a bludie daft duffer." He took the driver from Harry and toweled off the dirt.

Standing behind his wayward ball, Harry examined the fairway ahead with what would appear to an onlooker as a practiced eye. Mackegan did not know what to make of him.

"What do I use from here, Mackegan?"

"I wad suggest a 3-wood, sir, to gie us free o' this roughage and doun the fairway."

"Oops!" The second shot wormed forward an increment. Still in the rough. "Think I took my eye off that one. Maybe I moved my head. You happen to notice what I did wrong?"

"Weel, sir, I'm no ane tae gie advice; but I dae ken that wi' peerserverence a' things wull fa' intae place."

"My sentiments, too. Practice, practice, practice." This positive nature did not desert Harry even though two piteous shots had still left him 340 yards shy of the green on a hole measuring 370 yards.

Harry may be dangerous, Mackegan thought, a worthy candidate for the psychotherapeutic clinic. Best stay cautiously on guard. He stood back twenty feet from his charge, "Mak guid use o' the sel'same club, sir."

Fiona's instruction did not augment Harry's ability one iota. His next two shots were low rollers; the second dropping out of sight when it entered the Swilcan Burn. Mackegan took a long pull from his flask.

"I think my ball went in that river."

"Aye. 'Ti s nae but a wee burn, sir. I'll feesh it oot." Using a pitching wedge, Mackegan ceftly flipped the ball up and on to the fairway.

Harry dribbled it back in.

Mackegan jumped down into the burn and tossed the ball on the far side.

"Shouldn't the drop be over here?"

"Substantial leeberties air permitted whun playin' the Auld Coorse this late in the day, sir."

"I see what you mean," said Harry looking at the sun descending toward the horizon. He hurried his next series of shots: the first flew over the green; he topped two chips; the next landed nicely on the green; he then four-putted. The last a five-incher. "Yes!" he yelled. "Gimme five, Mackegan." They slapped hands.

Glowing from inside out, Harry looked back to the tee and recreated in his mind each stroke. "Well, Mackegan ol' buddy, how'd I do?"

"Admirable, sir." Tallying the scorecard, "Fifteen … only eleven strokes ower par fae the first hole."

"Wow. Really? Not bad. Not bad at all." He was genuinely pleased.

"Weel doon, sir, weel doon." Then to himself, "Weel doon as a thrice-roasted nut."

Clouds appeared out of the eastern sky and scudded across the low lying full moon. The wind picked up.

On the 2nd tee Harry's first swing was a whiff. With his second effort the ball scooted off to the right. Harry danced over to his ball. He was boyishly rhapsodic. "The most famous golf course in the world, and I'm playing it! Yes!" and struck the air with his fist.

"Desecrating it, belike," muttered the caddie before draining his flask.

CHAPTER 15

At that precise moment an aureate glow illuminated the interior of a large thicket three holes ahead. Uncannily, the glow was confined and did not filter out through the furze into the deepening twilight enclosing the Links. Two male figures from a bygone age stood within. The older man sported a patriarchal grey beard and wore a tweed jacket and plus fours. The younger man's attire was more in keeping with golf wear a generation earlier, and he was crowned with a Scotch bonnet. The attentive respectful young man was unearthly, the pale essence of a man, scarcely visible. The senior figure was a complete corporeal person and exhibited a nature both vigorous and strong-willed. These two souls were father and son: Old Tom Morris and Tommy, illustrious citizens of St. Andrews whose names and heroics will forever bring glory to our fair burgh.

Standing in the middle of the thicket, Old Tom was holding a golf club and discoursing with self-satisfaction: "… it's balanced by this wee dab o' iron that fell oot o' the nicht sky and dropped tae this verra spot. And this, Tommy," with a sweeping gesture, "this is Scotland's maist enchanted bit o' groun'."

"How sae, dad?"

"Where ye noo stand, lad, I unearthed the wee meteorite I've implanted in this driver. And close to hand Bishop Seaton fell under the blaws o' marauding Danes a thousand years syne. That sainted father's blessed blude sanctifies this plot. And deerectly aneath ower feet lies the holy spring which \… ."

"I see nae spring."

"Ach, ye were a wee bairn when I redesigned the Auld Coorse and covered the spring." Annoyed by the recollection: "Tae mony peelgrims came dipping intae its holy waters and held up play on the links. Noo, where was I? Ach, aye. The revered rowan o' ower forefathers floorishes here; hooiver, ane element was missin', the ane element that wad endow this charmed spot wi' suffeecient magic to roun' oot my task."

"Wha element, dad?"

Tom Morris proudly pointed to a tiny plant encircled with rowan berries. Its significance was lost on Tommy.

"Dae ye no ken, Tommy?' he prodded. The ectoplasmic young man bent down to peruse the botanical closely but could not identify it.

With jubilation, "It's the michty oak, son!"

"Wha I see is nae michty but a wee oak new-hatched frae a nut."

"Size is no important. It's its presence here that is essential. I needed jist a wee touch o' it. Ye see, Tommy my boy," with increasing excitement, "this wee oak, as ye deescribe it, was maist sacred tae the druids, an rightfully sae. And noo—God be praised—and noo its spreadin' roots hae commingled untae itsel' a' the mystical qualities o' this hallowed groun'."

Had Tommy been any less visible he'd have been as completely in the dark as was his understanding.

Holding the club aloft in triumph, "Tommy, I hae a' these qualities in this verra driver I've made fae ye." Then happily added, "This dandy bit o' wark is the trick ye need tae trounce that blasted Jones fellow!"

"But, dad, that wad be dishonest."

"Dishonest!? Nae, son. 'Tis but a slicht betterment. Listen, lad, Bobby Jones and his upstart compatriots had the benefit o' a technology far in advance o' owers. Sae why should we be stuck fae eternity wi' ancient implements when this braw number wull turn the trick prettily. Use the club, Tommy. Ye'll master Jones every roun'."

"Nae, dad, I'll no use sorcery to best Bobby. He's an honorable lad and my guid friend. I wull no stoop tae deceit. As it stands, I'm ane o' the verra few that dae beat him on occaseeon."

"Efter a' the years I've waited fae the arrival o' this wee oak; and efter a' the time I've spent putin' my hand tae the magic, and hae it come tae nocht."

"Ach, dear, dear dad. Yer time had been better spent wi' mair celestial undertakin's. Yer lads hae been missin' ye on the coorse. Ye've gang aglee. Departed frae yer guidsel'."

"How departed?"

"For ane, ye shouldna linked yersel' wi' Isabel Goudie. The wretched witch is incurably daft."

"Daft is she! It's dae tae her unsparin' assistance that I hae fasheeoned this magical club fae ye, my boy. Ye should no be unacceptin' o' the artistic temperament."

"Dad, ye maun ken she's an unrepentant loony. O' a' the mony executed witches in Elysium she singularly insists in walkin' amang us toasted tae a crisp and snarlin' like a veecious doig."

"Ach, lad, we are a' strange in ower ain way."

"Look at ye noo—flesh and bluid. Isabel Goudie hae turned yer haid. Nae Club Elysium soul has ever, tae my mind, allowed hissel' tae be materialized. Ye've gane tae far wi' this business. Baneeshment is a possibility, dad. Gie it some thocht. Remember it's God's grace that we air here. Dae no tempt His displeasure."

"It were a necessity, lad. Only a corporeal bein' could manufacture this club. It's like dinna exist in Elysium. Makin' it was nae easy task. Mony a nicht my een were lashed by this infernal whin; I've cut my hand in twa places, and they still smart. It's the first time I've felt pain these hundred years. And my progress was delayed twa nichts syne when a besotted caddie wandered intae my warkplace and peed on that verra ring o' rowan. He'll no dae that again. I tapped the blichter on the shoulder wi' my club while he was relievin' hissel' and frichtened the wits oot o' him. Ach, son, ye shoulda seen him. He bolted like a flushed roebuck wi' his tail awaggin'. I was hot on his heels a' the way tae the Road Hole. The puir deil wet hissel' frae his knees tae his shoon. I felt justified in houndin' him at the time, but noo I regret it and dae hope I've no caused him permanent mental anguish. I truly hope the episode may induce him to gie up demon spirits."

"I agree. Weel, dad, I maun gae noo. I hae a tee-time wi' Miss Wethered."

"Afore ye gae, wull ye no try it ance," he pleaded offering the club"

"Nae, dad. I'm sure it's a braw driver." Tommy drifted away, his voice trailing, "Ye ever were a master at yer craft." He evaporated into space.

"Ach, Tommy, Tommy, the greatness that's in ye is mair than goff. I'll no yet chuck the club; ye micht change yer mind."

Tom was not alone; a charred-limbed five-foot tall burnt log, smoldering and crackling, appeared beside him. The log spoke: "Yer bairn disna tak tae yer wa' o' thocht, mister."

"Ach, I wish he wad. Is he nae the greatest goffer o' a' time, Isabel?"

"Aye, surely he is 'at," she growled.

"My bonnie boy entered Elysium wi' clubs that dinna serve him weel. His reasonin' is unsoun'. He feels obliged tae remain true tae his ain era and thereby puts hissel' at a considerable disadvantage against these newer arrivals with clubs and ba's o' a maist superior nature. It is unfair tae him."

"Aye, and a father's pride."

"Shall we proceed, Isabel?"

"Aye, mister, 'tis the last phase: the cantraip."

"Verra weel. Corbies bleezin …"

"Nae, nae, no yit," was her surly interruption. "Ye maun hold ye club ower the buried spring. Mind, an agreement ower runnin' water is bindin', and can only be undoon the sel'same wa'."

Solemnly, Tom Morris with arms outstretched before him and holding the club across his open palms stood above the spring marked by the oak and ring of rowan. The crisp smoldering witch, Isabel Goudie, faced him, embers pulsating in parts of her.

When she spoke her voice took on a toneless, metallic quality. "The cantraip," she growled. "A' taegither noo."

Corbies bleezin cauld kail,
Rooks pick shellin-hill,
Green warms in the hairst aits,
Maukins in the kill.
Jinglan, inglan, jinglan, jill.
Gaberlunzie hae yer fill.

"Repeat efter me, mister: Water be me witness."

"Water be my witness."

"'Tis doon. The implement be charmed."

"How dae ye ken it'll wark, Isabel?"

"The power o' this cantraip be a kent specific syne the time o' the Picts. It alwa's warks as lang as ye dinna see a snail afore dawn."

"I thank ye, Isabel, wholeheartedly. I'd kiss ye but I'm afeared o' scorchin' m' lip."

"It were a pleasure warkin' wi' ye, mister. Ye are a trew and tangible frien'. Ta."

"Fareweel."

Tom took in the full measure of his creation; its weight, balance, feel and aesthetics. To his mind it attained perfection on all points. He took a proper stance and swung skillfully at a loose pebble, propelling it out of the thicket and high into the nearly night sky. The stone lighted on the fairway 300 yards away, in line with the pin. Everything felt right. Thoroughly pleased, he sat on a rock and began a final light sanding of the hickory shaft. He felt and admired its smoothness. He produced a pen knife and started carving his initials on the top of the clubhead, singing all the while.

Come under my plaidie, the night's gaun to fa';
Come in frae the cauld blast, the drift, and the snaw;
Come under my plaidie and sit down beside me,
There's room in't, dear lassie, believe me, for twa.
Come under my plaidie and sit down beside me,
I'll hap ye frae ev'ry cauld blast that can blaw;
Come under my plaidie, and sit down beside me,
There's room in't, dear lassie, believe me, for twa ...

CHAPTER 16

Mackegan had become quite tipsy and fidgety walking behind Harry as they advanced to the 5th tee. Harry continued in a state of bliss, unmindful of his caddie's mounting fear.

"On the links at nicht ..." spoke Mackegan, peering nervously about, "on the links at nicht there be ba's whizzin' aboot, and demon laughter and shoutin'."

"Baloney, pure baloney."

Mackegan stared the full moon in the face and shuddered. "On certain moonlicht nichts ... ." Golf clubs jostled as he hustled to be close to Harry. "On certain moonlicht nichts the Auld Coorse is taen ower by speerits. Aye. Their gaein' on hae driven braw lads tae strang drink." He uncapped his flask and shook it above his upturned mouth. He was profoundly disappointed. "No e'en a wee drap," he sniveled.

A large black cloud obscured the moon. Standing on the darkened 5th tee, Harry and Mackegan became shapeless figures. Harry peered ahead. "Where's the green?"

Mackegan, exasperated, "Ye canna see the green nor the flag this time o' nicht, sir. Ye canna see yer hand afore yer face. And if, perchance, ye were tae strike the ba' moderately weel, it'll no be foun'."

"You worry far too much, Mackegan. If we lose a ball, we'll play another. I brought plenty."

"Aye, like a' crazed mon, " he muttered, "nae sense but plenty o' ba's."

"Try to keep an eye on this one," Harry said, just prior to executing a forceful downswing. He ripped a low screamer off to the right.

Old Tom was in the middle of carving his last initial when he was bowled over by a wicked blow to the head. "Ay! Ay! Ayayayayay! Ohhhhh! Ohh!"

"Ay! Ay! Ayayayayay!" the sharp shrill cry issued out of the adjacent shrubbery. Mackegan threw down Harry's golf bag and dashed toward town for refuge. Harry, fraught with concern, hurtled blindly into the thicket. He fought his way through the tangle and fell headlong into a lucent clearing. He leaped up with Old Tom's club in hand. Deep concern and astonishment filled him as he beheld an elderly bearded man in plus fours whirling about in pain and vigorously rubbing his head.

"Oh! Ayayayayay!"

"Oh, m'God. I'm sorry. I'm so sorry."

"Ohhh."

Full of remorse, Harry approached the injured party. His presence startled Tom. In his dazed condition he mistook the golf club in Harry's hands for the object that caused the growing knot on his head. He shied away from a repeated attack. Nae! gae awa'!"

Harry advanced, proffering the club. "I'm awfully sorry, mister. It was an accident. How can I help?"

Tom, disoriented, "Nae, nae, ye daft Yank—the club is no mine."

"Not mine either."

"Than I gie it tae ye." Tom and the light dissolved into darkness.

"Hey, mister! Hey! Come back! Where'd he go? Yooohoooo!" Harry stood alone in the spooky gloom encompassed by complete silence. He slowly and cautiously groped and scratched his way back out of the furze guided by moonbeams piercing through the spiny branches. "Ouch! Ouch! Ouchouchouch!"

Mackegan was nowhere to be found. "Mackegan! Mackegan! Now that guy's up and vanished, too. What in blazes is going on?" Harry dropped Tom's club across his bag and brushed himself off. It was too dark to continue. He picked up Tom's club and tried to examine it in the moonlight. It was old, odd, and unappealing. He took a ball out of his pocket and dropped it on the ground. He addressed it with the old club; then struck it squarely. He picked up his bag and put Tom's club in it, and all the while the ball was still sailing over the fairway, landing and settling inches from the pebble hit by Tom. Harry had no idea of what had taken place after he struck the ball. He walked back to town.

"Well, I got to play the Old Course. Can honestly tell people I shot a 68. Don't need to tell them I played only four holes. Mackegan? Whatever happened to him? Got spooked, I bet. Hope the old duck I brained is okay. Had a fight with Brew. Had a date with Fiona. Wow. This has been some day. Darn it, I hate to leave this place."

CHAPTER 17

Morning in the old town was favored with sunshine. Little notice was given to Hamish Macpherson heaving golf bags and luggage into the awaiting van; Brew, Mal, Tony, and Gunther stood apart discussing whether to admit membership in their country club to Mr. Enzo Saltalamacchia, an uncultured immigrant who became a billionaire builder of tunnels and bridges. Brew, Mal, and Tony were against his petition; Mal, on the grounds that his boisterous aggressiveness ill-suited dignified society, and whose presence would intrude on close, long-established relationships among club members, some dating to pre-colonial times, much prior to the onrush of incompatible "undesirables" from the Mediterranean regions. Tony feared Mr. Saltalamacchia would sully the club's highly refined menu by introducing meatballs. Brew felt strongly that the builder would reduce the intellectual quality of conversation in the lounge and card room to an elemental level accented with a crude lingo and irritable gestures. There was also the belief among all that Mr. Saltalamacchia undoubtedly had connections with unsavory characters from one of the Boroughs.

Despite these antitheses, Gunther, who, bit by bit, was becoming more receptive to the world outside the restrictive conformity of his caste, reminded his friends that Mr. Enzo Saltalamacchia had donated millions to charities that assisted the underprivileged and poor.

In rebuttal, Brew and Tony agreed with Mal that the fellow's largesse would serve society better had he endowed business schools so that the world's cheap-labor pools would always have bright, shiny new capitalists on hand to hire workers out of them. Mal further suggested, and they unanimously concurred, how infinitely considerate it would be if Mr. S. purchased the adjoining truck farm and constructed for the club an additional nine holes. Such a gesture would certainly warrant a trial membership.

A blaze of energy in the person of Phil shot out of the Bishop Seaton Hotel.

"Listen, everybody! Guess what? Harry's staying here!"

All, save Hamish, were pleased as punch.

"Harry said he'd meet us at the airport in Glasgow."

Glee quickly faded from Brewster Payne when struck with suspicions of Fiona spending more time with Harry Golub: "She wouldn't ... she couldn't ... not him. Naaah."

"The guy's a hundred per cent idiot," spoke Phil. "Says he wants to polish his game here in St. Andrews. Can you believe it?"

"How does one polish what does not exist?" asked Tony.

Hamish finished loading. He slammed the door shut. "Gentlemen, we're off to Muirfield," he snapped.

"Let's get the hell out of here before he changes his mind," blurted Phil.

The telephone in Harry's room rang.

"Hello."

"Hello, hello, Harry? It's me, Sydney."

"Sydney, how are you?"

"Fine, Harry, wonderful even, couldn't be better. I'm calling to tell you I saw on the television a Scotchman in a plaid skirt, like you he looked, Harry, exactly almost. A spitting image even. Harry, he could be your twin."

"Was it during a Brewster Payne interview?"

"Harry, you saw it too?"

"That was me, Sydney. You saw me on TV."

"Oh, Harry, you are a celebrity person. You on the television? No kiddin'?"

"Yup."

"Harry you looked like a real Scotchman—the chief of a clan even. That's what the sports person said."

"Wade Diggs said that?"

"With you he was quite impressed, Harry."

Harry looked in the mirror and puffed his chest, "And those schmucks said you looked like a bonnie lassie. You're a Highland Baron, you are."

"What schmucks, Harry? What bonnie Lassie? And who's Baron?"

Coming to himself, "Tell you all about it when I get home."

"Everything's okay?"

"Perfect, terrific, great … bonnie."

"Bonnie, he says. That's good, Harry, you're learning Scotch already. My Ruthie sends her love. You keep enjoying up there. Things at the store ain't the same without you. You're a hard worker and a nice vacation you deserve."

"Thanks, Sydney, and thanks for calling. See you next week."

"Bye, Harry."

"Cheerio."

Sydney laughed, "Now he goes with the cheerio. Oh, Harry, such a mensch you are."

"… what could you possibly see in that twerp?" asked an incredulous Brew standing outside Fiona's front door.

Curious eyes from within the idling van curbside focussed on him.

"Many things, thank you," replied Fiona standing in the doorway, "all of them commendable."

"For instance?" he challenged.

"He is a gentleman, which you are not. He is considerate …"

"Aw, come off it, Fiona—he's a bumbling half-wit and you know it."

"I know no such thing. He is considerate. He has a sense of humor, in which you are totally lacking. And he is truthful—which you definitely are not. Shall I go on?"

Conscious of losing face in front of his friends he spoke more quietly and with a touch of futility, "He's squat, he's ... good Gawd, Fiona, Harry's a babbling idiot. I know you, you're using him to get back at me. Right?"

"What cheek. Never have you been so wrong. It seems you know absolutely nothing about me or Mr. Harrison Golub. So, really, you should not concern yourself with us." She stepped back to close the door.

Brew held it open and whispered, "But what about us? Last summer?"

"A grave mistake. Yesterday I discovered the truth about you.

"What truth?"

"You are a liar and a deceiver." She glanced down at the van. "And you chum around with the rudest people I've ever encountered. Maybe someday you'll see yourself for who you really are ... then maybe you'll change for the better. Meantime ... we are history. I wish you well."

Mal called out to Brew, "Macpherson says we're running late!"

"And I'm running late for work. Goodbye, Brew," and closed the door.

Aloud, so that all could hear, "I'll be back and we can straighten this all out."

He swaggered back to the van. With false bluster, "She'll come around. They always do."

"Looks like little Harry's gonna have free rein," Phil taunted.

"Shut up!"

CHAPTER 18

Walking briskly and cheerily through town and down along The Links, Harry felt free and easy for the first time since he left New York City a week earlier. Without a tight itinerary to adhere to and without Brewster Payne and his mates berating him, he was able to take pleasure in small things: the sun's brightness and warmth; the air's freshness sparked with the tang of salt; the cries of winging seafowl; and the click, crack, and thump of struck golfballs near and far. His spirits elevated to such a high pitch that he felt compelled to sing sotto voce in the range of a coloratura: "When a body meet a body, comin' through the rye …"

He blithely viewed everything around as if noticing them for the first time: golfers, Swilcan Bridge, happy tourists, quaint shops, the woolen mill store, the golf shop with a life-sized cut-out figure of an old-time golfer propped by the entrance. It struck a familiar note, as did the Cleek and Thistle a wedge shot ahead.

Harry entered the Cleek with the familiarity of a long-standing customer. "I'm home!" he called out.

Cam stopped mid-sip of his "tea" and Fiona ceased dusting the back bar. There were a dozen or so convivial patrons engaged in meaningful converse anent golf, Euros, and the good-natured rivalry between the Rangers and Celtics. "Harry, it is you, isn't it?" said a delightfully surprised Fiona. "I thought you'd left us."

Harry sat next to Cam at the bar. "Decided to spend the rest of my vacation here in St. Andrews. I cut loose of those clowns I came with until we fly back home."

"Aye, a bad lot they are, Harry," said Cam. "Yer good to be free of them."

"Sure, and Cam's right."

"I love this town and everything in it; even our good friend, Cameron Flett, master of pub and club." Harry patted Cam's shoulder.

"How sweet you are, Harry," said Fiona. "We were beginning to miss you."

She placed a cup of coffee before Harry and Cam slid over a bottle of scotch; Harry smiled thanks but no thanks.

Cam acknowledged a signal from one of the booths and got up to draw a pitcher of ale.

"Fiona, I'm gonna be here in town for a few more days. Is there any chance you could give me another lesson?"

After a moments pause, "Better yet, Harry, why don't we play later this afternoon. I'm totally free."

"When and where?"

"I'm partial to The Jubilee. Five suit you?"

"You're on."

She excused herself and delivered the pitcher Cam filled with ale to two men in a booth. Harry's eyes followed her with pleasure. Never in his life had he felt brazen enough to look so long and longingly at such a lovely creature. Her walk, her talk, her casual acceptance of him tingled his nerves. The men in the booth, Americans on holiday, flirted with her and she with them. All in good fun. She returned to Harry with a curious look.

"By-the-by, Harry, Cam said Angus Mackegan burst into the Cleek last evening frightened out of his wits again! Said he was caddying for you. And that you hit a ghost with a golf ball. Is it true, Harry?"

Amused by her gullibility, "Hardly a ghost ... just some odd old duck wearing knickers."

"He said it was the very same ghost that chased him two nights past."

"The old geezer might have chased me too if the tables hadn't turned on him. I got in the first blow … didn't mean to. It was an accident. My ball slid off the end of my club and bonked him. I tried to help, but he dropped his club and ran off somewhere. I wanted to give him back his club but it was too dark by that time and I really didn't want to wander around out there looking for a mad man, so I came back to town. Boy-o-boy, I sure hope he's okay."

Harry's tale gripped Fiona with keen interest. "You have his golf club?"

"It's in my bag."

"How does it look?"

"It's a funky old thing."

"Cam, I believe Harry actually saw Old Tom."

"Aye."

"What is it with you people and ghosts? You two and my caddie. Pull yourselves together, there are no spooks on this golf course or anywhere else on this planet."

"We beg to differ," said Fiona in a solemn tone, "there have been far too many sightings of spirits over the years to simply ignore these recent encounters out-of-hand."

"Aye."

Harry, cynically, "And there's a Loch Ness monster, too."

"Nessie does exist," pronounced Fiona. "Mind, Harry, you are in the land that gave rise to Halloween."

"Aye," spoke Cam, "Scotland boasts the world's largest variety of other-worldlies."

Harry shook his head at vanished reason.

Fiona looked Harry square in the eye and counted off, "Ghosts, goblins, elfs, fairies, ferlies, kelpies, witches, warlocks … ."

"Never heard of some of these things," said Harry. "You guys are putting me on, right? I mean, really, ferlies, warlocks … you're making this up. Warlocks? What are warlocks?"

"Male witches," said Cam.

Let warlocks grim an' wither'd hags
Tell how wi' you on ragweed nags
They skim the muirs, an' dizzy crags
Wi' wicked speed.

"Robert Burns?" asked Harry.

"Aye."

"It is odd, Harry, don't you think, that Cam and I, who have not seen a spirit, are believers, and you who have seen the ghost of Old Tom, are not?"

Harry acquiesced, "There's no arguing with faith."

The Cleek was brought to capacity with the arrival of a cheery party of two mixed foursomes from Cumberland.

"Think I'll explore town a bit," said Harry, vacating his seat, "maybe treat a goblin to lunch."

"Watch he disna curdle yer milk," warned Cam from behind a puff of pipe smoke.

"You guys are nuts."

"Five, then, Harry?"

"Gotcha, Fiona. See you then."

"Ta."

"Ta."

CHAPTER 19

Harry strolled back up The Links amused and puzzled by Fiona and Cam's impaired logic—"Ferlies, warlocks ... Peter Pan." Again he eyed the life-sized golf figure propped by the golf shop door—"It's him!" He looked at the sign above the display window: TOM MORRIS GOLF SHOP. Harry glanced through the window to see if indeed Tom Morris was minding the store. The only person he saw within was a saleslady. Once inside he studied his surroundings with the same trepidation he would have had he entered a bat cave. Everything appeared in order—no supernaturals, disembodied or otherwise, no mystical light, no weird sounds— only items pertaining to golf were stuffed into this tiny shop: clubs, balls, towels, tees, books, bric-a-brac, pictures, handsome silver flasks, and countless curious articles. The fortyish, smartly-dressed saleslady was busily shuffling papers and working a calculator behind the counter. Above her, for sale, was a calligraphic sign: "If I Could Chose Just One Golf Course To Play Forever, It Would Be The Old Course Here In St. Andrews—Bobby Jones."

"Good afternoon, sir, how may I help you?"

"The large picture outside?"

"Yes. Tom Morris."

"I can swear I saw that very person last night."

Without any sign of wonder, "And where was that, sir?"

"On the golf course."

"The Old Course?"

"Why ... yes."

"I fancy you did see him."

"Wait a minute—Old Tom has been dead a hundred years."

"Still ... ."

"Still? What do you mean, still?"

"It's not widely known outside this area," she spoke quietly and with assurance, "but Tom Morris does indeed haunt the Old Course at night."

"Have you seen him?" asked Harry, doubting her claim.

A little irritated, "I, myself, have not seen him nor do I wish to. Nonetheless, a responsible acquaintance of mine and her gentleman friend happened upon him during an evening stroll and saw him vanish into thin air—poof, like that," she flicked open the fingers of both hands.

"You're absolutely convinced it is not some local old coot impersonating Old Tom?"

"Quite sure," was the curt answer." Then, officiously, "May I show you something, sir?"

"No thanks," he left more perplexed than when he entered.

Once outside, Harry re-examined the picture, half expecting it to move. "Hey, old man, waddaya got to say for yourself? Not speaking, huh? Knew it." He walked off trying to grasp the source of the Scots' irrational acceptance of ghosts, goblins, and warlocks. "It's gotta be the whiskey, or something they put in the water."

CHAPTER 20

"Tee the ball higher this time, Harry," said Fiona standing aside scrutinizing his mechanics, or lack thereof, and trying to find a way to gather all his loose ends. She found no clue as to where to begin. Teeing the ball higher changed nothing for the better. Harry, as always, swung with malice aforethought, and, as almost always, the ball scurried off to the right. Glumly, they walked off the tee.

"Don't swing so hard," she chided, exasperation growing with every stroke. She could sense that Harry was a reprimand away from chucking the whole thing. For the tenth time she forced herself to be more positive. She held his head in her hands and had him take a few slower practice swings. "Good, Harry. Keep your head still. Swing easy." When next he struck a ball, using a 5-iron, it lofted 80 yards forward.

"Holy cow! What did I do right? That's one of my best shots ever." He wanted to hug Fiona but settled for a high-five. "Wow, you are an excellent teacher … first rate … top notch … A-one."

"Thank you."

And, after a while, Harry did indeed do slightly better than in the past. He felt less pressure to perform. He was able to concentrate on shot-making and not on how others would react to his inevitable miscues. The area that showed the greatest improvement was around the green—chipping and putting. A slower backswing helped knock a stroke or two off each hole.

When they arrived at the Jubilee 5th tee Harry said, "It was on the 5th tee over there on the Old Course that my ball bonked the old coot last night. This is his club."

She examined it with fascination. "It's an old-fashioned club … looks new … unused. Lovely workmanship. I don't think Cam has produced a better. Shall we give it a go?"

"What if it breaks? The old guy will go Daffy Duck on us."

"Oh, bosh."

"Have at it, it's your funeral."

Fiona hit a good drive, "Nothing spectacular, about 150 yards. It does have a nice feel to it. Now you try."

"I have trouble enough with this one."

She took the club out of Harry's hands and gave him Old Tom's driver. "This one is a wee shorter than yours. It may be a better fit. Give it a go."

"Why not."

He studied the club knowing it would surely work against him. He had as much confidence in its ability to aid him as he had in Brewster Payne giving him mouth-to-mouth. To placate Fiona he followed his usual routine: got behind the ball to picture his intended line of flight; took two practice swings before addressing the ball. Fiona wasn't sure, but she thought she witnessed two smooth swings. Whack! Harry executed a picture perfect backswing and follow-through that shot the ball out and up over the fairway before descending and rolling to a stop over 300 yards away in direct line with the pin. Harry did not see his ball in flight or landing. Fiona, wide-eyed, shook her head in astonishment. Mouth agape she stared at the distant pinpoint of white.

"Well?" asked Harry, expecting the usual corrective: Keep your head down.

Speechless, Fiona pointed.

"It went straight? Good. Nice club."

"Harry! Did you not see your ball land?"

"Uh uh."

With the concentration of a scientist about to confirm or disprove something dubious, Fiona teed two Maxflis, poised at the same height. Without a word she took the club from Harry and drove one of the balls. It traveled approximately the same distance as her previous attempt. She handed the club back to Harry and pointed to the teed ball. Harry gave a very-well shrug of his shoulders and proceeded to demonstrate a few faultless practice swings. He then struck the Maxfli squarely. The result was a near duplicate of his previous shot.

"Now, did you see that one?"

"Nope."

Greatly agitated, "How could you not see it?"

"You told me to always keep my head still."

"Not for eternity, Harry!"

Harry, apologetically, "Doing that badly, huh?"

"You really do not know what you have just done—not once, but twice?!!"

Completely in the dark, "What?"

Fiona, nearly screaming with excitement, "Harry, you've smacked the feathers out of two balls … with that old club! Come along, I'll show you."

His short legs worked at a canter as he tried to keep pace with her longer strides. When she picked up her two drives Harry looked back to locate his. She walked ahead, "Come along; don't dawdle. My drives traveled about 150 yards … consistent with my own driver …"

"I know. Those were great shots."

"You think those were great," she stopped and grabbed him by the shoulder and pointed ahead, see those white specks together straight ahead?"

"Yeh."

"Those are the ones you hit with that old club."

Looking back to the tee, "No way."

"The golf balls you hit were mine—Maxflis. Go on and see what those balls are."

Harry was not sure she wasn't playing him for a fool. He reached gingerly for one of the balls half expecting it to explode or turn into a white mouse. It was a Maxfli. And so too the other. Stunned, he looked back to the tee. "I landed here? I don't believe it."

"Believe it Harry. I can prove it to you." At mid-fairway she again teed two balls. Using the same club she played back to the tee. The ball made it half way. "Now you. Same direction."

Harry was still not convinced things were on the up and up. He obliged her and cracked the ball with a sweet swing. The Maxfli landed and rolled up onto the tee. Harry was dumfounded.

"Now you know."

Harry was speechless. He inspected the club, stem to stern. There was nothing he could point to that would explain the magnificent shots he played.

Fiona dropped another ball, "It's about 180 yards to the pin, Harry, let's see what happens when you hit it from this shorter distance."

Fiona noted that Harry's hands gripped down on the shaft and his swing adjusted automatically for correct distance. The ball flew to the green and rolled pin high six feet from the hole. They jumped up and down, hooted and hollered. They danced and skipped to the green, golf clubs clattering.

"The club is magical, Harry. There's no other way to explain what's happening. And, Harry, the club works for you only."

For Harry, the beauty of it all finally sunk in. "Old Tom must have been out of his gourd to give me this baby." He kissed the club with more than ordinary affection. "Come to think of it, he was out of his gourd."

"I think Cam should have a look at it, there may be some trick to it after all."

"Good idea. Let's go find out."

CHAPTER 21

Cam's dusty workshop in back of The Cleek and Thistle smelled strongly of wood and tobacco. In one corner was a lathe, in another corner stood an old wood stove. Golf clubs and parts of golf clubs were jammed into all recesses. Cam, apron-clad and sucking his pipe, was at his workbench examining the old club, with Harry and Fiona looking over his shoulder. Cam rubbed his thumb over the carved initials, TM, on the clubhead. He drew attention to the unfinished M, "Harry, m'lad, you must have hammered Old Tom about here."

"So Tom Morris made it?"

Cam reflected during a long pull on his pipe. He leaned his head back and puffed a nimbus of smoke above them. "Until the day he died, Old Tom was still making long-nosed woods … like those," nodding toward an opposite wall. "But this beauty is of a fairly recent design; however, it has been put together the old-fashioned way, by hand, using old fashion materials. Clearly, a club of this design should have a steel shaft, and the soleplate should be made of aluminum or brass." He pointed out the parts described, "And what we have here is hickory and ram's horn. The clubhead, except for this screw, is constructed from a variety of local woods: thorn, hazelwood, and inlays of rowan and oak. The implanted screw serves no function that I can see; it's most likely an aesthetic touch. Unusual make for Tom, and yet … I'm sure he made this club. The initials cinch it."

"What causes the club to perform as it does?" asked Fiona.

"Old Tom put magic in it."

"Why does the magic work only for me?"

"Old Tom gave it to you."

"Out of his mind when he did it. I know he didn't mean for me to have it."

"Tommy!" blurted Fiona.

"Tommy?" Harry asked.

"He made it for Tommy, his son."

"But Tommy's dead too," said Harry.

"So?"

"So?"

"He meant it for Tommy's spirit," said Fiona. "Many golf-loving spirits play the Old Course on moon-lit nights. Old Tom would make this club for none other than his beloved son."

This had become deeper than Harry could fathom. "Cam, tell her she's talking nonsense."

"I'll no tell her different from what I myself believe."

"Whoa! Where am I, never-never-land?"

"You'll have to work that out for yourself, Harry," said Cam flatly. "Meantime, here's your wonder club. It's worth its weight in rubies. I'll not be wagering you on the links."

Harry hugged his club with possessive pride. He wandered about the confined space looking at clubs in various stages of completion. He pick up a completed wooden putter. It was a thing of beauty. Cam was a skilled craftsman.

Fiona drew her uncle aside, "Cam, do you think you could make a three and five wood to match Harry's driver? I would like to make a gift of them ... from us."

"Bonnie idea. The one thing I cannot duplicate is the screw. Still, when done he'll have a near perfect matched set."

"Thanks," she kissed him.

"Anytime, dear heart."

"Harry, Cam likes the design of your club, would you mind awfully if he copied it?"

Handing it over to Cam, "Not at all."

"You might make a set for display," said Harry, "I bet you'd get a lot of orders for them."

"Probably not right soon, but if you become a major's champion I'm sure I'll have more orders than I could handle by myself."

"Fat chance of that happening. One magic driver does not a golfer make."

"It would if you could pitch and putt a little better," said Fiona. "And I can help you there—it's the strongest part of my game."

"This is beginning to sound exciting," said Harry dreamily. Snapping out of it, "And scary too."

"Buck up, Harry," said Fiona. "Mind, think positive. Go for broke, and we'll see you back here for the Open."

Harry again imagined himself walking up the 18th, victory in hand, the gallery cheering—"Harry! Harry! Harry!"

"By-the-by, Harry, when … Harry … Harry!"

"Oop, sorry. I was about to putt out at Shinnicock for the course record."

"Good, Harry, you're wandering in the right direction," said Fiona. "When do you leave us?"

"Day after tomorrow."

"My-o-my. Cam, will that give you enough time?"

"Yes, lass. I have all the parts; it's just a matter of piecing them together. Not to worry."

"Harry."

"Yes, lass."

"Your quest for the gold begins tomorrow," She poked Harry on the chest with her finger. "Are you up for it?"

"Yeees!" Harry snapped to attention.

With the no nonsense attitude of a drill sergeant, "In the morning … o-eighthundred … pitch and putt lessons … same place … be on time."

"Aye aye, sir, er lass. Will there be anything else?"

"No. Carry on."

"I can hardly wait."

"Good. Off with you now, Harry. I'll be assisting Cam for a bit here and then I'll be busy in the Cleek for the remainder of the day."

"See you in the morning with bells on."

"Forget Belzon, come alone. Ta."

"So long, Fiona, Cam."

"Ta, Harry, m'lad."

Cam, as soon as Harry exited, "Who's this Belzon bloke."

"Not a bloke at all, just a silly bit of nonsense." She set about tidying the shop while Cam, engrossed with the magic club, took measurements and notes.

CHAPTER 22

I am reminded of the time in a far-off land when I myself performed a bit of magic with a borrowed golf club. It occurred during the year in which I was troubled with much mental anguish over a series of losses: the passing of our beloved George V; the demise of Auchterlonie, my pet Scottie; the unanticipated retirement of chef Bangaloree; the sapping of life's zest; and deuce knows what all, when I resolved, after a perusal of Kipling's *Kim*, to traverse if need be the whole of India to find myself.

In sweltering Bombay I attended out-of-doors classes in Krishnamurti Jenkins' dusty roadside ashram; at a Calcutta fakir institute on the banks of the Ganges I was broiled and basted; and I got all twisted up and addled by heat and unenlightened twaddle uttered by members of the Madras Fellowship of Theosophistical Yoga. These and similar institutes availed me naught. Still was I adrift, encumbered with yet more losses—my funds and my senses.

British officers, I am told, found me dancing and singing a ditty in the outskirts of Mysore.

Oh! sure the world is all run mad,
The lean, the fat, the gay, the sad,—
All swear such pleasure they never had,
Till they did learn the polka.

First cock up your right leg so,
Balance on your left great toe,

96

Stamp your heels and off you go,
To the original polka. Oh! ...

The soldiers said I was crazed, malnourished, foot-weary, bug-bitten and rank. They sat me in the far end of a lorry and drove me away from the feverish heat to an Ooty infirmary high in the Nilgiri Hills. A meal of oatmeal and bangers, my first substantial food in a month, was given me which I dispatched with uncommon relish. After a long, hot bath and shave using sweet-smelling soaps from Selfridge's, I studied myself in a mirror. Eureka! Greatly to my credit I beheld an Englishman—a true, blue, mighty slender Englishman. India, be praised: I entered your confines bereft of contentment, and you cast me down to your lowest depths of privation so that I might appreciate how well off I really was back in the Isle of furze, gorse, and heather. Although a little worse for wear, I had come full circle.

You may well ask where all this is leading? Ooty, yes Ooty it was where I performed my most memorable shot on a golf course.

It began as most of my days did—unplanned. One morning after much lolling about convalescing, I felt the sudden urge to face up to a strenuous round of golf on the local course. There I fell in with a trio of Hindu chaps on holiday from Seringapatam. We hired the services of the requisite number of caddies plus a ball-spotter. Why this last fellow was insisted upon was not immediately made clear to me for I noticed that the fairways were wide open and seemed for the most part free of hazards. With four players and four caddies the possibility of losing a ball seemed unlikely. The spotter spent a good deal of time scanning the forest as though taken with the flashes of brilliant plumage flitting from tree to tree.

The early sun was aglow in all its majesty. The shiny dew had all but lifted. The hills were alive with the sounds of birdsong and macaque chatter. A well-tended tea plantation neat as a formal English garden rose up a slope to the right of the 1st tee; and to the left and below stood the dense Nilgiri Forest.

The Seringapatamanis were dismal players but jolly companions displaying gentlemanly traits and a rudimentary grasp of
English—"Veddy, veddy good strike, sah," was their polite response
to each of my shots. The caddies, to a man, were among the most
obliging and efficient I have had. The ball-spotter had little trouble
locating balls. My efforts of course were always in line with the
pin.

Upon reaching the 8th tee we were greeted by a loud rushing
crash about a three-wood's distance ahead, and this was followed
on the instant by shrill warning cries from our ball-spotter as he
fled away from what appeared to be a huge chestnut hurled from
the forest and rolling with increasing speed across the fairway.
Closer scrutiny revealed that it possessed four legs, tail, rippling
muscles, and wide-spread horns. Right off I knew what it was.
There before us was the aggressive beast that stumped me on my
first crack at the *Sunday Times* crossword—14 Down, four letters,
Tamil Nadu buffalo? "Gaur! Gaur!" the Hindus sought cover. The
giant bull was fast gaining on our ball-spotter. His only chance
rested with me. Everyone has a secret reserve of ability and I had
to call upon mine. With calm reasonableness I teed up a new ball.
I placed the ball back in my stance so as to produce a low trajectory, took dead aim—taking into account a slight up-draft and
the celerity of the assailant—then swung the borrowed driver with
as much force as an invalid could muster. The ball exploded off
the tee like a rifle shot. It zoomed low over the fairway on target
… and then it developed a horrid fade and knocked the feet out
from under the ball-spotter; a coconut palm halted his roll. The
bull skidded to a stop a scant few yards from his prey and eyed me
quizzically, not more than a choked-down nine-iron away. The
ball-spotter ducked behind the palm and eyed me helplessly. "Stand
firm!" I called to him, "not to worry." I teed another ball, and the
gaur—possibly thinking I was reloading my Enfield— turned and
stormed back into his forest sanctuary. The ball-spotter gathered
himself and hobbled up to me swearing eternal gratitude with

promises of offerings in my name to several of his deities. I told him Ernest Spectre had never felt more honored.Only heaven knows what we are capable of in a pinch, and I do believe Heaven interceded on our behalf that fateful morning. I finished alone and did rather well for a fellow on the mend. Scored in the mid 90s as I recall. Would have done better had the borrowed driver not developed an irreversible fade. Ahhh ... forgive me, I seem to have neglected our good friend Harrison Golub.

CHAPTER 23

As agreed, Harry and Fiona met that next morning eager to match the long- and straight-shooting Tom Morris driver against The Jubilee links course and any treachery it may reveal to the vainglorious. As far as the driver was concerned The Jubilee offered no hindrance whatsoever—long, straight, and true flew each shot. Long, straight, and true, that is, for the first six holes. Harry was oblivious to his surroundings, he hurried ahead to each lie eager to lace into the ball and watch its unerring flight. When they neared the 7th tee Fiona pulled Harry up:

"We know for certain," she spoke quietly for a small but growing gallery of spectators followed them, "we now know for certain that your drives have missile-control, all well and good, but I'm uncomfortable with all these people following us, what about you?"

"I've been so wrapped up with what I've been doing I hadn't noticed them. Wow, there must be ten people there. How do we get rid of them?"

"Here," Fiona handed Harry a three-wood.

"What if I whack the hell out of the ball with this?"

"Harry, get real."

"You're in for a big surprise, watch this." Harry's form and swing reverted back to his old way; the ball, though struck fairly well, traveled a mere 80 yards in the air. A faint choral groan emanated from the rear. "Man, that was darn good," Harry boasted to the onlookers. They thought not.

"Well done, Harry. From now on in I think we should lay aside Old Tom. It's chipping and putting we have to master, so choose the iron you feel most comfortable with and we'll use just that and the putter for the remainder of the round."

"Comfortable with?"

"Come now, Harry, pick a number between seven and nine."

"Eight."

"Brilliant choice."

Thereon Harry used his eight-iron on all shots off the green. Convinced the little fellow's booming drives were a fluke, the gallery deserted him after his tee shot on the 7th. On the whole, Harry's chipping advanced from hopeless to passable. By the end of the round he felt he understood the mechanics of chipping and putting. Fiona, through gentle prodding and positive reinforcement, was able to instill in him a small measure of confidence and a desire to persevere with his short game.

Afterward Harry walked Fiona to the Cleek and Thistle where she was scheduled to work for the rest of the day. She had to work longer hours, for Mr.Cameron Flett was busy constructing clubs for Harry, and they had to be finished before he left the following afternoon. Fiona told Harry she would see him off at the bus station. He hired a taxi and rode back to his hotel thrilled by his recent experiences and already regretting that they were coming to an end.

Brew and Phil, their vacation also ending, completed their final round of golf at Troon on Scotland's southwest coast and were standing behind the 18th green watching the final approaches of Mal, Tony, and Gunther.

"You lucky, lucky dog," griped Phil handing over an hundred dollar bill. "Lucky, lucky, lucky. Beat me by one lousy stroke."

Brew kissed the bill, placed it in his wallet, shoved the wallet into his back pocket and patted it, smirking all the while. "I gave you two strokes, so you really came up short by three," he spoke offhandedly, insinuating the match was a conclusion foregone.

Not to be totally bested, Phil smiled with marked insolence, "Do you think little Harry's making it with ... what's her name ... Fiona, is it?"

"Impossible." The directness of the query rattled Brew for an instant. "Why the sudden interest in Harry Golub?—do you miss your old roomie?"

"Good gawd, no. Just curious. Aren't you?"

"Not in the least."

"We'll see Harry tomorrow. I'll ask him how he got along with the girl that dumped you."

Brew bristled, responding with clenched teeth, "One of these days I'm going to ask myself why I put up with you."

"I've been asking myself the same question for years—and you know what?"

"What?"

"Haven't a clue."

I think at this juncture of my narrative you have formed some idea as to why these fellows are companions. To me it is evident. Their friendship—and I'm not sure that that is the correct word—was sustained by the opinion that each felt superior to the other—with blind judgement and self-glorification thrown into the mix.

Petrarch, I believe—or was it Plutarch?—said, and I paraphrase, that a conceited individual develops such a vicious habit of mind that it eventually turns upon one's closest friend, especially when that friend doesn't fully accept the warm personal gift of himself. And there you have these Connecticut Yankees categorized by Plutarch—or perhaps, Petrarch.

CHAPTER 24

Harry arrived early at the bus station giving himself ample time to make the necessary connections to Edinburgh and then on to Glasgow by train where he would rejoin the Brew crew for their scheduled evening flight to New York. For the tenth time he paced from the end of the loading platform and out to City Road where he scanned both directions expectantly. It was then that he saw Fiona marching up the hill with a golf club in each hand—a one-person parade with batons at the ready. Her appearance elicited in him a feeling quite like those he had as a child watching the Macy's Day Parades along Fifth Avenue. Upon seeing her he actually clapped and hopped for joy.

"I'm so glad to have caught you up," she puffed, handing him the golf clubs. "Cam and I want you to have these as mementos of your holiday here with us. Cam made them. Now you have a matched set."

With speechless gratitude Harry examined the 3- and 5-wood, exact replicas of Old Tom's driver. "I don't know what to say."

She tapped him lightly on the forehead with her finger, "Thanks, will do nicely."

"Fiona, they're beautiful, gorgeous, perfect ... boy-o-boy they're beauts. A million thanks to you and Cam ... for everything. I'm gonna miss you guys."

The terminal loudspeaker blared the last boarding call for Edinburgh.

"And we'll miss you, Harrison Golub from New York City," hugging him.

Harry, the last to board, hesitated before entering the coach. He was full of scrambling sensibilities. He wished he could hang back a little longer and tell Fiona how much her friendship meant to him; how much he appreciated her standing up for him against Brew and his bunch; and how he cherished every second he was with her; and the golf, and the jokes, and the walks, and the poke on the forehead and the hug. He could not find his tongue. He boarded the coach on the verge of weeping. He wiped his eyes before sitting by a window. Fiona stood alone on the platform waving to him. He waved back with a wan smile as the coach slowly rolled free of the station and out on to City Road for the hour-long drive to Edinburgh's Waverley Station.

CHAPTER 25

Ah, Manhattan. The gossip, the escapades, the drama, the foibles, the tumult, the hoi polloi ... the delis. Many a tale I could tell of my experiences there—literary and otherwise—over a period of six decades. You would be dazzled by the scope of my acquaintances among New York's fashionable and urbane sophisticates—especially the theatre crowd. But I fear if you indulge me in that wise I should be a long while getting back to my accounting of Harrison Golub. Perhaps, later, after a friendly round together we might relax on the terrace in the gloamin' with a wee dram. Dear me, I've slipped into the local jargon. Oh, well, when in Rome, what?

By-the-by, did you happen to know Jerome Kern? ... Irving Berlin? ... the brilliant Gershwins? ... the bewitching Edna St. Vincent Millay? ... Mel Ott?

Pity. Friends of mine.

No matter. In future I shall introduce you to them. Best return to the matter at hand, what? Right you are.

Harry and Gunther sat side-by-side on their passenger flight back to New York.

"Are you well, Harry?" Gunther asked.

"Why do you ask?"

"You look glum. I've not known you to be so quiet. And, you haven't had a bite to eat."

Harry dropped his seat back and turned away, "Just tired."

Gunther shrugged and went back to reading *The Financial Times.*

At this point, I thought—end of story. Bear with me. The best is yet to come.

We pick up our tale after the passing of a fortnight. Fiona and Cam were engaged in a mid-afternoon game of cribbage on a picnic bench overlooking the beach. Fiona became pre-occupied. Cam, pipe teeth-clenched, was counting out:

"… and a pair are six." He pegged, then picked up the kitty. "A treasure! Fifteen two, four, six, and a double run of eight is fourteen."

With a cheerless smile, Fiona's gaze followed Colin Mackay and Jean Forsyth, his betrothed, strolling together along the strand. Each seemed charmed by the other's idle chitchat, taking no notice of running and barking dogs, children shouting at play, and squawking seagulls.

"You're deal, love," spoke Cam pushing the deck of cards to Fiona.

She did not respond. Cam followed her gaze. Colin spotted them and he and Jean waved. Cam and Fiona returned the greeting.

"If that fine lad can hold up to pressure," said Cam, "he could be the new Montgomery. He has the makings."

"Aye, I wish him well, he's a splendid fellow." Fiona picked up the Joker and stared at it sadly. "Jean's a lucky gal."

"What's troubling you, my pet?"

She sighed, "Nothing, nothing at all, really."

Setting aside the cards and cribbage board, Cam made a place for the picnic basket. He began unloading it. "What have we here? Bless my soul—currant scones, my favorite. Ham, grapes, apples and Stilton. A feast for a ploughman."

"I packed it for you, Cam, I'm not the least hungry."

"Are you not well, my pet?"

"I'm fine, really," she said perking up a bit. She turned the Joker face down.

"Harry?"

"Why, Cam ... why didn't I encourage him?" She was near tears. "I do miss him. He's a good man—funny, generous, thoughtful. And I know he likes me and ... I shall never see him again."

"Aye, lass, I too liked the man from the start. True, there's a huge amount of goodness in him. I could tell he was quite taken with you."

"I know he's fond of me. But coming over here was his first venture away from home. He romanticized everything about his holiday in Scotland. Now that he's home ... oh, bother it all." She turned away to dab her eyes.

Cam uncapped a flask and filled two tea cups. "I have a strong feeling we haven't heard the last of Mr. Harrison Golub. Your lovely self and Old Tom's driver will draw Harry back to St. Andrews." He topped his tea with a splash of Scotch from a half-pint bottle and raised his cup, "To you and Harry."

She patted his hand.

CHAPTER 26

At that very moment, in lower Manhattan, Harrison Golub was working the floor of Levinson's Sporting Goods, a spacious high-ceilinged store replete with all sorts of athletic equipment and exercise apparatus. The golf section was in the rear with a net-enclosed mini-range running along the wall some 60 feet.

All sales personnel were assisting customers. Harry's charges were Alfred, a precocious pre-teen, and his mother. Alfred gripped, weighed, and fanned the air with one tennis racket after another; each in turn was summarily rejected with disdain.

"Maybe I could show …" Harry began.

"I know what I'm doing—leave me alone," ordered the boy sharply.

"I only …"

"Geez! didn't you hear me?"

"You must excuse Alfred," said the mother addressing Harry, "he is a tad willful at times, but I've found that it's best to let him go about his business or there's the devil to pay. And, really, the little dear does know what he wants."

Alfred finally settled on a top-of-the-line racket. He examined it, eliciting an air of racket insight far beyond his years. His expression suggested that this very expensive tennis racket just might be the one to match his high standard of utility. He performed a few spirited two-handed backswings. His mother watched every move with pride and delight. Harry stood by to make sure Alfred didn't upset things or injure himself.

Alfred made an unanticipated hop backward to return an imaginary lob, which he attacked with an energetic double-handed overhead smack, only to have the follow-through obstructed by Harry's groin. Harry gasped and winced. Doubled over in pain, he repeated in short breaths—"Ah ha!"—twenty or more times.

The imp faulted Harry for his injury, "You shouldn't stand so close. Gimme some room."

Harry looked like Quasimodo ridiculed as he shuffled behind a table display of tennis balls and peeked out to watch Alfred resume his mimic court actions.

The boy's mother joined Harry, "I'm quite thrilled over Alfred's progress at tennis. He's taken to it like a shark to water. I feel in my heart that my little darling will master the necessary skills to become another John McEnroe. What say you?"

"He's got the right attitude," said Harry through clenched teeth.

"He does, doesn't he? Alfred's a natural."

Alfred had a racket in each hand turning them over and back, seeming to evaluate their balance.

"Which one do you prefer, Alfred?" his mother asked.

He tossed them aside on the carpeted floor, "Neither, they both suck."

"Come along then." Alfred took his mother's hand and they walked out of the store.

When color returned to Harry's face he straightened up. He took deep breaths and scanned the store for unattended customers. He noticed three men at the end of the golf range taking turns chipping off the mat with a wedge. They saw him approach. It was too late for Harry to ignore Phil, Tony, and Gunther.

"Lunch time, Harry!" sang out Sydney coming down the aisle that separated soccer from basketball equipment. Sydney was a tall, loose-fit man in his mid-40s. He was casually dressed in a red cardigan and blue tie—the tie distinguished him from his employees. He was a man who seemed happy with himself and with the world around him.

"Lunch time, Harry. So you want to join me?"

"Can you wait a few minutes, Sydney?"

"For you I can wait, but only a few."

"See those guys at the range?"

"Yes."

"The stuffed-shirts I went to Scotland with."

"You don't say. They do act kinda uppity."

"Gimme a minute. Better see what they're up to."

"A sale's a sale, Harry, even to a stuffed-shirt," said Sydney as if postulating the company's creed.

"Hi, guys," said Harry using his standard salesman greeting.

"Why lookee here," announced Phil, "it's Harrison Golub, golfer extraordinaire."

"Phil ... Tony ... Gunther."

"Good to see you," said Gunther, civily.

"So this is where you hang out," said Tony. "Nice store."

Sydney worked his way forward by rearranging table displays. He was eavesdropping.

"Show me a first-rate pitching wedge," asked Tony.

"This is our newest best seller," said Harry handing him a club.

"You mean you're not promoting Brew's clubs?" questioned Phil.

"We do, and they're fine clubs, but Tony did ask for a first-rate wedge—this is it."

"How the hell would you know, anyway?" scoffed Phil.

"Try it yourself," Harry said.

Tony handed the club back to Harry, "Demonstrate it for us."

Harry was not cowed. He dropped three balls on the green mat. The skeptics stood abreast with arms folded across their chests prepared to witness the expected blunder. Harry took two practice swings and then proceeded to chip each ball within four feet of the 15-yard marker.

"Surprise, surprise," said Phil in an offhand, belittling way.

"Nice touch, Harry," said Gunther.

"Looks like your game has improved, at least here in the store," said Phil.

"A bit," answered Harry, "enough so that I could kick your butt any day of the week." Harry stunned himself by blurting this unreasoned remark. Even Sydney was taken aback.

"Why, Harry," Phil slithered up to him, "would you care to put money where your big mouth is?"

"Sure. How much?" Harry was emboldened beyond repair.

"I'll go easy on you—hundred bucks."

Harry paused a second, "Make it $500 and it's a deal."

Sydney knocked over a display of golf shoes; luckily they had soft spikes.

"You're on," grinned Phil.

Covetousness lit Tony's eyes, "How about me, Harry?"

"The more the merrier. You too, Gunther?"

"I think you should reconsider, Harry."

"$500, Gunther. Take it or leave it?"

"It's your money, Harry, why not."

Phil rubbed his hands with unrestrained glee, "Name the time and place."

"I'll leave that up to you."

"My country club, okay?"

"Suits me."

"In Stamford, Whitewood Country Club. Sunday? We already have a two o'clock tee time."

"I'll be there."

Overcome with malicious mirth, Phil and Tony wandered off.

"I shouldn't have to warn you, Harry," said Gunther, "Phil's a scratch player. Often Tony and I shoot in the 70s, low 80s. You know that."

"I'm gonna win."

"No offense, Harry, but we've seen you play. You don't have a ghost of a chance."

"Thanks for the warning, Gunther, but you and those two meatheads will each be out 500 smackers come Sunday."

"I have a feeling you're putting us on." Gunther moved off. "I'll be surprised if you show up."

"So long, Gunther. Sunday, two o'clock."

Harry spun on his heels counterclockwise with his head clasped in both hands. "What have I done!"

A bemused Sydney stood by his side. "Harry, I didn't know you became a Tiger Woods all of a sudden."

"What I suddenly became is enormously ... gigantically ... grossly ... dumb ... dumb ... dumb."

"That explains it."

Trying to compose himself, "Sydney, I can't go to their country club by myself—would you come along ... as my caddie? Please?"

"An honor it would be, my meshuga friend. I've never caddied before and I've never been to a hoity-toity country club. Oh, Harry," deeply serious, "can you afford to throw away $1500?"

"Nope."

Harry dropped a ball to chip, and dubbed it. His pained expression was mirrored in Sydney's face.

CHAPTER 27

Harry's impulsive bravado had caused his work to be undermined to such an extent that he avoided hobnobbing with Sydney, fellow employees, and customers so that he might steal away to practice chipping and putting, which he fell to with a determination that bordered on mania. Losing face and $1500 weighed heavily on him. He was unsure of the continuing efficacy of Old Tom: Would the club be his ace in the hole? Or were its powers limited to Scotland? to St. Andrews? would it perform in Connecticut? "If only Fiona were here," he muttered more than once.

Sydney empathized with Harry over the rash wager. If Harry believed that concentration on chipping and putting would somehow ease his defeat—so be it. Come Monday he would again be himself.

CHAPTER 29

The Whitewood Country Club's forbidding entrance sign—posted within a ring of Mayflowers—was the size of a tabloid newspaper with the club's name no larger than a sober headline, and a sub-head: "members only." Harry drove his five-year-old compact motorcar along an elm-lined lane with mansions on either side set back by an acre or acres of lawn. At the end of the road they drove onto a large car park. The imposing Mt. Vernon look-alike clubhouse stood off to the right and up a slight grade. Farther off to the right and attached to the clubhouse was a terrace and an adjacent putting green with a few golf carts on standby. Harry parked his small car between a Hummer and a Rolls Royce. At this point Harry and Sydney were fish out of water. They gaped like groupers peering out of an aquarium at highly polished vehicles and perfectly groomed grounds.

"Whaddya think?" wavered Harry.

"Fancy shmancy," Sydney intoned. "Are you nervous?"

"Very."

"Me, too. Wanna go back?"

"Don't tempt … Oh oh—I see the roosting buzzards over there," he pointed to the putting green.

They got out of the car. Sydney looked over the Rolls. Harry checked the sky in all directions looking for thunderclouds. There was not a wisp of nimbus to be seen. Harry popped the boot of the car, pulled out his golf bag and made sure Old Tom was accounted for. He sat on the bumper and put on his golf shoes. Sydney did not know what to do with himself other than to stand in place and look conspicuous.

Phil, Tony, and Gunther stood leaning on their putters and talking with Mal. "Here comes the pigeon," said Phil with sinister glee, nodding in Harry's direction.

"I really didn't think he'd show up," said Gunther.

"Who's that joker with him?" asked Tony.

"Looks like someone I saw at his store," said Gunther.

"I never expected to see Harry again," said Mal.

Harry greeted them heartily, "Hi guys—Mal. Ready to rumble?"

"Ready and willing," replied Tony, licking his chops at the sacrificial goat.

Mal pulled Harry aside, "You're playing my friends for ... have I got this right, $500 apiece?"

"Yep."

"Mind I get in on the action?"

"If you're smart you'll bet on me."

"Ahh ... I don't think so, Harry. I want to bet you that *you* lose."

"The more the merrier. The going rate is $500. Can you manage that?"

"Oh, yes," he patted his pocket, "I have it right here."

"Fair enough," said Harry looking around. "Where's Brew? Maybe he'd like to get in on this, too."

"I'm sure he'd be delighted, but he's enroute to a tournament in Oregon."

Harry walked over to Sydney and put his arm over his shoulder, "Fellows, this is my friend Sydney. He's volunteered to be my caddie."

Sydney was ignored by all but Gunther who shook his hand.

A loudspeaker squawked, "Phillips ... Phillips, your party is on the tee!"

"Let's get this fiasco over with," announced Phil hopping into his golf cart. Gunther and Tony also had golf carts. Harry and Sydney walked behind them to the 1st tee.

"Harry, what do I do?" asked Sydney shouldering Harry's golf clubs.

"Just stay close to me, except when I'm swinging."

"That I can do, Harry."

"Harrison Golub," said Phil with derision, "as guest you have the honors."

"Thank you, thank you," answered Harry, feigning coolness.

Everyone watching Harry practice-swing his three-wood looked like a bobblehead doll, for they were witnessing the same inept swing they remembered seeing in Scotland, and there was no way that that swing was going to give them competition.

"Nah, too close. Let's have the three-iron, Sydney."

"Two hundred and eighty-eight yards to the green is too close," said Tony to Gunther, "what a jerk."

In an effort to avoid contracting the heebie jeebies, Harry set up to his ball in haste, and as quickly flailed at it. To no one's surprise he topped it. The ball wormed ahead 50 yards. Phil and Tony could not contain their guffaws.

"Great shot, Harry," said Tony, "six or seven more like that beauty and you'll be on the green."

Phil faced Harry, "You were dead before you started, pay us now and save yourself more embarrassment."

"Nope. I'm gonna win."

"You're not only an idiot, you're an idiot's idiot."

Sydney spoke up, "Why don't you shut your mouth and play the golf."

Phil responded, "Hear that, Tony? Why don't we shut our mouths and play the golf." Phil smashed a powerful drive down the left side of the fairway, "Well shut my mouth."

Tony, reveling in the moment, addressed his ball with studied confidence and sent it beyond Phil's. Gunther's ball though not struck squarely rolled onto the first cut about 210 yards out.

Mal waved to his friends, "Meet you in the clubhouse." He eyed Harry with a look of utter puzzlement, "Do you enjoy humiliation?"

"Wouldn't know. Never experienced it. What's it like?"

"You'll soon find out. I'll be waiting for you with open hand."

"Better have 500 smackeroos in it."

"What a dreamer."

Sydney relieved Harry of the three-iron and bagged it, "Harry, if we make a break for it now we could be out of here before their golf carts catch up to us. Whaddya think?"

"Oh, ye of little faith. C'mon, pull yourself together."

Phil, Tony, and Gunther were standing by their lies looking back at Harry and Sydney coming down the fairway. Harry stood behind his ball as though calculating the distance to the pin. He then plucked a single blade of grass and tossed it above his head and immediately lost sight of it. Sydney was impressed with Harry's routine. But it was with trepidation that Harry extracted the driver from the bag. "Sydney, if I don't hit this ball well, it's all over. We're too far from the car to make a break for it so keep your fingers crossed. He kissed Old Tom and set it behind the ball without a practice swing. He looked ahead at the flag, then down at the ball. He made a picture perfect swing and follow-through. The ball rose and soared over Tony's golfcart and landed softly on the green, coming to rest two feet from the pin. Phil and Tony looked on in disbelief. Sydney's jaw dropped. Gunther's eyes were following a nuthatch circling an elm tree trunk. When he turned about, Harry and Sydney were standing by, for he was next up to take a shot.

"Sorry, Harry, I didn't see your ball."

"It's on the green, Mr. Gunther," said Sydney. "Such a shot I have never before seen. Harry, that's the best shot I've ever seen you do."

"Sydney, that is only the second shot of mine you've seen."

"So, who's counting."

"Well done, Harry. Well done indeed," said Gunther with a broad encouraging smile.

"How in hell did he do that?" Tony asked Phil. "Over 230 yards to the green."

"Even an idiot can get lucky once in a blue moon. It's a fluke."

Gunther's bump-and-run second shot also landed on the green. Tony's rolled into a greenside trap. Phil overshot the green. Harry putted out for a birdy. Gunther parred; Phil and Tony bogied.

Harry replaced the pin and looked at Phil, "Fun, huh? We've played only one hole and you're already two strokes down."

"There's 17 more holes, you're not likely to win another," he snapped.

The second hole was 167 yard par three. Harry teed off using his driver. The ball stopped four feet past the hole.

"Great shot, Harry," said Gunther.

"A hole in one you almost made, Harry," said Sydney.

Tony and Phil were dumbfounded.

Gunther's shot landed a few feet short of the green. Phil's settled pin high in the left hand rough. Tony overshot the green and his ball came to rest under a bush. Harry birdied, Gunther parred, Tony and Phil bogied.

Standing on the third tee Harry marked his card, "Two holes … correct me if I'm wrong, Phil, but it looks like you're four down."

"Screw you, Golub!" was the venomous response.

Harry's next drive on the par five third hole traveled 300 yards.

"Wow!' exclaimed Gunther.

"Hunky-dory," said Sydney.

"Lemme see that club," demanded Phil, snatching it out of Harry's hand. With a look of distaste he examined it. He gripped it, swung it, and examined it again. "Looks like some castoff you picked out of a Salvation Army dumpster."

"Works for me."

"Mind if I try a shot with this relic?"

"Why would you want to waste a shot on a Salvation Army relic?"

"Why not?"

"Go for it," Harry said with a trace of reluctance.

Phil stroked his usual length drive but sliced it wide. He looked at the club with contempt and flipped it to Sydney. He teed up another ball.

"What do you think you're doing?" Gunther asked.

"What does it look like I'm doing? I'm about to tee off."

"You just did."

"That last shot? I was only trying out Harry's stupid club."

"If your ball had had a good lie you'd have taken it," Gunther disputed him.

"Bull."

Phil's drive sliced further than his previous shot. "Dammit, Gunther, whose side are you on, anyway?"

"Harry's."

From that point on Phil and Tony knew they were in for a bad time. They were frustrated in their attempts to beat Harry. The only person with whom they had played against that had Harry's ability was Brewster Payne. If Harry had any weakness in his game it was an occasional mis-hit with a short iron. He seemed to have mastered the woods, even to the point of regulating nearly exact distances between 100 to 300 yards. Actually, the only wood he ever played was the driver. His new found ability had them completely baffled. At the end of the round Phil and Tony refused to shake Harry's or Gunther's hand.

"Harry, you're another Tiger Woods," said Sydney with pride.

"Yup, those few extra days in St. Andrews really paid off," he announced.

Gunther tallied up the scores: "Tony, 87; Phil, 91; myself, 79; and Harry, you got a 71—one under par. You win hands down. Great round. Congratulations."

Phil pulled his head into his shoulders and attempted to slink away.

"Hold on, Phil!" Gunther caught him up, "Forgetting something?"

"Yeh!" stung by the impressiveness of a sudden thought, he turned about wild-eyed and sinister, rushed to Sydney, pulled Harry's driver out of the bag and broke it over his knee.

"Noooo!" howled Harry in horror. He charged Phil and they fell to the ground and rolled down a slope. Loungers on the clubhouse terrace were drawn to the affray. Tony and Gunther pulled Harry away. Phil stayed on the ground and pounded the grass. He was, for the moment, unhinged.

An officious pair materialized on either side of Harry. One of them spoke: "Sir! Please leave these premises at once."

"I'll see that he leaves," said Gunther and escorted Sydney and a distraught Harry to their car. "Harry … Sydney … please accept my apology for the unconscionable behavior of my former friends—and myself." He started to laugh, "You really stuck it to us, Harry. Amazing, simply amazing."

Harry seemed not to be listening. With a half of Old Tom in each hand he walked ahead as though he were a funeral procession of one.

"I'm truly sorry about your club," said Gunther. "I could tell you favored it highly. But the good news is you are $2000 richer. None of us brought $500 along because we knew you couldn't possibly … !"

Harry perked up, "I knew it—you guys are gonna welsh on me."

"No, no, I'm prepared to write you a check for the full amount—$2000. I'll collect later from the soreheads."

Gunther picked a check out of his wallet and filled it out on the roof of Harry's car. He handed it to Harry.

"Thanks, Gunther, you're all right after all."

"A real honest-to-goodness gentleman," added Sydney.

A mournful pallor continued its hold on Harry.

"You can buy a lot of drivers with $2000, Harry," said Gunther, trying to extract Harry from his grief.

"It can never be replaced," he groaned.

"Somehow, I feel," sympathized Gunther, "that everything will right itself by morning." He patted Harry on the back in an effort to buck him up. "When things cool down here I'd be honored to have you and Sydney join me as my guests. Sincerely, will you?"

"Sure. Why not," said Harry, cheerlessly.

"Likewise," responded Sydney.

"Then it's a deal. I must say I don't for the life of me know how you were able to attain such a high level of proficiency at golf in such a short period."

"Every minute at the store he practices with the golf," said Sydney. "He's a go-getter, my Harry."

"You should seriously consider entering tournaments," said Gunther offering his hand. "Thanks for a most exciting and enlightening afternoon. Sydney."

"So long, Mr. Gunther."

"Bye, Gunther."

With Gunther out of earshot, Sydney asked, "Do you think the check is good?"

"What am I gonna do, Sydney? Look at my club."

"Harry, Harry, club shlub. Forget about it. You can have the best driver I got in the store … for half price. Think what a player like you could do with a fancy new big-head driver—oy, Tiger Woods, watch out."

"Thanks, Sydney. You're a good guy. I feel lousy—would you mind driving?"

"Sure, Harry, no problem."

Harry was about to change his shoes when he chanced to fit the two halves of Old Tom together. He could not believe his eyes. They magically, seamlessly reattached. "Holy moly! back in business. Ta dah!"

"Whatsa matter?" asked Sydney with his head thrust out the car window.

"Nothing. Everything's terrific, wonderful, magical." Putting away his golf clubs and shoes he danced and sang: "When a body meet a body, comin' through the rye." He jumped in the car, "Drive on, Sydney ol' bean."

"That's my Harry, you're yourself again. Now I recognize you. And what a golfer yet. And a cool customer under the pressure."

Leaving behind Whitewood Country Club Harry became philosophical, "Golf, Sydney, is an ancient and noble game. Humility, it teaches, and good sportsmanship, and self-control."

"You don't say."

"I do, and I did."

"On you a big head don't look so good."

"Touche."

CHAPTER 29

I feel obliged to confess that Harry's rude golf opponents were of a type not unknown to me. Permit me to acquaint you with an affront I received from an ill-mannered Camelopardian, and how, with quiet dignity, I put forth a response to good effect. If memory serves, it happened sometime in the winter of 1922 when all London was stalled by a bitter freeze which forced sensible people to stay put indoors. Ensconced I was in the Camelopard smoking room completely under the spell of a redolent, smoldering belvedere when I was rudely alerted to a sound that crossed the bounds of propriety. Ned Nottleby was in his cups blissfully humming Gustav Mahler's Kindertotenlieder in every key but the proper one. I had no quarrel with Mahler, but I did with Ned's irritable rendition reverberating in a room set aside for musing. There was nothing for it but to discharge an oblique rebuking glance that quite stunned him. He gaped back at me with a prolonged confounded look, then his eyes took a turn around the chandelier which imbalanced him and he slumped back onto a chesterfield and passed out.

The following day a sobered Ned Nottleby had no recollection of my sharp reprimand, nor who the devil was Gustav Mahler. The upshot was that he never, in my presence, repeated his insufferable humming.

In comparison, there was little prospect that a mild or strong rebuke from Harrison Golub could have altered the overbearing natures of the Brew crew. Only the threat of protracted discomfort of a kind suffered by the likes of Isabel Goudie could compel them to adopt a more worthy social sensibility. Fortune had shined upon them, for they were saved from such a fate; thumbkins, dousings, and auto de fes have not been sanctioned by the authorities for some years. And poor Harry, though he may have thought so, was not free of his tormentors.

A few days after the successful match at Whitewood Country Club, Sydney had formulated an idea or two respecting Harry's future in golf. From his office window he looked down on the showroom. Business was slow at that moment; the sales staff were talking among themselves, and Harry was alone chipping golf balls. Carlos, the delivery boy from the neighborhood delicatessen, flew into the store with bag in hand and raced directly up the stairs leading to the office.

"*Hola*, señor Leevinson, for joo I have sandweeches and extra peekles."

"Thanks, Carlos," he signed the bill and tipped him. "On you're way out ask Harry to come up like a nice fella."

"Gracias. Sure theeng, I tell eem. Adios."

"Adios."

Sydney bit a kosher pickle and savored it. He went to the window and watched Harry guide Carlos through a few wedge strokes. Carlos could not get the hang of it and handed back the club and left. Harry took a final shot and headed for the office.

"Harry, I got us a deli. Sit down. You're favorite—pastrami on rye."

"Thanks, Sydney. Awful slow day."

"Slow shmo, what of it? We can talk. Concerning you, Harry, I got some ideas."

"Ideas?"

"How's your pastrami?"

"Ummmm."

"I watched you closely with the golf last Sunday, and I watch you putz around here. Harry, you're good. Very good."

"Thanks."

"So I think maybe you should become a golf professional."

"Been thinking the same thing."

"No foolin'?" Sydney was delighted.

"Not professional—amateur."

"Amateur shmamateur. Nobody pays attention to amateurs."

"Ever hear of Bobby Jones?"

"So who hasn't."

"Francis Ouimet?"

"Yes."

"Both amateurs."

"No foolin'?"

"No foolin'."

"They never turned pro?"

"Never, ever."

"Harry, you could be as good as them."

"No way. All the same I'd like to enter tournaments, only ... I don't see how unless I find a sponsor."

"Harry, Harry, look no further. I'm your sponsor. That's what I wanted to tell you," he wiped mustard from his chin.

"Could be expensive," he warned.

"What's expensive?" he blurted, as of no consequence. "Together, Harry, we could make a killing."

"How?"

"How? If you do good with the golf ... let me market Harrison Golub products. We'll be partners, even-steven. Whaddya say?"

"It's all your money up front?"

"You bet."

"Who would buy Harrison Golub products?"

"I noticed how good you are with those handmade wood clubs. Nobody uses wood clubs any more, but they'll want them when they see how good they can be in the right hands. You know how golfers are, anything new or unusual that they think will improve their game they'll pay good money for, especially for drivers. I bet every golf nut has half a dozen drivers at home in the garage. They're never satisfied. It's a disease; am I right, or am I right?"

"Where you gonna find wood drivers?"

"We'll ask your friend in Scotland to make clubs for us exclusively. He'll be happy, we'll be happy."

Thoughts of Fiona swam in his head. "Nice ... nice. You pay all expenses, right?"

"Happily, Harry."

"You're on," Harry sat back and put his feet on Sydney's desk. "Okay, sponsor, get me a tournament."

"I'll get on it today." He swept Harry's feet from his desk, "Lunch is over; back to work."

Harry popped up, tossed the remnants of his lunch in the wastebasket and headed for the door.

"Hey, Mr. Amateur, if it's slow on the floor you should maybe putz around to keep in shape. Starting now I got a big stake in you."

CHAPTER 30

Full of ginger, Harry seized every occasion to develop his short game. It was safe to assume that his new found success with the long accurate drive was the momentous happening in his life. Prior to the advent of "Old Tom," his happiest golf moments—if we are to judge by what he disclosed to Fiona—were winter Sundays home alone watching golf tournaments from the tropics broadcast on the telly. The game absorbed him all hours. Faith in the efficacy of Old Tom, wedded with his modest short-game, filled his sleep and awake time with dreams of derring-do. A skins-game against Jack Nicklaus, Tiger Woods, and Brewster Payne in Cabo San Lucas in February was his most recurrent fantasy. He, Jack, and Tiger always shared prize money, whereas Payne always came up empty-handed.

Habits he had formed over the years changed markedly. Sundays and the few evenings a week he had set aside for dining out or for taking in a motion picture show were shunted in golf's favor. He played rounds on public courses lying within a 50-mile radius of his Manhattan apartment. Often he found himself motoring through unfamiliar tracts of Long Island, Connecticut, and New Jersey.

At all courses Harry arrived as a walk-on single. The judgement of starters and marshals who paired golfers for a round was that Harry, on first sight, fit the profile of a duffer; whereupon, he was often paired with chaps of "equal ineptitude." These unions were not bothersome, for Harry genuinely liked people, regardless of their handicaps. Needless to say, the high-handicappers he played with were awed witnesses to a masterly exhibit of adroitness and skill in the form of a roma tomato. The brilliance with which he controlled woods off the tee and fairway were like nothing they had ever beheld. And of course their natural curiosity over the little chap's odd-fangled wooden clubs emboldened them to ask if they too might have a go with one of them. Harry usually handed over the 3-wood; though some insisted on the driver. Although his clubs never improved their shot-making to any degree, yet a few did offer to buy his driver. Surely, if someone the likes of Harry could perform such extraordinary feats of power and control, it had to be the woods he used. One brutish fellow followed Harry to the car park after their round and insisted he sell him his Old Tom outright for ready money. It was a situation that required artful handling. Harry told the fellow that his clubs were prototypes on loan and that if he checked with the pro shop later in the season they were sure to have them for sale. To avoid further prying, Harry made it a point to not play the same course twice.

After a fortnight of jauntings far afield, Sydney informed Harry that he had scheduled him to play his first tournament in the state of Connecticut in two weeks time. Tournament golfers have caddies—ergo, he needed a caddie. But whom could he trust? Three people, only, knew the secret of his empowered driver—himself, Fiona Huntly, and Cameron Flett; and how many of the unliving knew, he had no way of ascertaining, nor would he care to find out. Any caddie he hired was bound to be inquisitive after noticing how dependent he was on his driver with all shots outside 100 yards to the hole. That would not do. Launching a career as a competitive golfer hinged on one other person. It was a long shot; he would telephone her straight away.

CHAPTER 31

On Sunday morning, Harry, in fuzzy flannel pajamas, sat on the edge of his bed fidgeting with a business card. He tapped his slippered toes nervously—they barely touched the floor. Every second or two he glanced down at the telephone on the bedside table. Next to the telephone was his most prized souvenir of Scotland, a framed photograph of himself and Fiona in front of the Tommy Morris memorial stone. Under the table was a stack of Sports Illustrated magazines featuring golfers on their covers. A few of the covers had been framed and hung on the walls. Also on the walls were poster-sized photos of Jack Nicklaus, Francis Ouimet, and Marilyn Monroe.

Ahhh, Miss Monroe, a goddess. Upon my soul, even now her image is enough to turn me into a dreamer of flattering and impossible dreams. Could there ever have been a more delightful spectacle than those few seconds of extemporaneous coquetry on a New York sidewalk when she braced herself above a subway vent and held down the skirt of her flimsy white dress billowing from a cool, uprushing, underground gale caused by a passing train? The very picture Harry had on his wall. She looked radiant in her joyous playfulness, and as opalescent as a pearl; delicate as an orchid; soft as down; etcetera ... etcetera ... etcetera. That vision, even now, has been one of my most haunting memories. Were I a pagan I'd have raised an altar to Marilyn Monroe, and I would make no excuse for doting before it—even allowing for the fact that she was not a golfer. And to be completely aboveboard, I have never pried into fantasies Harry or Sydney may have had in regard to our mutual inamorata. Forgive me. Allow me take a moment to disentangle myself ... .

Harry's bedroom. Yes, well, beside the objects mentioned, you would not be surprised to find that the room was strewn with knickknacks, the bulk of which made reference to golf.

Harry picked up the snapshot of himself and Fiona from the table and blocked out his image with the business card and gazed wistfully upon Fiona. He replaced the photo, took a deep breath and dialed the number on the card. The toe-tapping increased to a drum roll accompanied by fife-like whistling. The telephone rang.

"Cleek and Thistle."

"Is this Cameron Flett?" asked Harry.

"The same."

"Cam, this is Harry Golub from New ... ."

"Harry, m'lad, how is everything?"

"Great. Is Fiona there?"

"She's on holiday in Aberdeen. She'll be saddened to have missed your call."

"Darn. Cam, in a couple of weeks I play my first golf tournament."

"Splendid, Harry. I think I can guess the best part of yer game—and the best club."

"That's still our secret?"

"Yours, mine, and Fiona's."

"I need Fiona."

"And she needs y ... ."

"I need a caddie."

"Caddie?"

"And instructor."

"Instructor? In America?"

"Yes."

"You want me to tell Fiona Huntly to go off to America where she'll be your private instructor and caddie?" he questioned, half comprehending the idea.

"I know it sounds crazy but I can't trust just any ol' caddie with my club—you understand?"

"I do, Harry, but will Fiona?"

With desperation, "Please tell her she'll be well-paid. If she agrees, I'll send her $2000 and a plane ticket to New York. My sponsor and his wife have a beautiful house on Long Island overlooking the Sound. They have a lovely room for her. I need her desperately."

"Aye, Harry, that I'll tell her."

"Have her call me." Harry gave his number.

"Got it. It's engraved on the bar."

"Thanks, Cam. Love your clubs. Things go well here maybe I'll get to play in Scotland."

"I'd like nothing more."

"So long, Cam, thanks a million."

"Ta, Harry," and hung up. "The little dickens did not forget m'lass."

CHAPTER 32

Earlier that evening members and their guests were gathering for cocktail hour in the lounge of the staid Whitewood Country Club. Mr. Brewster Payne sat alone flipping through the pages of Gentlemen's Quarterly while nursing a vodka martini on the rocks. Gunther and a lady friend sat at a nearby table. Gunther was persona non grata with his old mates. His falling out with them was inevitable. Their elitism had become more unprincipled and vicious, and the consequences of their actions were mostly unpleasant. Animosity on both sides came to a head when Mal, Tony, and Phil reneged on their wager with Harry. They expressed particular resentment to Gunther for his taking it upon himself to make good their bets with Harry without having their approval. Only when Gunther threatened to go before the membership committee and expose their attempt to defraud did they reluctantly pay up.

Brew had just received a second drink when Mr. Malcolm Baldwin joined him looking puzzled and alarmed. "Brew, Phil just showed me the roster for the Greater Bridgeport Open— guess who's on it?"

"P. T. Barnum."

"Close, but no cigar. Are you ready for this?"

"Shoot."

"Harrison Golub."

"C'mon."

"Harry Golub. I tell you the little twit can play."

"No way. What's the joke?"

"No joke. Ask Phil, ask Tony. He took them each for $500."

Gunther leaned back in his chair and addressed Brew, "Harry also took me for the same amount—and Mal, too."

Brew and Mal turned their backs to Gunther and lowered their voices.

"He beat you, too?"

"Well, not exactly. I didn't play. Mine was a side bet. Dammit, Brew, he carded a 71 on our course!"

"Are we talking about the same Golub? The pathetic jerk that nearly ruined our Scotland trip?"

Gunther again intruded, "Actually, fellas, it was *his* Scotland trip, and we ruined it for *him.*"

"Do you mind, this is a private conversation," grumbled Mal.

"Just trying to keep the record straight," said Gunther smiling and winking to his lady with whom, it appeared, he had made privy to the whole affair.

Brew and Mal moved to a distant table.

"Again, are we talking about the same Golub?"

"The very same."

"Why he's terrible."

"Not anymore. He outdrove Phil and Tony on every hole but one."

Brew was nonplussed by the appalling strangeness of it all. "It can't be true."

"Well, if you like you can see for yourself. Phil's also entered in the Bridgeport. We haven't anything on that weekend. Let's go down with him and check out Golub."

"Where's Phil now?"

"In the sauna."

"C'mon." He stood up, gulped his martini, "I have to talk to him."

They crossed the room with a sense of urgency.

"There's something not kosher here," fretted Brew as he passed by Gunther's table.

"Believe me, he's kosher." Gunther's response startled everyone in the lounge.

CHAPTER 33

After a focussed eight hour session chipping golf balls in Levinson's Sporting Goods store in downtown Manhattan, Harry arrived home tired but pleased with his progress in that area. He was ready to settle in for a quiet evening—supper, then the telly until he began to nod off. It would be a night much like all other nights before he found himself a golfer. He hung up his jacket, put on slippers, popped a frozen dinner in the microwave, and pressed the message button on the kitchen telephone.

As of late he added a new detail to this routine. He grabbed a putter from the umbrella stand, dropped a ball on the hall carpet runner and putted to the far left hand corner, then putted back to the right corner; back and forth, long and short.

Sydney's playfully teasing voice entered mid-putt: "Harry, this is Sydney. You did good today with the wedge at the store. Now that you're home you should practice with your putz. Remember Harry, a well stroked putz is a happy putz. Goooood niiiiight."

"I'm putting, already."

"Mr. Gobul," the machine spoke, "Congratulations, Mr. Gobul. You have been pre-selected to receive a free one-time-only membership in Manhattan's exclusive He-Man, She-Woman Parlor of Exercise and Massage. Mr. Gobul, this offer … ."

"Stinks." Harry punched it out.

The microwave beeped and Harry was about to extract his dinner tray of meatloaf, mashed potato, and peas when he heard Fiona's voice: "Hellooooo. Harry. Are you there? It's Fiona."

135

"Fiona!" Harry stood over the phone.

"Cam gave me your message. Sorry to have missed your call. I was off visiting family. Imagine, Harrison Golub a tournament golfer, and myself a caddie … ."

"Yes!" Harry punched skyward.

"Sounds like a daft adventure. Well, I'm game. I've not been to America. You must be sure to be there when I deplane. Send the ticket and … and ta, Harry."

"Ya whoo!"

The remainder of the evening was devoted to gratifying thoughts of Fiona, and not all of them innocent.

CHAPTER 34

For days after Fiona's call, Harry became—if you believe it possible—a more fanatical golfer. He left no time for anything else. He practiced when he could; reread instruction books from his own library and borrowed teaching videos from the public library, which he watched evenings until he fell asleep.

Surely such resolute efforts deserve to pay dividends. Few individuals have crossed my path demonstrating the stick-to-itiveness of Harrison Golub. One does pop into mind, although his quest lay in a different direction entirely, and that would be the Scottish explorer, Findhorn Pittenweem, my old Harrow classmate.

Weemy spent the better part of four years, and the better part of his inheritance in trying to capture the elusive three-inch boa constrictor, mbondowoshobogowasi. The reptile was first brought to the attention of the Royal Zoological Society in 1798 by Mungo Park. Park had trapped two specimens—a blue male and a pink female. And before presenting them to the Society he had brought them along in a little wooden box to a garden party in his honor on an estate outside of Edinburgh. The venerable Duke of Athol, a Society member and one of Park's expedition sponsors, was also in attendance and very keen to see the "wee warms."

Park thought to show the mbondowoshobogowasis first to the lovely Lady Lavinia Kirkoswald for whom he had developed a deep affection upon hearing her deliver a heartfelt discourse on "God's Creatures, Great and Small" on behalf of the Midlothian

Antivivisection League. When he displayed the contents of the unlidded box, she did not know what to make of the pink and blue helix inside. She looked puzzled. Park said that they were mating snakes. Upon hearing "mating snakes" she fainted dead away. In an attempt to break her fall, Park dropped the little wooden box. He carried Lady Lavinia to a shady spot wherein to attend her. A doctor appeared, and with smelling salts revived her. With a start, Park remembered his fallen charges and ran back to where they had been unceremoniously dropped. In doing so he flushed two robins onto a tree limb. He noticed one had a pink tail sliding down its gullet; the other wore a smug expression. Mungo Park's mbondowoshobogowasis were no more.

The Duke of Athol believed Mungo Park's "wee warms" were a hoax, and Park himself a charlatan. Lady Lavinia Kirkoswald refused to acknowledge she had ever laid eyes on the creatures and forbade mention of the subject altogether. Furthermore, to add insult to injury, the Royal Zoological Society rejected Park's paper entitled: The Life and Habits of Africa's Smallest Herpeton: Boa constrictus ittibittimungoparcus.

Findhorn Pittenweem, a direct descendant of Mungo Park, was determined to sail to the Dark Continent, capture the elusive mbondowoshobogowasi and produce it before the Royal Zoological Society and salvage his great-great-great-uncle's reputation. And indeed in 1923 he set off for Niger in French West Africa.

Well, the long and short of it is, Weemy turned over every rock along the banks of the Niger River for 100 miles either side of the settlement of Gomba and never laid bare a hidden tiny boa. But in that nearly four years of moil he was able to amass a bushel basket of diamonds. When back in Scotland, comfortably established on his family estate near Findochty, he commissioned a statue of Mungo Park and it stands facing south on a precipice above the North Sea, and has since served as a beacon for migrating worm-consuming birds to and from the African continent.

Findhorn Pittenweem undertook an arduous quest, and although he failed in his appointed mission, he nonetheless persevered beyond what anyone should have expected and returned home a far wiser and a far wealthier man than he had ever imagined. In Harry I saw Weemy's pluck. And how far that pluck would carry him in his singleness of aim remained to be seen.

At this point we find Harry, with Sydney, each attired in a business suit, waiting in a crowded British Airways arrival area at the John F. Kennedy Airport terminal in New York. Harry, fidgeting about, had his visibility impaired by ranks of people also awaiting arrivals. He bobbed above heads and shoulders in a frustrated attempt to view Fiona. Eventually the crowd thinned as disembarking passengers departed with their welcomers.

"She's here! There she is!" he pointed her out to Sydney.

"The one in the green outfit?"

Fiona appeared with a handsome young man carrying her luggage.

"Who is that guy with her?" Harry wondered aloud. He felt a sudden chill in the bones followed by gloomy forebodings as the man talked familiarly with her. She seemed not to be paying her fellow traveler any mind as she anxiously scanned the assortment of faces before her. She caught sight of Harry waving wildly. She clapped her hands together, joyously happy that Harry was there to greet her. She relieved the man of her luggage, thanked him, and rushed to embrace Harry. Harry's face flushed beamingly from pleasure and timidity. The young man was distinctly disappointed to have missed out on such a tasty dish, especially to a roma tomato. Disgruntled, he sniffed audibly and went on his way.

Sydney appraised her. He was clearly impressed with what he saw.

"I was half afraid you would not be here," she said all atwitter, "but here you are in the flesh, Harry Golub. I am so happy to see you."

"Wow!" said Harry, "this is really something."

"And you, Harry, you look so proper in your fine suit."

"Nothing much, just an old castaway."

"A what?"

"Castaway."

"Castanet."

"Cast a line."

"Casta diva."

Sydney stood in bafflement.

"Cast a glance."

"Cast a …"

"Ahem," said Sydney holding the bags, "Have I been … cast aside?"

"Bravo," Fiona turned to the speaker. "Not at all, not at all. You must be Sydney?" He smiled broadly and nodded yes. She kissed him on the cheek. "I feel as if I already know you, Sydney. Harry had nothing but nice things to say about his good friend."

"Harry, why didn't you tell me about Fiona, and what a beautiful creature yet?"

"This is a nicer reception than I should have imagined."

"Unfortunately, I have to go back to work," said Harry. "When Sydney's away I have to lock up the store. Sydney will drive you to your new home. Ruth, his wife, is very happy about your staying with her and Sydney."

"My Ruthie likes company, and boy can she cook food like you never had."

"Thank you both for making me feel so welcome."

"Speaking of food," said Harry, "tonight Ruth doesn't cook, we're all going to eat out—Little Italy. I'll meet you there. Umberto's, my favorite. Okay with you?"

"Fine, Harry. Hope I can stay awake; jet lag, you know."

"If Sydney does all the dinner talk—he usually does—dozing off could be a blessing."

"Always a kidder," Sydney spoke to Fiona.

They hailed a taxi and motored to the parking lot to get Sydney's car. Harry then taxied off to the store.

Fiona was still in a state of excitement as Sydney wheeled his Cadillac away from the airport. "New York from the air is so impressive. The skyscrapers, the Statue of Liberty."

"You ain't seen nothin' yet. You're gonna enjoy your stay here, Fiona. You'll find New York the most interesting city in the world. I should know, I've been to Miami—no comparison."

CHAPTER 35

And indeed they shared a most satisfactory Italian dinner. Fiona became noticeably tired halfway through the meal; and after a few sips of wine became increasingly drowsy. The traveling, the excitement, the long hours, and the heavy meal had taken its toll. The one certainty clear in her mind before leaving Umberto's was that she had been with warm, intimate companions.

Harry insisted he drive her back to her new home even though Sydney and Ruth were going there straightaway. It was his way of demonstrating that her being in America was his responsibility, and that he was eager to do whatever was required to make her feel at ease. Not to mention that he wanted to spend every spare moment with her; and this he would not admit even to himself.

On the drive back Fiona kept nodding off; when she did, Harry, unnoticed, glimpsed at the lovely lass with longing. How could he ever hope to have such a beautiful woman look upon him with the same warmth of emotion he felt for her? He was, don't you know, a roma tomato. That's what he wondered each time he glanced at her. When she snapped awake for the thirteenth time, Harry spoke:

"Sorry, Fiona. Never registered till now how many hours you've been awake. You need a good night's rest. Probably shouldn't have gone so far for dinner, or stayed so long."

"Bosh, Harry, I had a wonderful time," she yawned and snuggled deeper into her seat.

In a instant she dozed off, and her head fell on Harry's shoulder. Her proximity made him tense for a few seconds, and then he was overcome by an inexpressible pleasure. Fionas chrysanthemum hair smelled faintly of lilac and lemon. Feelings entirely new pleased and confounded him. Later, when he assisted her from the car in Sydney's driveway, she clung to him as much for support as out of affection.

"Thank you, Harry," she yawned. "It's been a splendid evening. I'm sooo tired." She kissed his forehead, the part of him she could reach without exertion. "Good night."

He helped her to the door. "Good night. Sleep tight." He bounded down the steps, "Glad you're here." He turned to wave, but she was already inside closing the door.

CHAPTER 36

In order to minimize his sponsor's voiced concerns over employing a non-professional as his coach and caddie, Harry had embellished Fiona's skills in those areas in such a way as to make Sydney believe that his marvelous play was entirely due to her tutelage. How could it be otherwise? The proof was in the pudding. So that when she had arrived in New York a few days prior to the Bridgeport Tournament, Sydney accounted it timely and fortunate for all concerned, and doubly so when he saw how lovely she was.

And Harry, upon meeting Fiona at the airport, became so smitten by her charms that golf, his one ruling passion, was at that instant unseated and the lass from St. Andrews was placed on its vacated throne. She was unaware of her elevation; indeed, his bashfulness and fear of rejection prevented him from expressing the awe and homage royalty merited. He was so smitten that he discontinued his public course jaunts and instead visited her at Sydney's home where everyone spent evenings playing parlor games.

At work Sydney had noticed Harry daydreaming, an occupation ill-suited to a salesman. He also took into account Harry's diminished interest in practice. As his sponsor, Sydney felt it necessary to prod his negligent friend every now and again to pick up a wedge. He began to wonder if he had been too hasty in offering Harry the wherewithal to set out on a venture that was beginning to bog down now that he had become moonstruck.

But he needn't have worried. Everything started to come to-gether on the drive to Bridgeport for day-one of the two-day tour-nament. Spirits were high. Harry was focused; Fiona was eager to participate; and Sydney was glad to finally get moving on the first phase of his scheme to launch Harry Golub golf products. That he had so much faith in Harry was more a testament to their friendship than to any real knowledge he had of the game or of Harry's ability to play the game.

As it turned out they couldn't have asked for a finer day in southwest Connecticut—70 degrees, a lot of sun, and a modicum of disturbed air. Upon arrival Harry had gone into the clubhouse to change for the match. Fiona and Sydney stood among a large group of spectators horseshoed around the 1st tee. Fiona hadn't noted that Phil was one of the three golfers that had just teed off to polite applause, nor had she known that Brewster Payne and Mal Baldwin were also among the 1st tee spectators.

Harry, carrying his clubs, showed up smartly dressed in new golf attire with a Levinson's Sporting Goods logo sewn onto the shoulder of his shirt and on the front of his baseball cap. He looked very ill at ease.

"Loosen up, Harry," Sydney spoke. "It's only a game."

"Tiddlywinks, checkers, and pin-the-tail-on-the-donkey are games," was Harry's retort. "This ..." he waved his hand around, "... this is an event. Look at all these people!"

"People, shmeeple," said Sydney. "What's to worry. They're here like you—to have a nice day. So, Harry, have a nice day."

"Easy for you to say."

"Harry!" Fiona chided.

"Huh?"

"Am I your caddie?"

"Uh huh."

"I carry the clubs," she unburdened Harry. She pulled a base-ball cap out of the bag's pocket and adjusted it on her head. It, too, had the Levinson logo.

Brewster Payne gave his companion an elbow poke, "Get a load of this! The little twerp is really here."

"Now do you believe me? Say … am I seeing things or is that not your gal from St. Andrews?"

Brew was astonished, "Fiona? This is becoming more bizarre by the minute." He pulled Mal along and they eased over toward the Golub group.

An Official standing near the registration canopy called with uncertainty to the unathletic, squat man, "Mr. Harrison Golub?"

Harry perked up, "Yessir!"

He pointed to the table under the canopy, "Please sign in, sir. Your group is next off."

"This is it," said Harry. Fiona followed him, and Sydney, not knowing quite what to do on his own, followed her. They stood outside the canopy. Harry was introduced and shook hands with two strapping young men—his first round opponents. They were handed scorecards. Harry tended to loosen up with people who were civil to him and his opponents presented themselves affable blokes.

"Yoiks!" Fiona jumped and turned around wild-eyed and holding her pinched bum. And there stood Brew wearing a gosh-it's-great-to-see-you look. Fiona was not amused. "Don't you ever do that to me! You heathen. I could have you arrested."

Sydney was in the dark.

"Mellow out, Fiona," he attempted to soft-peddle his gaffe, "all in good fun. Why are you here?"

"Never you mind. Just go away."

"You can't mean that. We're old friends. Remember Mal, here?"

With cold disdain, "I never want to see either of you again. Never!"

Brew was stung, embarrassed, "Bitch."

Sydney walked between them, "Be good fellas and leave us alone."

"Who's this clown?"

"No one to concern you," said Fiona. "Now go!"

"Yes," Sydney held his ground, "please go."

Brew scrutinized Sydney like he was a foul substance. He then reached up and tweaked his nose roughly.

"Ahhhh!"

Still holding on, "You should not stick your big schnozz in where it is not wanted, mister."

Fiona pushed Brew away. "You rotter! You had no call to do that."

Harry saw the disturbance and hurried over to confront Brew. Mal saw him approach and dragged Brew away, "Let's go. Now!"

"Heathens!" Fiona shouted after them, causing people nearby to question their faith.

Fiona looked on with fellow-feeling as teary-eyed Sydney tried to rub the pain out of his throbbing proboscis. "Who was that crazy grabber of noses, anyway?" asked Sydney. "Such a schmuck."

Harry arrived, "That who I think it is?"

"I hate him!" snarled Fiona bitterly.

Sydney, in the dark, "Who was he?"

"That moron, Sydney, was none other than Brewster Payne-in-the-ass."

"The golfer?" Sydney was shocked.

"The very same," answered Fiona.

"Why should he give my nose such a grab?"

"Because," said Harry, "you are my friend, and he hates me."

"Now I hate him also."

"Sydney, I'm so sorry," commiserated Fiona.

"Not to worry, little lady," he inhaled deeply, "it's still a functioning organ."

The public address speaker seized everyone's ear: "Attention, please! Will Misters Berger, Bianco, and Golub report to the 1st tee!"

Bianco and Berger were already on the tee when Harry joined them.

Fiona handed Harry his driver and winked, "Good luck, Harry." She stood off to the side.

Berger and Bianco teed off ahead of Harry. The spectators responded with moderate applause for their above average drives.

All eyes were on Harry. He took a deep breath, "Well, what ever happens, happens." He was unable to concentrate. He stood at the back of the tee and tried to survey the 329-yard par four hole. All that lay ahead was a greenish-blue blur. He took two trifling practice swings. He tossed a blade of grass in the air and neglected to follow its drift; it fell straight down. He took two more aimless practice swings. He was about to tee off when he realized he had forgotten to put on his golf glove. He pulled it from his back pocket and his score card flew out. He retrieved it and put it in a different pocket. He took two more practice swings. Now he was ready. He turned a complete circle looking for his ball. He neglected to tee it up. He began to shake.

Sydney called out from somewhere in the crowd, "Break a leg, Harry!"

The misapplied encouragement was just the ticket he needed to keep from being weak-kneed to the extent that when he teed up his ball he didn't fall over. He managed to do it, stood back of the ball and took one practice swing. The gallery was not at all impressed with the little fellow and rather wished he'd get on with it.

Brewster Payne observed the clownish pre-swing routine with knowing amusement. His smirk widened in anticipation of Harry's inevitable muck-up. Mal Baldwin had no such misgivings. He stood ready with an "I told you so."

Harry finally stepped up to the ball. His swing—to use the oft-repeated phrase—was smooth as silk. At the crack of the squarely-struck ball all eyes attended its soaring flight. Onlookers gasped. Brew's smirk was supplanted by an involuntary gulp. He stood transfixed, flabbergasted. "I told you so," he heard someone say. The crowd roared when the ball landed just short of the green.

Thrilled spectators turned to one another questioning whether each saw the same phenomenon—a plus 300-yard drive on line with the pin. The squat, silly little man had out-driven his two opponents and everyone else they had so far seen. Berger and Bianco looked down the fairway; then looked back at Harry. Things did not seem to add up. They shrugged. Golf has reasons of its own. So be it.

Harry, breathing more freely, tipped his cap to the enlivened gallery and handed Old Tom over to his relieved caddie.

The threesome of Berger, Bianco, and Golub marched down the 1st fairway with an army of spectators tagging along, including reporter Craig Rudnik, who was taking notes furiously.

As you would expect, Harry's monstrous wood shots were on the mark throughout the match. The few mis-hits, with mid- and short-irons, kept him from appearing super human. The day ended with Harry in second place, carding a 3-under par 69, two shots behind a pair with 67s. Harry's beaten opponents and their caddies congratulated the miniature John Daly and Fiona for their fine play and their good sportsmanship. Sydney, much to his delight and profit, ran up on the 18th green and hugged his investment and showered him with praise. Cheers and good wishes greeted Harry as he made his way through the crowd signing autographs. He glanced at the leaderboard and saw his name in second place. He pointed to "PHILLIPS."

"Poor Phil—he didn't make the cut. Wonder how he's taking it."

CHAPTER 37

Phil had played directly ahead of Harry's group and could not have avoided hearing cheers associated with his shot-making. When Phil made the turn at the 9th-hole the leaderboard had posted GOLUB 2-under par after eight holes. It looked for all the world like he might come in with the day's lowest score. Phil was struggling at that point, and things got worse when jealous rage accompanied him thereafter.

He struck every lie with malice aforethought. When his ball went astray, he bullied his caddie. From then on no one in his group offered him the slightest courtesy. He had no defenders; no friend. He brooded: How could Fate have squandered her largesse on trashy, miserable little Golub, a man beset with so many inadequacies? There was nothing to commend Harrison Golub. He was not, like himself, rich, well situated, an Ivy leaguer, a member in good standing in a number of clubs and societies, nor was Harry tall and well-favored. And yet he blamed this non-entity for stealing the continuity out of his life.

After his match, Phil fled the tournament grounds rankled in the extreme. He drove away oppressed by a feeling that he was of no account to anyone, and that maybe, just maybe, he had never cut a very good figure after all. Where did he start to go wrong? Try as he might he could not harness his mind's galloping parade of past misdeeds which stretched back to his bratty childhood.

Poking along on the parkway he was overtaken by a puerile agitation that moved him to sing.

Twits, nitwits, and dodos rule;
The world embraced an utter fool,
Why not the likes of me-eeeee?
Why not the likes of me?

After having sung the ditty through several times he thought it could be much improved with horn accompaniment.

Twits (Beep!), nit (Beep!) wits (Beep!), and (Beep!) do (Beep!)
dos (Beep!) rule (Beeeep!!!).

Angry drivers honked back and shouted obscenities at the singing, beeping driver poking along the busy road. A sense of futility and friendlessness enveloped him. He pulled over to the shoulder and parked. He gazed at the rear ends of cars going nowhere at the same speed, and they somewhat corresponded to the life he had been living. This would not do. He needed a destination, a goal, an objective. Phil needed help. He tried to empty his jumbled mind by listening to the drowsy drone of traffic. He settled back to permit the blighting effects of pride to ebb from him. He wept. Within an hour's interval he experienced a striking alteration in bearing.

Bantering young voices and small splashes reached him from beyond an embankment of shrubbery near at hand. He left the car to investigate. Two contesting teenage boys were skimming stones over a small pond. Phil returned to his car, opened the boot, pulled out golf clubs, golf shoes, umbrella, box of golf balls, and a couple of trophies. He lugged the lot over to the startled lads and deposited them at their feet. He spun around and hied back to his car and drove off without saying a word. He settled back comfortably; brought the car up to speed; and diffused a vast substantial smile of relief and broke into song:

Ah! Sweet Mystery of Life
At last I've found thee,
Ah, I know at last the secret of it all.
All the longing, seeking, striving, waiting, yearning, —
The burning hopes, the joy and idle tears that fall!
For 'tis love, and love alone, the world is seeking;
And 'tis love, and love alone, that can repay!
'Tis the answer, 'tis the end and all of living, —
For it is love alone that rules for aye!

CHAPTER 38

Harry and his friends were caught up in the car park by an untidy stranger. He had a press pass pinned to the pocket of his wrinkled shirt. He spoke with the quiet assurance of an uncle who was accustomed to having his way.

"Quite a show you put on, Harrison," spoken in a soft monotone.

"Thanks."

"I'm Rudnik, Craig Rudnik."

"Whoa, Craig Rudnik. of all people. Say, I read you column in the Post."

"Really."

"I especially liked the series you had last month on old-time golfers ... but, you left out Francis Ouimet."

"We strive to please. Can't mention everyone, can we? May I ask you a few questions?"

"Ask away."

"Are you familiar with anabolic steroids?"

"Do you mean, have supplements enhanced this perfect physique?" Harry flexed every muscle in his body, and, not surprisingly, still looked like a roma tomato. "Waddaya think?"

"Had to ask. Tell me then, how'd you ever develop such a powerful, perfect swing?"

There was an uneasy pause, "I ... ah ... took a great many lessons from a little known coach in St. Andrews, Scotland."

"And who was that?"

"Who was that?" Fiona shook her head, no. "I ... er ... I can't tell you who, Mr. Rudnik, the coach hates publicity. That's the reason sh ... he's known to so few golfers."

Writing away, "I like it. A mysterious Scot. Good. What make of driver do you use?"

"Pardon me, Mr. Rudnik," Sydney pounced in. "I'm Sydney Levinson, Harrison Golub's manager. I think I can answer that question. We had the clubs made special by a Scotchman clubmaker. Presently we are negotiating for exclusive rights to handle his products at Levinson's Sporting Goods. So, until it's a done deal we cannot tell anyone. But, and you have my word on it, when it's finalized, you, Mr. Rudnik, will be the first to know. You have the word of Sydney Levinson, L-E-V-I-N-S-O-N," he motioned Rudnik to write it down, "Sporting Goods—downtown Manhattan." Sydney was very pleased with himself.

"May I see the driver?" asked the reporter.

Harry looked to Fiona. She shrugged and reluctantly handed it over. "*This* is the club you used out there today?" he asked half expecting some sort of joke.

"Yep. That's it."

"I'm really amazed, Harrison, that you're able to get so much distance out of this old-style driver. You must be awfully strong?"

"He's mighty strong," offered Fiona.

"Indeed," walking away. "I'll be keeping an eye on your progress. Good luck tomorrow."

"Thanks Mr. Rudnik," Harry looked relieved.

"Thank *you*, Mr. Rudnik!" called out Sydney.

Fiona patted Harry on the back, "You handled that very well."

Sydney rubbed his hands together, "Things are happening. Let's get a move on! I got big deals to make for Harrison Golub products." He turned to Harry to give him serious counsel. "To-night, my boy, get lotsa rest. Tomorrow you have to be fresh like a daisy for the final last round." He walked ahead to the car.

Harry took the clubs from Fiona and they walked arm-in-arm behind Sydney.

"Did you enjoy yourself out there, Harry?"

"I had ..." a long pause, then a shout. "I had the greatest! the most fantastic! magnificent time of my entire life!"

CHAPTER 39

Within the illumined spirit-thicket the shades of Tom and Tommy Morris were joined by the shade of Francis Ouimet.

"Am I late?"

"Nae," said Tommy, "She's no yet arrived."

"Ye kinna expect punctuality frae a haff French female," grumbled Tom. "A trew Scot wadna be sae derelict o' dewty. She's maist likely in a dalliance wi' ane o' her guid fae nothin' court-iers."

A woman's voice sang out from the shadows: *"Me voici!"* Mary Stuart, Queen of Scots, appeared in their midst straightening her flounced silver-and-gold brocade gown, and then took a moment to fuss with her lustrous red hair. A singularly attractive monarch she was, and well aware of her allure and rank. She sat on a throne-like rock, adjusted her ruffled lace collar, and signaled those present to stand at ease.

"Salut, mon beau esprits."

"Greetings, your majesty."

Adopting a severe mein of dignity and power, Mary Stuart spoke ex cathedra: "We have summoned the St. Andrews Old Course *conseil d'etat* at this time to discuss the most efficacious manner in which to proceed toward having returned to our elysian *franternite* an enchanted golf club ..." she paused to glare at Old Tom, "that one of our number—against all rules and regulations—surrendered during a fit of monumental *stupidite* ..."

"Stupidity!" Tom resented the charge. "Stupidity, ye say, madam! I was brutally attacked and disarranged. Stupidity? Ye are unjust, madam."

"Ssh! Shush!" warned Tommy and Francis.

The queen continued, "... surrendered to a New World mortal of limited capacity, one Harrison Golub, Esquire, from New York City, North America. Gentlemen, you have had sufficient time to consider the dilemma confronting us, and, we dearly trust, its resolution."

Francis Ouimet stepped forward, "If you will permit me your gracious majesty, beloved Queen of Scotia, protector of the faith, most honored ..."

"More to the point, *Capitaine* Ouimet, more to the point." And muttered to herself, *"Mon Dieu* these colonials do go on." She looked expectantly into the far darkness. "We must proceed apace, gentlemen, for we have what promises to be a pleasurable foursome shortly—Bothwell, Darnley, Signor Rizzio and ourself."

"Indeed," said Old Tom in an aside to Tommy, "they a' shared her bunk and now the loftty duffers wull share the same bunker."

"A' at ance?" marveled Tommy.

"Not all at once, Master Morris." She had overheard the comments. "Not all together." She paused for a moment, reflected, smiled. She returned to the problem at hand, "Will you please continue, Francois?"

"Thank you, your majesty. Due to Tom Morris' magic golf club, Mr. Golub is on the road to becoming a formidable champion golfer. His proficiency will advance considerably with each outing. At this moment, in Bridgeport, Connecticut, on a course I have played numerous times ... it was there that I ..."

"More to the point!" admonished Queen Mary. *"Ma foi,* Francois, you'd try the patience of a stone."

"Sorry, your majesty. I have it on good authority that Mr. Golub will be invited to participate in this year's British Open, which you all know is to be held on this very course in six weeks time."

"Trew."

"That is sae."

"Merveilleux."

Movement in the far darkness drew everyone's attention. It was Bothwell pacing. Mary wiggled a finger at him to be patient. He was joined by Darnley and Rizzio. All were wearing kilts, and preening.

"Ahem!" Francis got her attention. "Your majesty, when Mr. Golub arrives in St. Andrews, Tom could then approach him and ask for the club back."

"That's right!" The suggestion pleased Tom. "He'll listen tae reason, or I'll strangle the bugger and tak it back!"

"You cannot do that!"

"Sacre bleu!"

"Ye kinna tak it back, dad. It maun be gien ye freely."

Mary, with contempt, "As you freely surrendered it to him."

Tom held his temper, "I couldna be held responsible fae my actions at that precise moment. I hae been toppled heidlang by an errant ba'. My wits were scrambled fae a wee. When my guid sense come back—the brute and club were gane."

"True."

"Trew."

"No excuse," pronounced the queen.

Tom, with forced calmness, "Neirtheless, I'll see it back." Then, with mounting fervor, "But a', can ye no appreciate what a splendid club I've created? Because o' my craftsmanship—and a daub o' hocus-pocus— the wee duffer Golub wull be renown throughout goffdom as anither …

"Bobby Jones!" shouted Francis Ouimet.

"… Tommy Morris," finished Tom.

"Come alang!" Bothwell was brusque. "Come alang, m'lady; tee time. Dawn hies apace."

"Oui, James," she cooed, "be with you presently." She addressed the assembled, "Well then, *messieurs,* it appears we are *en*

rapport. The magic golf club will be returned to Elysium this summer." She stood, "If there is no other business …" Ouimet stepped forward and was glowered at. He retreated. *"Finir de parler.* Dismissed. *Au revoir."*

With her skirts grabbed up, she ran over to the gentlemen-in-waiting and patted each on the head: *"Un, deux, trois! Allons, mon amours!"* The exalted foursome passed trippingly through the shadowy whin.

CHAPTER 40

From Bridgeport to New York City they were so exultant over the day's success that Harry, Sydney, and Fiona had difficulty getting words in edgeways. Each was commended repeatedly for his and her role in Harry's extraordinary first day on the professional golf circuit. But after depositing Harry at his apartment Sydney refrained from engaging in further chatter with Fiona as they drove through Manhattan. He had mistaken her pensiveness for fatigue and thought it best to let her rest. The lengthy drive to and from Bridgeport, the early wakeup call, and toting a full golf bag 18 holes should have worn her out.

Driving out of the Queens Mid-Town Tunnel and onto the Long Island Expressway brought them to the last leg of their long trip—a trip only to be repeated in the morning.

Fiona had something on her mind, "Sydney."

"Yes."

"Sydney, you've known Harry for a long while?"

"Let's see … Harry came to work for me … um, ten years ago. A godsend, he was. Nobody works harder than Harry. He likes what he does. With the customers, he's great; a real schmooser. Oh, and what he doesn't know about the golf, ain't worth knowing."

"Yes, I do know that about him."

"Singlehandedly he turned our golf department into our biggest moneymaker."

"Would I be correct in saying you know him better than any-one?"

"You would be correct."

"Do you think Harry likes me?"

"Like you? And why shouldn't he like you? Of course he does. What a question."

"I mean ... does he *really* like me.?"

"Ahhh, you mean *that* way like you. Ah haa." Sydney thought for a moment. "All these years I have never known Harry to have a real girlfriend—never talked about one even." Something jabbed his memory, "Ah, yes ... we both have a thing for Marilyn Monroe."

"Marilyn Monroe," Fiona was amused and charmed by the revelation.

Sydney spoke confidentially, "Please don't tell Ruthie about me and Marilyn—I don't think she'd understand.'

"You're secret is safe with me." Fiona felt certain that the disclosure of Harry's "thing" for Miss Monroe would somehow work to her benefit somewhere down the line.

They were almost home.

CHAPTER 41

Sydney begged off going along to Bridgeport the next morning claiming that mounting bits of business at the store demanded his immediate attention. Really, there was nothing so urgent that it could not have been postponed another day or two. His remaining behind in New York was a ruse used to allow Fiona to have Harry to herself for the day. If any female could coax the girl-shy little chap out of his shell, it would be Fiona. Sydney hoped with all his heart that she would succeed.

As you should have gathered by now, Sydney was a man of generous disposition, and, moreover, a man who rather relished playing the role of Cupid in this instance. Not being in Bridgeport was a great personal sacrifice, for he looked forward to watching his friend's brilliant play, which continued to amaze him.

That Harry had the largest spectator-following at the tournament came as no surprise. Word had spread concerning the little man with the big swing and prodigious drives. And he did indeed live up to his newly acquired celebrity. He was tied for first place after 14 holes, but things began going to pot on the 15th green. His assurance with Old Tom was a given; he simply addressed the ball and the magic came into play. Nothing could alter the result—a long, straight shot. But with the irons he was his true self, and therefore often at the mercy of his insecurities. Lack of close mental application while playing was a major fault in Harry. As he was about to chip onto the 15th green his mind cluttered—as it often did—with flashes of pre-shot points that must be executed in order to pull off an effective shot. For the most part he had managed passably, and, much to his credit, was in the way of improving incrementally.

When he initiated his chipping down-stroke an utterance from the hushed crowd caused him to foozle the shot.

"Golub golub."

Heads turned in the general direction of Brewster Payne, who also turned his head to look behind as though the heckler were somewhere in that vicinity. After an uneasy interlude all eyes returned to Harry whose ball was away. Somewhat rattled at this point, he hit a 30 foot putt much too softly and it came up short by 10 feet. Onlookers gasped. He was still away. His next putt fell prey to another "Golub golub." The ball went four feet beyond the cup."

"Shut up! Quiet!" yelled the crowd in the direction of Malcolm Baldwin.

"Will who ever is making those fowl noises, cease!" called out Brew from the opposite side of the green.

The spectators agreed: "Yeh, cut it out! Shut up! Cool it, stupid!"

Harry saw Brew and knew the actual source of the harassment. Fiona was incensed. Brew gave each his nastiest smile, and with a flick of his fingers bid them continue. Harry finished the hole and fell back three strokes from the lead.

Gunther followed Mal over to where he joined Brew. He spoke menacingly to the two hecklers. "If you turkeys gobble one more time I'll wring your scrawny necks."

"We don't know what you're talking about," said Mal with mock innocence.

Brew snubbed his erstwhile friend and sauntered away.

Harry, still shaken, three-putted each of the final holes but managed to finish alone in fourth place. Harry was ecstatic. The crowd applauded its appreciation of his fine play. Brew, still a presence, caught Fiona's eye and blew her a kiss. She responded with a sour look. Harry grabbed her at that moment and gave her a huge hug. One of the first in line asking for an autograph on his program was Gunther.

"Thanks for showing up, Gunther."

"Wouldn't have missed it for the world, Harry. I don't think you need worry about the turkeys anymore. I think I put the fear of God in them."

"Appreciate it. You got my invitation to the party, right?"

"You bet. See you then. Take care—you, too, Fiona."

Signing autographs and receiving handshakes and pats on the back—one on the backside— Harry worked his way through the crowd. After staying for the short ceremony for the winner they were anxious to leave for New York and relate the day's happenings to Sydney, but they were held up in the parking lot by reporters demanding interviews. Rudnik was among them. The reporters essentially asked the same questions Rudnik had asked the previous day and received the same answers. When they left, Brew showed up.

"Golub golub."

Harry spun around, resentful, confrontational, "Yesterday, it was nose grab day for you! Today, you're a dumb ass turkey! What kind of a jerk are you, anyway?"

"This kind," and Brew decked Harry with a sharp blow to the jaw. Harry was knocked senseless.

Fiona knelt at his side. "Harry! Harry, say something." She patted his face.

"Oh, ohhh," he moaned.

With arms folded across his chest, Brew looked down on the pair with bitter scorn.

"You heathen!" she barked at Brew making her words sound like a curse. She turned to her fallen hero, "Harry, speak to me."

Harry saw Brew glaring down on him, "Oh, ohhh."

Brew spoke derisively to Fiona, "Is that the best you can do?"

"He's one hundred per cent above the likes of you."

"At this moment he doesn't look to be above anybody."

Harry groaned, "What happened?"

"The guy's a total loser," said Brew over his shoulder as he walked away.

Fiona screeched after him, "Go to bloody hell!"

"You're a couple of losers. You deserve each other."

"We do indeed."

Fiona pressed Harry's head to her breast. Brew glanced back at the scene of his triumph only to see the fallen adversary receive ministrations from the fair maid who once thought well of him. He felt a fleeting tinge of self-reproach before he shrugged his shoulders and marched off tingling with malicious pleasure.

Sensing Brew's departure, Harry revived.

Fiona cooed soothingly, "Haaarry. Are you okaaay?"

Harry sat up manipulating his jaw, "I think so. Whoa, that smarts."

She assisted him to his feet. "I surely hope we never encounter that horrid beast again."

Harry brushed himself off, "We can't avoid him if I continue to play tournaments."

"I wish I knew how to cast spells," said Fiona as she brushed off his back. "I'd turn Mr. Brewster Payne and his loathsome accomplices into mud-puddle toads."

"I like that. Work on it, would ya."

"Abracadabra," she chanted, "Brewster Payne-in-the-arse and his mates are bug-eyed warty toads in a mud puddle. Abracadabracazam! There. That ought to do it. Sound right to you, Harry?"

"Ribbet, ribbet!"

"Blimey, now I have to kiss a frog and turn him back into Prince Harry."

"Oh oh, time to go," and he jumped in his car.

CHAPTER 42

Not that Harry's tournament play had proved a distinct success; not that his star was in the ascendant; not that he courted praise; no, Harry gave a party out of the sheer enjoyment of doing it. The first he had ever given. Too long he had been something of a recluse. His garrulous nature, his odd stature, and his unintentional lapses in the social graces had on first acquaintance contributed to a large extent on his having been slighted socially. And those repeated snubs had conspired to chip away at his self-esteem. But the new Harry found that his getting up and out in the world allowed right-thinking people an opportunity to know the real Harrison Golub—garrulous and squat, a bit rough around the edges, yes, but the fact remained that he always was a man with a good heart, a sense of fun, and respectful of his fellow men.

Harry's once lonely apartment was jammed with happy people, new and old friends, fellow workers, neighbors. Making sure everyone was having a good time, he ran around dispensing drinks and jokes, and introducing guests. Fiona and Ruth balanced trays of canapes as they wove through the animated crowd. Sydney had a few men cornered in the kitchen and was attempting to drum up orders for Harrison Golub golf clubs. Bette Midler's recorded voice sang in and out of the babble. Harry answered the doorbell.

"Come on in, Gunther. Glad you could make it."

Gunther handed Harry a package with a bottle in it, and stepped inside, "Wow, Harry, this sure looks like the hot place to be in New York."

Harry took Gunther's jacket, "Make yourself at home."

"By the way, Phil sends his regards."

"You gotta be kiddin'."

"Believe me, Harry, he's a brand new person—you wouldn't recognize him. And, get this, he says he owes it all to you."

"Me?"

"Yup. He said the humiliation of your beating him nearly drove him insane. Then he said something about cars in the fast lane to nowhere, which I didn't quite follow. He says he's stopping to smell the roses, feed the pigeons—and not step on ants."

"Whoa."

"Yeah, he's still got issues to work out. I think he's still a little crazy ... but in a good way. Anyway, he quit golf and the country club and turned to God and AA. Not only that, he's got Tony thinking along the same lines. Weird, huh?"

"I'll be darned. Well ... give them my regards, will you?"

He gave Harry's shoulder a tap, "You're one in a million, Harry." He went over to join Sydney.

Sydney was in the middle of a sales pitch. "Harrison Golub drivers are individually crafted with loving care by theee master club maker in all of Scotland." He handed the club around. "Ain't she a beaut? The place you can get this is Levinson's Sporting Goods only."

Fiona relieved Harry of Gunther's jacket and took it to the bedroom. She laid it on the bed with other wraps. Her attention was drawn to pictures on the wall. Almost all were signed photos of golfers. There was an enlarged old photo of Francis Ouimet as a lanky young man wearing knickerbockers and a tam, and leaning on a golf club. She picked up a framed photo from the bedside stand. It was herself and Harry posed in front of the Tommy Morris memorial. An unexpected delight. Since her arrival in New York nothing had been more agreeable than happening upon that photo, in that room, in that apartment. She now knew exactly where she stood with Harry. She replaced the photo. The one displayed item that did not fit the links theme was a glossy promotional photo-graph of Marilyn Monroe; the famous one from The Seven Year Itch where she holds down her skirt over a subway grate with itching Tom Ewell gawking in the background. She studied the picture, then, imitating Miss Monroe's pose, uttered a soft, steamy "Wheeee."

Back in the living room Sydney had corralled half a dozen new auditors. He read from a newspaper clipping, "'Move Over John Daly, by Craig Rudnik.' This Rudnik I know personally. He is the authority in the universe about the golf. So what he says is bibli-cal. 'Move Over John Daly. I never thought I'd say that, but I'm forced to proclaim what these eyes marvelled at over and over these past two days at the Bridgeport Open. What I and a gasping throng of spectators witnessed was the booming power of newcomer Harrison Golub of New York City, a muscular little dynamo who stands tall in the tradition of those other Dukes of Distant Drives—Tiger Woods and John Daly. Immortality awaits … .'"

Harry greeted two more women guests and took their wraps into the bedroom. Fiona was perusing pictures on the wall.

"You have many grand things in this room, Harry."

"Glad you like them." He picked up the photo of himself and Fiona from the bedside stand and shoved it in the drawer.

Fiona saw his action reflected on the glass of a framed picture of Byron Nelson. She closed the door and sashayed flirtatiously to him. He was unnerved by her sexy forwardness. He swallowed hard and attempted to direct her attention to a display of odd-shaped putters in a line leaning against the wall.

"A couple of these are 150 years old."

"Putters? Fancy that," she said in a throaty whisper inches from his ear. He moved distractedly around the room with Fiona dogging his every step.

Utterly at his wit's end, Harry kept turning away from facing Fiona and pointed out various items of his collection. "I guess you noticed … I collect … I collect golf memorabilia … see … golf pictures, books, programs … balls, clubs … autographs … ."

Softly in his ear, "I have Jack Nicklaus' signature on Uncle Cam's business card at home; would you like it for your collection?"

"He's a great guy, Jack Nicklaus," Harry said moving toward the door. She cut him off. "I met him during a Pro/Am at Shinnecock a few years ago."

"A fine chap, indeed," she said and maneuvered him up against a wall, her face very close.

"My all time favorite golfer is …"

"Bobby Jones?"

Harry shook his head no; their noses flicked He slid down the wall. Nose to nose she traveled with him.

"Dow Finsterwald?"

Harry's voice cracked, "Fran … cis, Francis Ouimet."

"Ahh, yes, Frances Ouimet. She was brilliant."

"He. He put golf on the map in the United States."

"Francis was a cartographer?"

"No … oo. He was a 20-year old caddie from Boston who won the 1913 U.S. Open."

"Oh, that Francis Ouimet."

Harry sidled to his left and found himself wedged in a corner. "Later, this same Ouimet became … became the first American elected Captain … Captain of St. Andrews Royal and Ancient Golf Club."

"St. Andrews? A charming place. Have you been there?" Fiona leaned into him and blew lightly in his face.

Harry swooned. "I don't know what a captain does at St. Andrews, but it must be a great honor."

"Must, surely." She pursed her lips and lowered her face to Harry's. He was bug-eyed with panic.

The door flew open and Sydney entered. "There you are, Harry. Ruthie and me looked everywhere for the pickles. You know we gotta have pickles with pastrami sandwiches. Did you forget them?"

Harry ducked under Fiona's arm and hurried to the door. "They're in the cupboard over the ice box." Sydney smiled approvingly to Fiona and followed Harry out.

Fiona opened the bedside stand drawer and took out the photo. She sat on the bed and studied it. She replaced it on top of the stand.

CHAPTER 43

On the heels of his unlikely success in the Bridgeport Open, and the glowing media coverage he received—especially from highly respected golf columnist Craig Rudnik—Harry became inundated with all manner of offers and proposals. Many contacts were cranks wanting him to join them in some business scheme or wanting to represent him as his agent. Two were proposals of marriage. Most were invitations to upcoming tournaments, for it was widely held that his presence would assure a larger group of spectators. Harry's star had risen with the speed of a comet.

I dare say much of his appeal had to be due to the nature of his game. He was a walking contradiction—an unimpressive, roundish little chap capable of howitzer drives. He was a phenomenon, repeating again and again physical impossibilities. And to realize he accomplished such feats with what appeared to be antediluvian woods.

His high finish in the Bridgeport qualified him for the New England Invitational, which he attended in Brattleboro, Vermont. Harry won the tournament in a three-hole playoff. The following weekend he finished third in the New York Open held at Bethpage. And the week after, Sydney flew down with Harry to a P.G.A. qualifier in Myrtle Beach, South Carolina which he also won and lowered the course record on the final day. Fiona stayed behind to keep Ruth company. They watched the final round on the Golf Channel. They cheered Harry on, and they giggled at Sydney, a befuddled, out-of-place caddie. But following each round Sydney wrote up dozens of orders for Harrison Golub clubs.

CHAPTER 44

And then, Hollywood called. The voice on the telephone wanted Harry to appear in his own life story. "Harry baby, don't worry about the acting part, trust me, a piece of cake. I know a natural when I see one—and baby, you're a natural. You got box-office written all over you. Just like Jackie Robinson and Audie Murphy, they played themselves and they were terrific. Harry, trust me, you are so you. Already we have a title," said the impassioned voice on the phone, "this oughta grab yah: The Harry Golub Story. Catchy, right? We're gonna roll all the way with this and take it to the top, baby. Already we got the perfect director. Already we got hot screenwriters lined up. Already we have a cool mill set aside for you. Are we ready, or are we ready? All we need from you, Harry, is a yes. Do I have a yes? Harry baby, talk to mama."

Harry baby would have none of it.

Sydney tried to persuade him otherwise. "Harry, think about it. This is too rich to pass up. Harry you should grab the bull's horn, grab when it's hot the iron, grab and run with the money. Grab at life, Harry, grab at life. In this world you gotta be a grabber," he exhorted, then quickly covered his nose.

Harry was adamant. Fiona backed him. Sydney showed his exasperation by yanking his hair with both hands.

To my mind Harry made the correct decision. The secret of his club should stay secret. But that aside, he also avoided poten-

tial heartbreak; Hollywood would have bollixed his story to such
an extent that he would not have recognized even a part of himself on screen. Movies, unlike theatre, permits too much input
from too many egos; and not all of those egos have talent. The
original script is never the finished product. I know. I've been
grist for the Hollywood mill. I have a woeful tale in that regard if
you will allow me a few words.

You may recall a play entitled *The Air Out There.* I wrote it
and am pleased to remind you that it captured the Joseph Jefferson
Prize for the best drama in 1920. The play was optioned to Eminent Studios of Hollywood with the proviso that I undertake the
writing of the screenplay there on the Hollywood lot under the
watchful eyes of director, producer, cameraman, and son-in-law
of the studio head, Marcus Selfisch. There was of course no dia-
logue, this being the era of silent cinema; even so, I was required
to draw descriptions of characters, and set forth scenes, settings,
and stage direction. *The Air Out There* was a simple story and
rendering it into a motion picture didn't seem to offer any ob-
stacles. I think a synopsis of my play and then that of the resulting
screenplay should give you a fair idea of how a true work of art
can be bastardized by a miscellany of uncultured butchers.

The drama, *The Air Out There,* is as follows

The year is 1888. Dr. Humphrey Van Weyden, Boston's
leading authority on respiratory ailments, prescribed the brac-
ing air in the mountains above Flagstaff, Arizona as the essential remedy for inflating the flagging lungs of the beautiful, 19-
year old dental assistant, Ruby Mobie. To attain full benefit
from the salubrious nature of the mountain retreat it was necessary that Miss Mobie sojourn there for a full year.

Miss Ruby Mobie was a bold, resourceful young woman,
and surviving alone in an abandoned fur trapper's cabin in the
wilderness presented challenges the city girl was willing to explore. When an adolescent, Ruby devoured James Fenimore

Cooper's Leatherstocking Tales. Often she had envisioned herself coursing forest glades and deer trails as Natalie Bumpo. Now she had the rare opportunity of putting her well-informed outdoorsmanship to the test. She embraced the trapping trade. Sightings of snakes, wolves, and grizzly bear added zest to her sense of adventure. A diet of berries, trout, squirrel and beaver tail served her well through the summer. With the onset of cold weather she descended, with her burro, Gordo, down to Flagstaff to trade beaver pelts for provisions to lay in for the winter.

When Ruby returned to her log cabin she discovered a Mexican senor comatose in her bed. He had been shot in the leg and shoulder. The man had one arm only. Recognition was immediate for she had studied his wanted poster on the Flagstaff mercantile store window. He was none other than El Pistolero del Uno Brazo—the one arm bandit! It never entered her mind to collect the two dollar reward offered for him, dead or alive. Ruby was never one for profiteering from another's misfortune.

There lay the stricken intruder. Being a conscientious member of the medical profession she set about treating the patient. First, out of habit, she examined his teeth. She thrilled to note he had the most perfect canines she had ever probed. And all accounted for. After sponging El Pistolero clean she believed he was the most devilishly handsome one-armed Mexican she had ever laid eyes on. So striking he nearly took her breath away, which in her condition might have been fatal. It was a clean flesh wound to the shoulder which she cauterized using her bowie knife, the blade heated red hot. He flinched but did not waken. However, it proved trickier business digging the bullet out of his upper thigh because it was exceedingly close to a vital organ. After two days of fever and chills and delirium he rested comfortably. When fully recovered he let it be known—neither spoke the other's language—that his happiness was in forever serving Ruby Mobie with undiminished love. And she reciprocated. And so the cabin fever they experienced throughout the winter was not the cabin fever experienced by sourdoughs. With the melting of the snows the happy pair made their way through a gauntlet of bounty hunters to the safety of La Paz, Mexico, El Pistolero's birthplace.

That summer Dr. Humphrey Van Weyden received a post-card from Mexico with the picture of an albino seal poised on a rock above the blue water of the Gulf of California.

All is well. Lungs full. Thanks for everything. Sincerest good wishes, Senora Ruby Mobie Pistolero and family.

THE END

That, my friend, is merely a cursory glimpse of my play and in essence my screenplay. But never would you recognize it as such on the silver screen. The Hollywood simpletons ravaged my beautiful drama to such an extent that the only resemblance to the play and the motion picture was the title, *The Air Out There*.

The Eminent Studios completed version went along these lines.

The year is 1912. Ailing dentist, Dr. Richard Moby, urged by his family physician to take to the open seas in order to restore his diminished vigor, enlisted as ship's surgeon on the 50-foot sealer "Ghost" for a year-long voyage to the colder parts of the North Atlantic in pursuit of fur seals. Within a week out of the home port of Boston, first mate Buck Stellar informed the crew that peg-legged Captain Baja had ordered the Ghost to change course to the Sea of Cortez wherein he hoped to encounter and destroy El Gordo, the great white seal who had chomped off his leg below the knee, below La Paz, beneath the Pleiades.

Able to stave off three mutinous attempts, and a nine-day battle against the elements in the roiling cauldron of the Magellan Straits, Captain Baja, through sheer force of will and a primed shotgun, eventually brought the Ghost and crew to

the heart of the Sea of Cortez. For three days the ship lolled in
still waters and sweltering heat. At six bells on the fourth morning, able-bodied seaman Humphrey Van Weyden shouted from
the crow's nest, "Ahoy! Ahcy! Thar she bobs! The Great White
Seal!"

"Man all boats!" commanded Captain Baja. "Go to it,
mates! A cask of Amontillaco to the lad that nails that bloomin'
limb lubbin' b_s_a_d!"

And indeed all men save one, the ship's surgeon, Dick Moby,
rowed out to harpoon El Gordo. The sinister seal drew the
rowboats two miles away from the Ghost whereupon he
turned and rammed them. All hands were lost, and a few
legs to boot. Bloodied but triumphant, El Gordo flopped
up on a rock, basked in his glory, and barked at passing
yellowfin tuna.

Dick Moby, left to his own resources—but now in robust
health—proved himself an able navigator. He sailed the Ghost
round Cape Horn and up along the east coast of South America
without a hitch. But, off Cape Hatteras, he was blown north-
northeast by a steady gale and ran headlong into a breaching
blue whale which caused the Ghost to take on water, list,
founder, then sink. Mobie managed to swim out to a floating
hatch door and hang on. Adrift for two days he was sighted
and rescued by a pleasure ship on her maiden voyage from
Southampton to New York, the Titanic.

THE END

I ask you, where in all that balderdash is my play? They muti-
lated it. Not cricket, I say. So it made the studio a lot of money
even though a Variety review commented that "*The Air Out There,
Stinks.*" That's hardly the point. Who's to say that my screenplay
left as it was would not have made a lot of money? We'll never
know. And that is why I never again ventured beyond the Hudson

River. Hollywood? Pfaw. You can have it. Not good form anyway you look at it. Let this be fair warning to men of good will, do not go there, you'll not find contentment.

On my soul, I do believe I have again fallen prey to my penchant for moral digression. I do hope you haven't found me overly prolix. Again, to Harry. We shall listen in on two Elysian souls who in this instance shall serve as a Greek chorus catching us up to date on particulars concerning our protagonist.

CHAPTER 45

For St. Andreans it was the dead of night, but the dead of night was their time to be out and about on the moonlit links where no intruding, off-putting city clamor was heard, just the sound of the eternal measure of the sea.

Tommy Morris and Bobby Jones, two of a galaxy of notable souls in our abode of delight, were idling on a bench adjacent to the 13th—known locally as Hole o'Cross, coming in—notorious for its strategically placed Coffin Bunkers, and for the gaping Lion's Mouth pot bunker in front of the green. A winsome threesome had just quit the tee and were heading down the fairway looking smart in their athletic prime—"Babe" Didricksen Zaharias, Dorothy Campbell, and Joyce Wethered.

"Bobby, what hear ye o' yer countrymon, Harrison Golub?"

"Home folks say he's doin' mighty fine," replied Jones in a curious Georgia-Harvard drawl which caused him to sound like a homespun sophisticate.

"Dad's charmed club is servin' him weel then?"

"Must, by golly. He's one of the favored in the U.S. Open."

"Fancy that." Tommy stood and rehearsed swings with his hickory-shafted brassie. "Golub maun hae raked in a pile o' money."

"Not a red cent. And he'll not turn professional."

"Why sae? Nowadays top goffers mak' millions o' pounds."

"In many ways Harrison Golub is a gentleman. He's fully aware of the advantage he's had over his opponents. He simply doesn't feel justified in acceptin' prize monies."

"There's honor in that. But ye ken he's deprived the trew winner o' his trophy and glory. Dae ye no find that troublin'?"

"Yes, by gummy, I do find it troublin'. I need not remind you that an instinct for fair play is not deep-rooted in everybody. I'm afraid Harry has fallen into that category of high handicapper who welcomes any advantage to lowering his scores without questioning whether it's on the square. I have known good men, men of unyielding character, who, in an effort to win a close match, have cast aside all the principles of a lifetime. In all else they remained good men. Golf can try a man's soul. But I think the good in Golub outweighs the bad."

"Hoo sae?"

"The advent of Harrison Golub, Golfer, has given an enormous boost to the game's popularity in the States, especially among those people who had shunned outdoor activity due to personal girth or awkwardness which they found to be embarrassin'. Harry's their poster boy. His influence was strong enough to lure stay-at-homes to put off a twelfth viewing of a *Gilligan's Island* episode on television and get themselves out to golf courses and drivin' ranges. There they rediscovered the benefits of fresh air and exercise; their mental health also improved. For these reasons alone I give Harry considerable credit."

"Aye, a guid mon in that. But ye ken, Bobby, the langer he maks use o' Dad's driver ... I'm afeered he'll no come to a braw end. His High and Michty Sel' disna allow Elysian wares amang the quick unless He confers them."

"Let us hope, for the good of Harry's soul, we can resolve this matter at our next privy council."

"Aye, for what sha' it profit Harrison Golub if he gain the U.S. Open and lose his soul?"

"Amen." They stood on the tee.

"In nae sma' way Harry reminds me o' yersel'—a perfit gentleman, a gifted American amateur goffer who wins mair than his share o' tournaments."

"Shucks. You are exceedingly kind, Tommy, however Golub's gift is from Old Tom—mine, such as it is," he pointed up, "emanates from an even higher Personage."

"Mine tae," he seconded reverentially.

"Tommy, do you reckon He'll favor us with His presence on one of our rounds?"

"Nae likely any time sune, He disna care fae the game any mair."

"How odd. You've see Him play—how'd He co?"

"As ye'd expect, a picter-perfit swing. He connected brilliantly wi' every club ... save the ane-iron."

"The one-iron?" Bobby was incredulous. He inspected the one-iron in his hand.

"The last time We played taegither He said He wad no play anither roun' wi' me until He mastered the ane-iron. And that be an hundred year syne."

"That long ago. Well, He must be mighty busy. No time to hone his skills, I expect."

"He's the time, nae doot aboot it, lad. He manages tae attend cricket matches in Jamaica, and India and Pakistan."

They looked at each other and weighed the preposterousness of His attraction of cricket over the royal and ancient game.

"Borrrin'," they pronounced in unison.

From above, a pleasing Voice addressed them "Have a sublime game, gentlemen."

"Thank Ye, Sir."

"Thank You, Sir."

Tommy teed off with a furious brassie drive which caused his scotch bonnet to fly off. Bobby drove with his one-iron; a smooth easy swing that produced a soaring shot that landed beside Tommy's ball on the fairway. Bobby kissed his club and put it in his bag.

"Smarty pants," said the Voice from above.

The happy golfers snickered on their way down the Hole o'Cross, coming in; they were in every way content.

CHAPTER 46

On the eve of the U.S. Open, outside Boston, the Country Club dining hall bustled with good-natured banter. Busy waiters in black uniforms flitted from table to table like starlings. Harry entered with Fiona and Sydney and were immediately directed to a far table. The players present were the golf world elite. Harry knew many by reputation but had never personally met any one of them. On the other hand, the professional golfers were well aware of the new fellow in their midst. Rudnik's Golub articles were syndicated worldwide, often accompanied by photos of Harry next to a normal-sized person to illustrate the incongruity of his powerful drives with his obvious anatomical deficiencies. While wending to his table Harry received a number of polite nods of greeting from faces he recognized on television. He responded to each nod with unexpected familiarity: "Corey, what's happenin'?" "Ernie, how's it goin'?" "Tiger, nice shirt." "Vijay, nice seein' ya." "Hey, Justin, see ya on the 1st tee." All reacted with bemusement. One table recognized in Harry a character in the mold of Lee Trevino and Fuzzy Zoeller, a jester who could add much needed levity into a tour that some thought had become much too serious.

Harry was held up by a grip on his sleeve by someone he didn't recognize, "Harry, what's your power source?"

Harry whispered in his ear, "Chopped liver sandwiches."

The man hailed a waiter. "I would like a humongous chopped liver sandwich."

The waiter looked down his nose, "Regretfully, sir, not on our menu."

"Just as well, I hate liver."

Dashed if that waiter wasn't Shrewsbury incarnate. Shrewsbury, our man in the Camelopard smoking room, was a servant with a like disdain for impropriety. I had never known him to register a smile nor attempt to disguise his conceit. I was ever of the opinion that he functioned under the delusion that his calling was the most precious of all blessings, and that I was fortunate in the extreme to have been placed in his care. Indeed he was exasperatingly perfect in carrying out members' requests, but he let us know, by his manner, that he was our better. Shrewsbury walked a treadmill whereon he approached but never quite attained insolence. There were occasions when I have been torn between extending him the hand of gratitude or extending a fist to his haughty nose. The fact that I refrained from acting either way proved to my satisfaction that I was a true gentleman, and Shrewsbury a true snob. For these reasons, the Camelopard was, in the balance, the arena wherein Shrewsbury and I tested our tolerances.

When Harry and his party had seated, an elderly gentleman leaning back in his chair spoke, "Harry, I've tried one of your drivers and there was a 50 yard difference in my drive—50 yards less. How do you account for that?"

"Dunno. Maybe you should tighten your grip."

"I see you also give bad advice. I'm going to need to keep an eye on you," he scolded, then chuckled. "Just pulling your leg. Glad to have you aboard. Good luck this weekend."

"Thanks, Mr. Palmer."

Sydney spoke, "From Cam I got a call this morning. He sends his warmest regards to you, Harry; and to you, Fiona, his love."

"How dear of Cam—and how is he?"

"Fine. Better even than fine. He's hired six more clubmakers to keep up with the demand for Harrison Golub woods. Such a success I've never before been part of." He pleaded, "Harry,

Harry, with you I'm begging—turn professional. We could make millions Harry, think of it."

"No, Sydney," he answered calmly. "Things are fine as they are."

"That's my Harry," said Fiona patting his hand.

"I don't know why you always have to agree with him," said Sydney and quickly covered his nose. Brewster Payne was standing behind Harry. "Oh, oh, it's the grabber of noses."

Brew, not hiding his persistent hostility, looked down on Harry, "Looks as though one of these tables has been reserved for idiots."

Sydney, with a defiant note in his voice, blurted, "Maybe you should sit at the head of this table." He then covered his face with both hands.

Harry shoved his chair back. Brew put his hands on Harry's shoulders and held him down in his seat. "Later, Harry, later. You're looking well, Fiona." He walked back to his table where Malcolm Baldwin had been sitting alone observing the encounter with discomfort.

"What is it with that schmuck?" asked Sydney in extreme exasperation. "Will somebody please tell me what's going on here?"

Harry, flipped through his salad with a fork, "Brewster Payne hates me because I was not a good golfer ... and now he hates me because I am a good golfer."

Fiona addressed Sydney, "Brew and I used to be ... friendly like. Now he thinks Harry and I are ... you know."

"Are you and Harry ... you know?"

"Enough already with the you knows. Let's eat this good food. I gotta turn in early—I'm in the U.S. Open tomorrow. Can you believe it?"

"Here's to you, Harry," Sydney gave a toast. "For you in the tournament—lockheim." They clinked water glasses.

"If you win, Harry," Sydney said reprovingly, "all you'll get is a big vase. But, if you were a professional you'd get over a million dollars."

"Win or lose, I'm here to have fun."

"Fun, shmun. You can't have fun with a million dollars?"

Fiona and Harry looked at each other: "Naaaah!"

Sydney threw up his hands and surrendered.

CHAPTER 47

The scene I am about to deliver may give offense if your inclination is rigorous morality; however, if you have a mind and heart which affirms that Love is the richest joy out of heaven, then you shall look upon this romantic episode in my narrative as an ode to that joy.

After the banquet Sydney went to stay with relatives in Brookline. Fiona and Harry entered their separate rooms in an upscale Chestnut Hill motel. Around midnight, Fiona, in a short, frilly nighty examined her fetching self in the full-length mirror. She slipped on a blonde wig and adjusted it just so. She mimed a good imitation of Miss Marilyn Monroe acting enthralled over the ministrations of a suitor. Continuing her Monroe persona she lifted a tray bearing two cups of coffee, turned off the light, nudged the window drape aside and peered for a long while into the darkness. Satisfied that there was no one about she slipped out of her room and quietly shut the door. On bare feet and balancing the tray she hurried past four rooms to Harry's door. She looked anxiously around, then tapped.

"What is it?" Harry called from his bed where he lay propped up reading the Boston Globe sport section.

"Tea time," was Fiona's throaty whisper.

"I know, I know. 9:15 in the morning. I'll be there."

Fidgeting nervously, "Harry—it's Fiona."

Surprised and delighted, he jumped up and bounded for the

door. His first inclination when he opened the door was to slam it shut in the face of an imposter, but there was something in her manner and look that made him grab her and pull her inside. He checked wildly up and down the parking area, seeing nothing compromising, gently closed the door without making a sound. For a few seconds he stood listening with his back to the door. He opened the door a crack and peeped out. All seemed clear. Fiona stood at attention in the middle of the room holding the tray and watched his discomfort with amusement.

Harry could not bring himself to look upon the immodest, unshod, alluring blonde creature before him. He groaned and pushed his forehead against the door. "Good God, Fiona, pleeease, put something on."

"I have something on. Oh, turn about Harry, I'm not going to bite you."

She set the tray on the bedstand, and there again was the photo of them together. She sat on the edge of the bed.

She spoke coaxingly, patting the space next to her, "Come, Harry, my sweety. Sit here."

He tensed, but didn't stir. She rose, took his hand, led him to the bed and sat him down. When she sat beside him she patted his thigh. He swooned.

He began to tremble, "You shouldn't be here."

"True, true," she answered cooly.

"What if someone saw you come in?"

"Ah, what if … ."

Harry sidled to the end of the bed. She followed.

"Harrison," using her sexy, breathy Marilyn Monroe voice, "Harrison, my love, my sweet, my pet, I have a confession to make." She reached for the tray. "This is not tea," she whispered in his ear, "it's coffee. One lump, or two lumps?"

He responded innocently, "Can't drink coffee this late—it'll keep me up all night."

"Up all night, surely? That's more than one should expect."

Fiona lifted his chin with a finger. She caressed his head in both hands. He scrunched his eyes shut and clenched his teeth. She brushed back his hair and kissed him gently on the forehead, then on each cheek. His tenseness slackened. She kissed the tip of his nose; each side of his mouth. She kissed his lips softly, then fervently. His arms slowly, hesitatingly, moved up around her. She tossed away the wig and they rolled over on the bed.

We in Elysium voluntarily adhere to a code of good form. So whatever transpired between Harry and Fiona in his motel room on the eve of the U.S. Open in the glorious month of June beneath a new moon and within a stone's throw of Boston College may best be left to our imaginings. And there you have it.

By dawn the motel parking area was astir with golfers, caddies, and hangers-on. Contestants were preparing equipment for early morning tee times. A steady stream of cars and shuttle vans were motoring off to the Country Club. Brewster Payne, assisted by Malcolm Baldwin, was taking a final check before departing in a rental car. Mal was counting golf clubs, and Brew was placing his mark on golf balls with an indelible felt pen.

"... fourteen," Mal finished counting the maximum clubs allowed. "All Brewster Payne signature clubs accounted for and in tiptop shape. All set, big guy?"

"I feel good about this one, Mal ... real good," and deposited the balls with his identifying mark in the golf bag.

Clubs were tossed in the boot; the lid slamming shut worked on Mal as cue for an exhortational send off: "Let's go kick some butt, Brew Payne! You're the man!"

"Yeah, baby, let's get this show on the road. Look out Open, here I come."

As Mal pulled the car out of its parking space Brew caught sight of Harry in front of his room which immediately deflated his pumped up ebullience. Harry was all smiles and doing what appeared to be minimalist exercises: shallow knee-bends, and stretches that looked more like yawnings. He did buckle down to labor through three large deep breaths. Anything more would have overtaxed him. As they were about to pull away, Fiona stepped out of Harry's room wearing his clothes. She chucked Harry under the chin and then ran to her own room. Mal drove off unaware of the goings-on humming the theme from "Rocky." But, Brew, still glancing back, had eyes black as pitted olives stuffed with acrimony.

CHAPTER 48

Moments later, Fiona was sitting on her still-made bed in bra and panties, and with a towel wrapped around her head. She was donning slacks when somebody knocked on her door.

"Who's there?" she called out while fluffing damp hair.

"It is I, Harrison Golub, from New York City." He spoke in a manner eavesdroppers would accept as platonic.

"Please enter, Mr. Golub," was the formal reply.

Harry entered and leaned back against the door staring with fond pleasure at his half-robed caddie. "Miss Huntly, I presume?"

"By all means, Mr. Golub, presume as you will," she grinned. "And how was your evening?"

"I think, madame, I can say with perfect candor, I had ... THE TIME OF MY LIFE!"

"Shhh! Me too," she whispered. She pulled a collared shirt over her head which sported a Levinson logo and threw Harry a cap with H.G. Drivers on the front. Brushing her hair she walked to Harry and gave him a warm kiss on the lips. "Shall we go, darling?"

"If you insist."

And it's well that she did, for he would just as soon have stayed.

Just now I had a happy recollection, and it involved myself and Hetty Overdone, a distant cousin who at the time was sweet 16, and I, a year her junior. We met for the first time while on a visit to the country home of Boverton Haddox, O.B.E., a cousin who was not so distant from either of us. Boverton was a large fan of King George and wished to celebrate our monarch's 60th birthday with a royal bash featuring games and such, not unlike activities Americans engage in on their Day of Independence holiday: foxhunting, shooting grouse, croquette, archery, badminton, cricket, draughts, etcetera. The gathering constituted Boverton's extended family to the amount of some 60 guests, some of whom, out of necessity, found quarters in the surrounding villages. There was no golf to be had within 30 miles of Thorpwillow—Boverton's estate—so I was at loose ends, if you will, not at all willing to test myself in events to which I had shown no aptitude. Hetty was also disinterested in the planned recreations and as luck would have it, we met while meandering Thorpwillow's maze. I say met; we actually ran into one another rather forcefully when rounding a corner in that confusing and baffling yew-hedged network of pathways.

"Dreadfully sorry," she said in a voice having the quality of delicate chimes.

As I recall my response was a simple but well-meaning, "Oops." More I could not utter for I was struck dumb by her beauty and ashamed of my clumsiness.

"I didn't expect to find anyone here in this labyrinth," she said casually, readjusting her blouse. "Do you come here often?"

I nodded no.

"I was hoping you'd know the way out. Do you by any chance?"

I nodded no.

"Perhaps together we can find the way." She took my hand. "I'm Hetty Overdone, and you are … ?"

I nodded no.

"You must have a name; every one is called something. How are you called?" she asked with a sweet smile.

I pinched myself and responded, "Ouch … Ernest."

"Owchurnest? Unusual."

"No … I mean, just Ernest … Ernest Spectre."

"Very pleased to make your acquaintance, Ernest Spectre." Measuring me cap-a-pie, she remarked, "I'm surprised a healthy-looking young man like yourself isn't joining the others in sport."

"I'm not very good at anything other than golf."

"Golf! Oh, I am indeed fortunate. I'm having the deuce of a time getting the ball to rise above the ground. Please, Ernest, say you'll help me?"

"With pleasure. When will it be convenient for you?"

"Why this very moment. I'm leaving early this evening. I must go back to school, don't you know. Now do tell, what must be done to elevate the ball?"

"It appears that you are not allowing the loft of the club to do its job. Most likely your swing has a scoop to it which causes the club to come up on the ball before striking it behind and under. You're topping it, and thereby keeping it low to the ground."

"Would you be a dear and demonstrate the swing by standing behind, holding and guiding my arms and taking me through the proper unscooping procedures?"

"We do not have a club handy."

"I'm sure we should manage without one. Now, please," she motioned me behind.

I reached around and held on to her warm, smooth forearms; she leaned back against me. I dared not breathe; I dared not move. I froze and exuded what I believe is designated a cold sweat.

"This is all very well and good, Ernest, but there seems to be an absence of motion. Do try."

Slowly I lifted her lovely arms to the proper position for releasing the downswing. The imaginary club struck behind the imaginary ball at the bottom of the swing. In this manner, for a dozen or more times, we drilled.

"I'll try it on my own now if you don't mind. Watch me and do not hesitate corrections."

She was a good study. She performed faultlessly. I was beginning to believe I had a calling as golf instructor. "Jolly good, Hetty, you are a fast learner. I dare say next time you play you'll be surprised at your progress."

"Oh, Ernest, I'm so grateful." Then she embraced and kissed me hard on the lips. I tried to disengage myself, but she had drawn upon unmanifested reserves of strength. I felt myself getting weaker and weaker under the robustness of her gratitude. I was rendered a mewling babe; completely in her power. Then I received a sharp tap on my head.

"What the devil is going on here?" It was a large beefy man in riding habit with a quirt at the ready.

"Father! It's not what you think. Ernest was giving me a golf lesson."

"Do you take me for a fool, child. The lesson this fellow was giving had nothing to do with our noble and ancient game. Bless my soul, Hetty, can you not see he's a wheedling masher?" He turned upon me shaking his quirt, "Young brazen … off with you!"

I ran I knew not whither. For if you recall I was in a maze, and in it for hours before I stumbled my way out. Completely humiliated I returned discreetly to the manor and was informed by cousin Longinus Haddox-Iddings that the Overdones, overwrought, had left for home. I was also told, and this by Flavia Haddox-Iddings, that Hetty was a brilliant golfer who had already won a significant number of ladies' events, and was even then scheduled to participate in mixed doubles at Worplesdon with Joyce Wethered.

Why, you may ask, has this tale been brought to your attention? There was a point somewhere, but now I haven't the foggiest notion what it was. It may yet come to me. Could it have something to do with women's wiles? Something on that order I expect. What any of this has to do with Harry Golub and the U.S. Open I'd be hard pressed to tell you.

CHAPTER 49

The Open served as the turning-point in Harrison Golub's career. Harry played brilliantly. Had he not foozled a short-iron here and there, and had he not misread a few putts he'd have won handily. Spectators were dazzled by his woods play and quite puzzled over his rather ordinary ability with other aspects of his game. A gallant blast out of the deep rough by Vijay Singh resulted in a birdie on the finishing hole which clinched for him the trophy. Harry and Jim Furyk tied for fourth, four strokes back.

Harry was no longer a rumor coming out of the hinterlands, but a solid player on top of his game. Craig Rudnik wrote: "Happy-go-lucky, hard-hitting Harry Golub is one or two swings away from knocking the focus out of Tiger Woods." Along with Rudnik many analysts believed that by the time of the British Open in St. Andrews, a little over a month away, Harry would bring it all together—or words to that effect.

Fiona was proud of the way Harry handled himself in countless interviews throughout the week. Even at his giddiest he kept his wits about him by not putting too fine a point on his woods-play. Reporters were intrigued by the various facets of Harry's personality: his talkativeness, his outrageousness, his graciousness, his lightheartedness. And always, they commented on his stature. They pestered Harry and Fiona about their relationship, which they refused to comment on altogether. This added additional mystery to those already fascinated by the little fellow with exceptional qualities. That there was more there than met the eye could not be otherwise when Fiona and Harry were so frankly and innocently happy with each other. There was something touching in their interaction on the golf course. No one could recollect such a similar pairing among past golfers and their caddies. All golf aside, for Harry, Fiona was an asset of incomparable worth; for Fiona, Harry was … well, one of a kind. And they were in love.

The one person begrudging Harry his due was Mr. Brewster Payne. His inordinate loathing so affected his game that he missed the cut. He spent the last two days of the tournament stalking Harry around the course with the express purpose of giving him the evil eye, which he believed would cause him injury, or at the least blight his swing. It was his reading of the morning newspaper horoscope that suggested this approach to unmanning Harry: "Scorpio: Look square in the eye that which thwarts your passion, it will put you in the driver's seat. Avoid molasses and juniper berries." Scorpio was not Brew's sign, but it jumped off the page and took control of him. His own sign, Libra, was not in sync with his current frame of mind: "Today, anything negative would be ill-advised. Cool your urge to lash out. Consult your pharmacist."

Mal accompanied Brew and endeavored to talk him out of his Harry fixation. Every good shot Harry made, Brew belittled as having had a lucky bounce, lucky roll, fortunate gust, perfect lie. Mal felt compelled to remind Brew of the old maxim—"The more one practices, the more lucky one gets."— and that that was the source of Harry's "luck." Brew turned on Mal a threatening stare. That did not sit well with Mal, so he bit his tongue and watched the rest of the match without comment.

Harry's unwavering stance on maintaining amateur status was by far the most controversial issue in golf. No one thought it made sense. One of the sports writers calculated that had Harry accepted prize money from the day, two months earlier, when he joined the professional golf circuit he'd be just shy of half a million dollars—"... and that ain't chicken feed." He also noted that it was very unfair of him to deprive his lovely caddie a share of the winnings. The writer knew that Harry was not a wealthy man. Other writers and commentators suggested that maybe Harry wanted to eclipse records set by amateur, Bobby Jones. Then there was the fellow on ESPN television who intimated that the idea of performing under pressure of playing for high-stakes dollars panicked him. Those and other guesses further fueled the mystery surrounding Harrison Golub.

The tabloids saw Harry and Fiona as good copy for advancing their sales and made up the most glaring fables about them. One had him selling his soul to the devil and Fiona was part of the bargain. Another hinted that he took an undetectable anabolic steroid. Still another that he was hypnotized into believing he was the incarnation of Walter Hagen. There were countless others, but none were imaginative enough to really touch upon the actual source.

CHAPTER 50

Three weeks after the U.S. Open, a strange jittery man loitered outside Levinson's Sporting Goods store dressed in unbecoming attire; he might easily have been mistaken for a dustman. He peered in through the store window and surveyed the interior. Customers and sales staff were going about their business. Harry was chipping balls into a basket in the indoor range. Neither Sydney nor Fiona were on the floor. The man seemed to be biding his time.

Sydney and Fiona, meanwhile, were in the upstairs office looking down on Harry.

"Harry's getting awful good with the chip shooting," said Sydney.

"It's the best part of his game."

"No, Fiona, it's long driving."

"You're right—of course. What was I thinking?" She was commenting on Harry's improved, unenhanced abilities.

Carlos entered with a bag of delicatessen lunches and sought out Harry. Harry signed for it and headed for the office. From outside, the strange man watched him ascending the stairs, and he warily entered the store.

"Chow time," announced Harry.

Sydney cleared spaces on his desk to accommodate three people for lunch.

Intrigued by the odd fellow that had just entered the store, Fiona watched him casually walk the aisles to the golf department. The moment he picked up a Harrison Golub driver she recognized Malcolm Baldwin. He scanned the store nervously, hoping not to be unmasked. He hurried to the cashier, paid cash for the club, and ran out the door without his receipt.

"So, Harry," said Sydney while passing out sandwiches, "do my Scotland arrangements meet with your approval?"

"Whatever you say."

"Ah, food," said Fiona joining the others without commenting on Mal's bizarre behavior. "Cam insists we all stay with him—that suit you, gentlemen?"

"Perfectly," said Harry.

"Wonderful," said Sydney. "Then he can show me the clubmaking operation."

"I can hardly wait to be there," said Harry. Fiona squeezed his hand. "Back where my real life began—playing the Old Course and the Jubilee, finding Fiona, finding a magic clu ..." He caught himself up.

Not to worry, Sydney was deep into his reuben sandwich and not at all deep into the conversation.

"Yes, Sydney," continued Harry, "the magic clearness of St. Andrews air—you'll love it."

"Clearness shmearness, anywhere I can breathe. Ain't I got lungs?"

CHAPTER 51

The British Open was near at hand when the contingent from Levinson's landed in Edinburgh, Scotland, where they were met by Cameron Flett and driven an hour's distance to his St. Andrews home. There Fiona and Harry rested after the long trip, but Sydney, ever the keen businessman, would not be put off visiting Cam's new workshop in nearby Anstruther. The next afternoon they gathered for a pub lunch at Dunbar the Makar. The Poet's Pub was alive with the usual aggregate of rollicksome college students.

"Then, Sydney, ye approve of our operation?" asked Cam.

"And why shouldn't I? You make terrific golf clubs and they sell like hotcakes. People gobble them up as fast as we flip them out."

"If you're happy, then I'm happy." He turned to Fiona, "And speakin' of happy; good to have ye back, lass. Ye seem to be rosier than ever, or are these poor eyes failin' me?"

"I've never been happier," she patted Harry's hand. "Isn't that Colin Mackay sitting at the bar?"

"Aye, that's Colin. And that's his Jean over there tending tables. By the by, Harry, Colin's qualified for the Open, too."

"I recognize him," said Harry. "I wish him well. He's a nice guy."

"Aye, indeed, he's all of that," said Cam. He stood and raised his glass, "A toast to Harrison Golub and Colin Mackay, two excellent chaps.

It's good loftin' balls to the sky,
It's good hittin' honest and true,
It's good to play the Open in Scotland
And swing with a sweet follow through.
Harrison Golub and Colin Mackay—
Godspeed in yer Open debut.

"Hear, hear."

"Robert Burns?" asked Harry.

"With help from Cameron Flett," said Cam.

A student voice shouted Scotland's motto above the din, *"Nemo me impune lacessit!"*—No one assails me with impunity.

Other scholars displayed their little Latin.

"Jacta alea est!" trumpeted the classics scholar.

"Delenda est Cathago!" proposed the Sandhurst alum.

"Et tu, Brute," swooned the expiring thespian

"Gaudeamus igitur!" sang the music major.

"Terra firma!" stomped the agrarian.

"Tempus fugit!" belched the Newtonian unsure of himself.

"Caveat emptor!" was an aside from a business major.

"Tabula rasa!" the charwoman muttered.

"Etcetera!" sneezed the barman.

"Ibid.!" hiccuped the fresher.

"Fortuna favet fatuis!" yelled Cam.

"Hear, hear," responded the giants of learning, not exactly wise to Cam's leg-pulling.

CHAPTER 52

A clouded over Wednesday morning found Harry at the far end of a line of golfers on the practice range. Young Colin Mackay was next to him listening intently to Charlie Maxwell comment on mental preparedness for a major tournament: "Dinna gie yersel' airs, lad, and dinna sell yersel' short. Concentrate only on the shot tae han'. Tak' yer owen guid time. Haste mak's waste. Dae as I tell ye and ye'll no gae wrang." Brewster Payne, a few players removed from Harry, was telling Malcolm Baldwin a bawdy joke: "Did you hear the one about the farmer's daughter and the penguin?"

Spectators behind a restraining rope watched golfers at practice. After Harry hit a few long ones he put up his driver. Seeing him use his 8-iron, and only moderately well at that, the crowd moved away and focused their attention on Tiger Woods, John Daly, and Colin Montgomery.

"May I hae a ward wi' ye, Mr. Golub?"

"Sure," said Harry." He spun around, and no one was there. "Hello."

"Bide a wee till I gather m'sel'. Dinna be alarmed. We maun talk."

"I know that voice," said Harry guardedly.

A few yards away, near a shed, Old Tom faded in. "Dae ye now. Weel 'tis guid tae be remembered."

Harry stepped back. Old Tom beckoned him closer. Harry advanced warily. "You're not meshugana are you?"

Tom, slightly nettled, stood nose to nose with Harry. "Ye colonials hae quaint expressions."

Harry registered dread. "I mean you no disrespect, Mr. Morris."

Tom spoke pleasantly, "O' coorse ye wadna. Let us shak' han's and be friends."

Brew looked over and saw Harry shaking no one's hand.

"Laddie, I'll no beat aboot the heather—I maun hae the club back."

Old Tom reached for Harry's bag. Harry clutched it and moved away. Brew could make no sense of what was going on.

Harry pleaded, "I can't return it—not now! I'm playing in the Open tomorrow! Without the driver I'm helpless.'

Brew thought he was watching a dumb show.

Old Tom considered Harry's position. "Regretfully, Mr. Golub, the club was niver tae hae left Elysium. I gie it tae ye whan in a dazed state, lad. A grave, grave mistak' on my part. Ye maun return it me. There be consequences maist critical tae ye if ye choose tae keep it."

"Like what?"

"Yer life; yer efterlife," he expressed mournfully. "Maist uncomfortable."

"If you meant to frighten me, you have." Harry, in a dither, pondered his plight. Tom saw Brew approaching.

"Mr. Morris, please, may I keep it until after the tournament?"

"Is that a promise?" he spoke hurriedly for Brew was nearly upon them and looking on rather suspiciously.

Harry raised his hand, "Yes, sir, on my honor."

"Verra weel, then. Mind, keep yer ward, Mr. Golub." Tom faded out.

"Where will I find you?"

"The nicht following the Open—same place, same time."

"I'll be there. You can count on me. Thanks. Thanks a million."

"You're welcome, goofy," said Brew looking down on Harry.

"Well, if it isn't Mr. Wonderful, and it isn't."

Brew looked around, "Why do you talk to yourself?"

"I like what I have to say."

"Does your floozie also like to listen to your stupid babbling?"

"My what?!"

"Your caddie—the floozie."

Harry dropped his golf bag and threw a punch at Brew's belly. Brew was unphased by the tepid blow and smiled sadistically; then he doubled over in pain from an additional blow he received from a powerful invisible agency.

"It's unlikely he'll trouble ye henceforth, Mr. Golub," whispered Old Tom.

"Thanks," said Harry relieved.

"You're welcome," Brew aspirated, shuffled off trying to catch his breath.

Harry took out his driver and whacked a prodigious drive.

CHAPTER 53

"The most bonnie town in my kingdom," or words to that effect, was how Mary Queen of Scots regarded the quaint ancient burgh of St. Andrews. For most days of a year it is indeed a "bonnie town." Its University is the country's oldest—third oldest in Britain after Oxford and Cambridge—every year the bonnie town is made bonnier with a new infusion of matriculating bonnie lads and bonnie lasses which sustains the burgh's youthfulness and vibrancy.

Every five years or so, when the British Open is held here, the vibrant town is supercharged with statical electricity. The one and only time Harrison Golub entered the Open, a record crowd estimated over 100,000 spectators were on hand for the four-day event, an event many of us in Elysium agree is the finest game on the grandest links in the world.

Not a room could be let within 40 miles; no available parking spaces existed; long queues formed outside restaurants, pubs, and portable loos; and shops filled to the brim with shoppers. Temporary grandstands were raised strategically throughout the course to accommodate 30,000 viewers: the most prominent ones being those above the 18th green and the Road Hole green, and the largest one extending nearly the length of the 1st hole with flagstaffs spaced above bearing flags representing players' countries of origin. It was a sight to behold. The "grey auld toun" was transformed into a panoply of iridescent hues, and free and easy merriment, when

Open day arrived on a sunny, windless Thursday morning in July.

Perfect playing conditions for early starters, but those teeing off afternoons would invariably find the going less submissive when the roguish east winds arose sweeping and swirling across flatish, treeless links, deflecting balls from their targets and depositing them now and then into curse-worthy hazards—pot bunkers, whin, heather, and tall, rank, bent grass. Golfers need nerves of steel and a mariner's sense of windage to hold the mark, particularly on the final six or seven holes where fluctuating left-to-right crosswinds have on many occasions blown would-be champions off course and reduced them to also-rans. Another strategy is required altogether for the home hole which generally has the wind in one's face.

Tradition, the world's strongest players, hard to predict winds, intermittent rains, numerous hazards, a capricious terrain that gives rise to unexpected bounces, all combine to establish the Open on St. Andrews Old Course the sternest test of a golfer's skill and courage. To the winner goes universal admiration and the Claret Jug, golf's ultimate prize.

A greater than expected crowd forgathered early around the 1st tee. Already seven threesomes had begun their rounds when Harrison Golub showed up with Todd Hamilton and Justin Leonard for their 7:33 tee time. The media was very much evident. The ubiquitous Ward Diggs stood above the tee with his back to the Royal and Ancient Club House admiring himself in the television camera lens. In a huddle next to him the director was coddling the nervous, hyperactive first-time color commentator, Mr. Finn McRae, while an attractive make-up artist dusted the glow from his nose and at the same time successfully repelled his improper frontal advances. McRae, a burly, coarse fellow, was a recently retired popular footballer from the ranks of the Packers of Green Bay in the state of Wisconsin. If I heard correctly, McRae was a backer of lines. Diggs was cued to speak, and McRae directed to standby.

"This is Ward Diggs welcoming viewers to our widely antici-
pated, ne plus ultra, British Open. Need I mention that this is the
premier golf event? No." He gave a gentle cough into his hand as
though he were fine-tuning his instrument. He continued with
ponderous gravity, "We begin our coverage with the group below
us: Two past Open champions, Justin Leonard, and Todd
Hamilton. The final member of this group is the redoubtable
Harrison Golub, a product of New York City, from whom much
is expected in this his initial endeavor. Personally, I have yet to see
the highly touted Mr. Golub play, but I'm certain we have met
under somewhat different circumstances. Our threesome is due
shortly to get underway here in historic St. Andrews, the epicen-
ter of golf worldwide. Today golfers from over twenty nations will
pit their considerable skills against the wind-swept ..."

Finn McRae, wanting an introduction, showed his impatience
by waving like a minstrel at Diggs, urging him to step aside for his
endman presentation.

"... grandeur of this venerable Old Course with its deceptive,
insidious hazards. Hazards with forbidding epithets: Hell Bunker, The Coffins ..."

Craving attention, McRae elbowed Diggs to introduce him.
A light jab from an endomorphic backer of lines is no love-tap.
Diggs grimaced but held his ground, not firmly, but determinedly.

"... Cat's Trap, Grave and other such ruinations of concentration and character. Ooomph."

McRae rather forcefully nudged Diggs aside, "And right you
are Diggsie." He then proceeded to freeze up in front of the camera smiling uncomfortably while his face reddened. The camera
shot over to Diggs.

"That, ladies and gentlemen, is our color man for this week's
event, Finn McRae." Diggs spoke with the utmost composure
which cast the ineptitude of his partner in even darker tints.

Leonard was introduced by the starter and received loud applause. He drove safely onto the fairway. The same for Hamilton.

Judging from the introductory applause for Harry he was clearly the crowd's choice in that group. The warm reception raised expectations which made him more jittery.

"Try to relax, Harry darling," said Fiona. "Enjoy yourself. Isn't this where you most wanted to be?"

Harry spoke quietly, "What if things fall apart? What if Old Tom grabs the club out of my hand or puts the whammy on it?"

"I've always understood Old Tom to have been a man of his word," she guessed. "So buck up. Stiff upper lip and all that." She nodded toward the tee, "Darling, you're up."

Harry took a deep breath and delivered the ball, with roll, 320 yards. The spectators stood in stunned amazement, then, roared with delight. The ball lay less than 50 yards from the pin and 30 from the Swilcan Burn, the same burn he had continually knocked balls into the first time he played the course with Angus Mackegan as his caddie.

Harry, cockily, handed the charmed driver to Fiona, "This kid's good." He proudly walked on ahead.

Colin Mackay, standing by with the next group of players, called out, "Weel doon, Mr. Golub!"

Harry, waving to the cheering spectators, did not hear him.

"Thanks, Colin," said Fiona getting underway with Harry's bag. "And good luck to you."

Moving up on the tee and watching Harry's group depart were Colin Mackay, Nick Price and snarling Brewster Payne.

"Well, sir," Diggs addressed Finn McRae on camera, "what think you of Harrison Golub's swing?"

"To tell you the truth, Diggsie, I should have his swing and you should have a wart on the end of your nose," he said without cracking a smile.

"A wart?" shot back Diggs with a piercing stare. "Did I hear you correctly?"

"Only funnin', little buddy, only funnin'. Fan your fanny."

"Just as you please," he said by way of dismissal.

Auditing the proceedings, the director was pleased as punch. Too many viewers, he discovered, found Diggs insufferable, much too full of himself; so when the backer of lines managed to take him down a peg, he was pleasantly surprised. Recruitment of Finn McRae as foil for Ward Diggs had thus far proved to be a capital idea. Footballer McRae had gotten into the swing of things and was holding his own. The on-camera sportive exchange suggested more colorful repartee to come between the Verbose and the Gross. The director fancied higher TV ratings than when Ward Diggs was left to keep his own counsel.

CHAPTER 54

The day was Harry's. Even his iron-play held up as reflected in his low score of 66, which placed him in a three-way tie for first. Others with low rounds were early off the tee and in before the afternoon winds became a factor; among those were Brewster Payne and Colin Mackay.

After Harry had spent the better part of a hour in post-round interviews, he and Fiona set off for the parking area reserved for tournament personnel. Colin Mackay and his Jean were leaning against the wing of their motorcar chatting with a number of friends and locals. They waved to Harry and Fiona.

Colin called to Harry, "Yer burnin' up the links, Mr. Golub. Hae ye no mercy. Air ye no gien the rest o' us haff a chance?"

"Not if I can help it," Harry sang out cheerily.

Fiona laid down the golf bag and excused herself to go chat with Jean. Harry was happy with himself and filled with the glow of the day. He leaned against the car to wait on her for he dared not attempt to drive Cam's car on lanes that ran opposite directions from those at home.

Brewster Payne backed his car out of his space and deliberately backed over Harry's golf bag and drove off. Harry turned round upon hearing the crunch and was just able to catch sight of Payne and Mal Baldwin pulling away. His bag was flattened.

"I'll get you for this ... you ... you ... scribbledorpleditcher!" cried Harry. All eyes centered on him.

Fiona appeared, "What's wrong?"

"Look. Payne backed his car over my clubs and took off like nothing happened."

"Nooo," wailed Fiona bending down to inspect the damage. Expecting the worst, she slowly eased the driver out of the bag. The shaft was shattered. She was on the verge of tears when Harry took up all the pieces and immediately Old Tom snapped together.

Fiona could not credit her eyes. "How'd you do that?"

"No idea," Harry shrugged. "Does it itself."

Fiona hugged Harry around the neck with such verve that they nearly toppled. "Well, that was a fright. Damn that Brewster Payne-in-the-arse."

Harry thought for a moment, "Maybe he didn't know he smashed the clubs. Could be he was in a hurry to get somewhere … visit friends or something."

"Don't you be giving him benefit of the doubt. He'll not waste an opportunity to dishonor himself by abusing us. That's how much we're despised."

"You may be right. Anyway, enough of that, let's go see Cam and get another set of clubs."

"You're a good man, Harry Golub from New York. I bless the day I found you."

Even after having driven four or five blocks, Brew maintained his look of sinister glee. Mal's indignation finally gave voice, "That was low, even for you. Let me out."

"C'mon … no big deal."

"No big deal?! Harry's kicking your ass out there … and you resort to that? Stop the car. I want out … now!"

Brew pulled over to the curb on busy Market Street. Mal got out, held the door open and leaned in, "From here on in, you're on your own. One last bit of advice: go to hell, it's the one place you're sure to be appreciated." The door slammed. Mal marched back down the street.

Brew felt the pangs of remorse. He needed air. He got out of the car and walked. He wandered aimlessly through the "grey auld toun," himself looking and feeling very grey indeed. Unable, he was, to connect his thoughts or to pull himself out of his wretchedness. Eventually fatigue and heat overcame him. A cool blast of conviviality struck him broadside as he was about to pass the open door of the Poet's Pub, Dunbar the Makar. He hesitated. The combination of song, chatter, and laughter enlivened him. He entered. Standing room only. He was surprised that no one pointed a finger at him or confronted him for his recent and past abuses of common decency toward his fellows. Instead, Jean Forsyth, heading back to the bar with a trayful of empty beer glasses, yanked on his arm and directed him to a bar stool, the only empty seat in the pub.

"You're one of the chaps in the tournament, isn't that so?" she asked cheerily.

"Yes. I am."

"Thought so. You played in the group with Nick Price and Colin Mackay. I thought I recognized you. I followed your group around. You played brilliantly today. Can I get you something?"

"Yes, please. A beer would be nice."

"Beer 'tis." Jean directed the barkeeper, a portly, middle-aged man to serve Brewster Payne, while she refilled her tray with glasses of beer.

Brew looked about him. He saw an animated, fun-loving crowd of young people free from care. When he turned back to the bar a beer awaited him. He quaffed a third of it. He found its tang and coolness pleasurable. Pleasure, pleasure, he thought. The whole record of Brewster Payne's life was that of self-gratification and selfishness. If he deigned to indulge someone, reciprocity must be done on a usurious scale. For the first time in his life he was quite put out by his uncontrollable stupidity. To want people to look upon him with envy and crave his acquaintance, were blind desires. No longer among his friends was he first among equals. His friends? Within the short period of two months he had lost his companions, chums since childhood: first Gunther, then Phil and Tony, and now, Mal, his closest friend and agent. The aloneness he felt was the direct result of his incivilities. Harry Golub now, he had none of Brewster Payne's advantages in life, and yet he was far happier, far more popular, and more highly respected. And Harry was entirely free of all personal bitterness. Why was that so? It must be that Harry's whole record of life was that of unselfish generosity.

Jean tapped him on the shoulder, "I wish you well tomorrow, Mr. Payne."

And a few chaps at the bar, moved by good humor and bonhomie, raised their glasses to him, "Hear, hear."

Harry's play in the middle rounds were much like opening day's—brilliant, and accomplished in fouler weather. Continuous drizzle with occasional rainy periods. More than any other influence it was the wind that frustrated players, driving many out of contention. Some ancient sage wise to the vagaries of golf uttered this general truth: "Where there is no wind every man is a pilot." Be that as it may, in two days of squalls Pilot Harry Golub proved to be Golf's answer to Captains Cook and Magellan by sailing safely home with contenders far back in his wake

Harry's masterful consistency seemed to be unaffected by the strongish winds, winds often accompanied with rain. Not a few spectators and marshals thought they saw Harry's drives actually settle into his divots from the previous day's round. More apparent was his birdieing the same holes in each of the three rounds. And if these points were not enough to fill one with wonder, his scores surely should—66, 66, 66, for a 198 and a commanding nine-stroke lead, 18 under par, heading into the final day.

Harry had the stuff of heroes in him. The Old Course—his arena. The wee bloke came on the scene looking for all the world too transparently foolish to fool anyone. He did not cower, he did not boast, he did not swagger, he simply approached his business with a happy confidence, and leveled the field.

The sports world went wild with speculation: Would Harry Golub bring in the lowest score ever in The British Open? If he did, would that score ever be broken? One tabloid warned that the only thing that could waylay the juggernaut, Harrison Golub— barring injury—would be a bad marriage. To avoid that the paper recommended he propose immediately to his caddie since it appeared they already got along famously. Harry read the article and laughed at its absurdities; Fiona did not.

Light breezes and scattered clouds were predicted for the final round. This opened the way to lower scores for players with the ability to hit high-lofted shots onto greens softened by two days of steady rain without having to take the wind into account.

CHAPTER 55

Late on the eve of the final round it rained heavily, but within the spirit thicket all was a comfy glow. Bobby Jones and Francis Ouimet entered in casual conversation.

"… that sort of lie has always been a devilment for me, Francis."

"Bobby, try doing this next time you're banked against the fringe," demonstrated Ouimet. "Set your putting stance, then, using the leading edge of your niblick, tap the ball at the equator, and she'll roll as if putted squarely."

"How well I know. You played brilliantly today."

Tom and Tommy Morris entered.

"I tell ye, lad, that club o' mine …"

"Dad," interrupted Tommy, "that club is why we're summoned here."

From out of the whin burst Queen Mary, all business, "*Messieurs,* attend us! The St. Andrews Elysian Privy Council will come to order." She focused on Old Tom. "We'll not beat about the heather." She sat down, the others remained standing. "*Monsieur* Tom Morris, you, sir, were to retrieve the enchanted golf club. You have been willfully negligent. You're unseemly lack of initiative cannot be tolerated. We need not remind you that your indiscretion has introduced into Elysium an unnatural stressful circumstance, and placed the very soul of *Monsieur* Harrison Golub in jeopardy. What have you to say for yourself."

"Yer majesty," Tom was contrite, "I was near tae retrievin' it whan I was hindered in my conversation wi' Mr. Golub by the ruinous appearance o' a maist unwholesome fellow. I did, hooiver, gie Mr. Golub tae agree tae han' the club ower tae me efter the Open."

"Saints, preserve us!" she said rolling her eyes. "That will not do! Tom, certainly you are aware of the unsporting advantage Golub has?"

"Tom," Ouimet scolded, "with your club, and his own steadily improving skills, Golub is performing feats far beyond the capabilities of the best golfers."

Bobby Jones spoke, "At Golub's present pace he will establish records that may never be challenged."

Ouimet placed a hand on Tom's shoulder and spoke for all who played the game with integrity, "For the good of the game, Tom, and for a renewal of serenity in Elysium, Golub must be stopped by you. If not … I fear the Almighty is sure to intervene."

"Thunderbolt!" cried Queen Mary as though chucking a spear. Everyone fell back a step.

"The results could be calamitous for mortals caught up in your folly," Ouimet charged.

"I'm trewly sorry," said Tom. "I dinna wish the club in the han's o' the livin'."

"Ma foi" said the queen, still indignant. "This awkward situation should never have arisen had you refrained from dabbling in the poisonous intoxication of sorcery. Tom, before it's too late—get back the club."

"I shall dae my utmaist, yer majesty."

"Parole d'honneur?"

"Parole d'honneur."

"Bon. And, Tom, no more tinkering in the black arts. It is not proper to encourage infernal notions in Elysium."

Tom assented with a nod.

"We are adjourned," pronounced the queen, lifted her skirts and dashed off into the shadowy whin. "Oo-la-la! signor Rizzio. Naughty, naughty boy."

Bobby Jones and Francis Ouimet took their leave with Ouimet describing his recipe for New England fish chowder, "… haddock, cod, milk, buttah … ."

Tommy, with heartfelt concern for his father and the soul of Harrison Golub, "Hae ye a plan, dad?"

"I'm at my wit's end, son. I gie Golub my ward that he cad keep the club ontil the Open's ower."

The sky rumbled.

Tommy looked up, "I fear for him."

"Sae dae I, son, sae dae I. A trifling fool am I."

CHAPTER 56

"Check this out, Fiona." Harry, in pajamas, drew back his putter. Fiona was in bed reading, surrounded by newspapers. Wind-swept rain pattered on the windows. Harry's putt traveled about eight feet over the carpet and stopped on the other side of a beer coaster. "Kerrrr-plunk. Not bad, not bad."

"Very good, darling," she answered absently, more intent on reading. "All the newspapers say you will far exceed all Open records. Your skills are referred to as 'wondrous,' 'uncanny,' 'supernatural'—little do they realize how right they are."

Harry concentrated on another putt and did not fully catch what she said. "'Member a few months ago, I didn't know which end of the club to hold? Now ... what was it the Herald said? I'm destined to be an immortal ... something like that."

"Harrison Golub!" she chided. "Come back to earth this instant. Immortal, indeed."

"Humbled, I stand before you," he bowed. "Let's face it, without Old Tom I'm nothing." He sat on the bed a little upset with his hoodwinking the public. Fiona scooted over to him and smoothed his hair. "My low scores scared off a lot of players—but some are hanging in there giving it all they've got: Colin ... even Brew, he's playing the best golf of his career. I'm paired up with those two tomorrow. I don't deserve to win the British Open, or any tournament for that matter," his head sunk, pressured by a mind uneased.

"Of course you do," Fiona drew him to her bosom. "You are a good person, Harry Golub, and good persons deserve some good breaks."

Lightning fluttered the lamp lights, a thunderclap shook the house.

"My greatest break was finding you. What more could I ask for?"

"Even if it's true, it's always nice to hear," she said and pushed the newspapers onto the floor.

CHAPTER 57

Not a hint of atmospheric disturbance anywhere that glorious morning. Widely-dispersed puffy white clouds, a shimmering placid sea, radiant whin bloom, and a glistening, softened green-sward greeted the thousands on hand to witness history in the making in the person of one Harrison Golub.

With a commanding view of the Old Course from the press booth above the Road Hole green, Ward Diggs and Finn McRae kept up their running commentary of the match as they received up-dates from colleagues situated at key positions round the course.

"At this juncture, ladies and gentlemen," intoned Ward Diggs, "it would appear that Mr. Harry Golub of New York City has the British Open—if you will permit an American vulgarism—in the bag, signed, sealed, and all but delivered. An historical moment, an unbeatable record is being forged here today."

A crowd roared in the distance.

Diggs listened intently to his earphone, "I have been informed that Golub birdied the 13th. That means he presently stands twelve strokes up with five holes to play. This is indeed history in the making. One would need reach back into fables to find its equal in wonder: the tortoise beating the hare; Jack slaying the giant; Androcles uneaten by the lion."

"Or Scrooge McDuck flying an airplane?" offered Finn McRae.

"Yes, yes, Finn, a point well taken," said Diggs, not at all sure who Mr. McDuck is or was. "What have you to add concerning

Golub's phenomenal play?" A distant rumble from over the North Sea was barely heard above the hubbub of the crowds.

"Verrry impressive, Diggsie. Golub is nailing this baby down and is about to throw away the key. The little guy is sailing into the sunrise and leaving a wake of golfers in the dust. It's all over but the shooting. End of story."

"Phrases … well … well turned," stumbled Diggs. The rumble of thunder drew his attention across the links. "How strange. Ominous clouds are heading our way, it seems. There was little in weather reports I received this morning to suggest that inclemency was even a remote possibility. We are near to ending this tournament so I do not think a stoppage at this point would be a consideration … hang on, those black clouds appear goaded with whip and spur. We may be in for it after all."

The gallery cheered as Harry and Fiona, Colin Mackay and his caddie, Angus Mackegan, and Brewster Payne and his local caddie approached the par five 14th tee, the Long Hole. Distant lightning flashes and thunder drew scant notice, but a growing chill in the air did as people began buttoning up their shirts and jackets.

Having arrived early to get a good spot to watch golfers teeing off on the difficult 14th, Gunther, Mal, Phil and Tony stood together to cheer on Harry and Brew. The Brew crew had reconciled. Brew had sought them out and apologized profusely for his bad behavior over the years and asked for their forgiveness after having discovered that one cannot live independent of all persons. They had seen the errors of their ways, sought reconciliation, and were now happily reunited with a better developed social conscience. One of the reasons Brewster Payne was outplaying himself was that he was perfectly willing to listen to his caddie, who, by the way, had been highly recommended by Charlie Maxwell. An earlier Brewster Payne would not have allowed his caddie to have an opinion on anything. Jock Muckross, his present caddie, he treated as an equal. Muckross, whose skill in reading the

wind, distances, and locations for each shot, was part of the reason Brew was holding on to third place thus far.

"Brew never played better," observed Mal.

"He's got it all together," said Tony.

"Yeah, but no one—not even Tiger Woods or Jack Nicklaus—
has ever played a tournament as flawlessly as Harry," praised Phil.

"Uncanny," said Tony.

"Unbelievable," said Mal.

"Magical," said Gunther.

A few yards away Hamish Macpherson had as his charge for
the week, the Sultan of Gorselan and his retainers. All eight of the
Sultan's traveling wives were frittering away time back in the hotel. The middle-aged Sultan, an avid golfer, was in Scotland for
the first time. He wanted to witness the British Open firsthand,
then later match his 30 handicap against local and outlying courses
for the remaining three weeks of his planned vacation before re-
turning home to Gorselan for the births of his 34th and 35th
offspring. His Serene Worship was domiciled in the Bishop Seaton
where he had learned that a local lass was responsible for advancing Harrison Golub's success in the royal and ancient game. Stories the Sultan had heard were further verified by Hamish
Macpherson who had been acquainted with Harry for a week's
time a short while back and remembered him clearly as an incur-
able hacker. Macpherson, like everyone else in St. Andrews familiar with the story of Harry Golub, gave full credit for his speedy
progress in links play to Fiona Huntly's expert guidance.

Having seen Harrison Golub on day-one of the tournament,
the Sultan praised God. Here was hope after all, he too might
improve his game with the assistance of Fiona, for Harry was an
almost perfect image of himself, though his Serene Worship in-
clined more to the shape of the cherry than roma variety of tomato. Upon seeing how lovely Miss Huntly was, and that she
possessed the mystifying ability to flex the rotund, he became profoundly anxious to possess her. God is good.

The Sultan directed his scribe to compose an enticing letter to Miss Fiona Huntly. He approved its content, signed it with a flourish and put his seal to it. Hamish Macpherson delivered the missive to the Cleek and Thistle. When Cam closed the pub he brought it home to her. Fiona read the beautiful, round hand calligraphy on scented stationery: "Most honored, delectable. Scotswoman, golf instructor par excellence, God be with you. I, Adhem Ben Abou, his Most Excellent Excellency, Defender of Truth and Justice, Sultan of Gorselan and Loved of God, extend to you my heartfelt greeting. I shall be honored if you will accept my munificent offer to be my personal golf instructor. Upon favoring my request you will receive Zanadu, the world's largest pearshape-cut emerald, and appointment as first among my concubines. May my tribe increase. God be praised. Yours to share, Adhem."

Fiona had never heard of the Sultan of Gorselan, but she had known of the Zanadu emerald for it had once belonged to a famous old-time cinema actress— Marion Davies? Vivien Leigh? Margaret Rutherford?—she wasn't sure whom. Immediately, she wrote a polite refusal, recommended Charlie Maxwell to instruct him, and hand-delivered it to the hotel concierge. She told no one about the Sultan's extraordinary offer which amused her no end. And that is as far as it went.

There he stood among the gallery at the Long Hole tee looking sadly and longingly at Fiona. Generally I have no deep-seated opinions of correctness in matters of the heart, but I do find it ridiculous that the Sultan, a man professed to have 30 wives and over 40 concubines, should swoon with the face of a lovesick calf over yet another woman. Enough is enough, I say. Fiona never saw the Sultan. Once on the golf course she took little notice of anything other than Harry and the flight of his ball. Up to that point every shot from the tee, and every fairway-wood shot was on the money—straight and true.

Emotionally charged Sydney Levinson, and Cameron Flett, a man of quiet reserve, were also among those at the 14th.

"When this Open closes," Sydney chuckled, rubbing his hands together, "they'll be thousands of orders for Harry's woods. Hoopdee-doopdee-doo."

"Sydney, there are more orders now than we can handle."

"Handle shmandle—ain't the golf wonderful?"

Thunder clapped somewhere over the sea. The wind picked up. A gust of raw damp air thrust inside Harry's shirt and chilled him. Another, and louder thunderclap, shook the earth. Electrified air shot up along Harry's spine and spiked his nape hair. Dark, ponderous clouds, like muscular ogres with flashing eyes, writhed over St. Andrews Bay. Harry studied the sky as if trying to decipher cloud shapes: "... see yonder cloud that's almost in shape of a camel?" "By the mass, and 'tis like a camel, indeed." Actually what Harry saw was a lone gull buffeted by squalls against a background of fast-moving black clouds. A flash of lightning blinded Harry for a second whereupon he lost sight of the bird.

Fiona poked Harry from his reverie and offered him the driver. He stopped her with a gesture.

Colin and Brew stood off to the side; Harry had the honor. "We better get moving, Harry," said Brew. "There's an arsenal of thunderbolts in those clouds. I'd hate for this to be called off when we've only a few holes left to play."

"Sorry, sorry Brew. Fiona," he said, yielding to an impulse, and reaching out with a dash of recklessness, "give me the three-wood."

"Really? Are you sure, Harry?"

Harry spoke with resolve, "Time to get real, sweetheart."

"Whatever you say, darling," she smiled, agreeing fully, and showed a new sense of pride in her man.

Harry teed his ball, stood behind it visualizing its trajectory and landing. He took two curiously odd practice swings. He stepped up to the ball with new, and he hoped, increased capacities. Fiona crossed her fingers. It was not his best swing, it was not exactly his old swing, it was somewhere in between. He overswung and pulled the ball left a goodly distance but it rolled into the furthermost Beardies bunker; the first hazard he had thus far encountered. Spectators gasped; Colin and Brew were completely taken by surprise. It was Harry's first blunder. It had gotten to the point where everyone had expected him to avoid all bunkers as did Tiger Woods when he won the Open on the same course. Colin and Brew in turn boomed drives far down the Long Hole, safely onto the Elysian Fields, the most trouble free stretch on the course.

"Waddaya think, Fiona? Not bad, huh? With my three-wood yet." He was genuinely delighted at the distance he had achieved without supernatural assistance.

"You really laid into that one, Harry, but we've got a real piece of work ahead. The Beardies are deep and there's not a thing I can do to help you," she said sadly.

"Last time I was in one of those it took me a dozen strokes to get out. I don't know how I did it then and I have no idea how to go about it now."

"But you will try?"

"My damnedest." Unswerving in the path of difficulty, "Hey, this is really what it's all about—play what you get. It's what makes this game interesting, terrific, unique."

Harry climbed down into the bunker and was lost to sight. "Here goes nothing," rose from out of the depth. A "thwak" sounded and a light sifting of sand flew up—but no ball. A short pause and "Thumpf"—more elevated sand, no ball. Another thumpf and the ball rose an inch above the bunker's rim and returned to sender.

Harry's plight hung like a dark cloud over spectators championing the little man. And indeed it was the only dark cloud in the vicinity, for the approaching storm had inexplicably turned tail and rumbled toward Norway.

One would have assumed that being at the bottom of a pot bunker would have been a sore trial to Harry, especially when it seemed he was multiplying strokes to his game. But, in a cheerful voice he called up, "Hey, Brew, check this out. I've dug a hole large enough to bury myself." Brew peered down on Harry and had no words of encouragement for what seemed to him a hopeless lie, for Harry's ball had settled into a bowl created by his displacement of sand. "If I screw up again, bury me here."

"Up until this hole, Harry, you were burying us. So, yes, any one of us would be happy to fulfill your request," said Brew lightheartedly. "Pull yourself together, Harry. You can pull this off."

"What's happened to Harry?" Sydney asked Cam.

"He's doing his level best." Cam had guessed that maybe Harry had used a wood other than the driver off the tee. Now he was certain.

As Harry again stood up to his ball with concentration and determination deep in the Beardies bunker, the spirit of Francis Ouimet entered his body. Brew watched Harry's fluid blast pop the ball out of the hazard and onto the Elysian Fields. The gallery cheered wildly. Ouimet stepped out of Harry and vanished. Cheers were even louder when Harry climbed out of the bunker. And louder still when he doffed his cap.

"Great recovery, Harry," said Colin.

"I had the shovel ready," joked Brew.

"How on earth did you do that, darling?" asked Fiona.

"Believe me ... I don't know."

Diggs, back in the press booth viewing the monitor, "Well done, Mr. Golub. Have you ever seen a finer shot, Finn?"

"Yes I did. Two shots, actually. It was the time my teammate, offensive tackle Gary "The Beast" Robinson, took our placekicker and quarterback out to my favorite bar in Seattle after they had flubbed the game-winning kick in the playoffs against the Seahawks. Right between the eyes, he shot them both."

"Finn, I fail to see the significance of that horrendous episode with that of Golub's bunker shot."

"Hey, a good shot's a good shot, Diggsie, whether it's out of a cannon or out of a glass."

"Your intellect surpasses my comprehension."

On the 15th tee the leader board had shown that Golub had dropped from 12 up to 6 up after completion of the Long Hole. Payne and Mackay were tied for third behind Montgomery. Harry was last to tee off and again selected to use his three-wood. The weather turned fair and contained only the gentlest of zephyrs. Harry's drive down the left fairway was close to 225 yards. Prior to the advent of "Old Tom" he had never pounded one that far. Two more decent shots, followed by a fat chip and a three-putt, produced a double bogey which pleased him no end, for a six was less than half of what the old Harrison Golub might have expected.

Harry double bogied the 16th, too. Diggs, McRae, Mackay, Payne, and spectators believed that Harry must have injured himself in the Beardies bunker, for his quality of play had turned sour from that point. They all marveled at Harry's demeanor, there was scarcely any evidence of ruffled composure. He had to be in pain, they theorized. Never would they know how tinglingly alive he felt. Fiona knew, Cam knew—Harrison Golub was playing his level best and, all things considered, it was damn good golf.

The 17th—the Road Hole—the most feared hole on the Old Course is attended with many inconveniences, not the least of which loomed before Harry. Approximately 150 yards in front of the tee jutted the "Black Sheds"—very old structures originally used for storing and drying hickory. In order to land safely on the fairway, drives must fly over the middle of the sheds. It is a long par four and it is wise to lay up your second shot rather than chance dropping it into the notorious Road Bunker, small in circumference and large in depth. This greenside hazard has wrecked the chances of many who had hoped to finish well in the tournament. Getting out of that pit of torment in under three attempts is a worthy achievement and a high tribute to one's skill. At the green's opposite side runs the dreaded paved road from which the hole derived its name and a good many other designations usually attended with harsh oaths, for if your ball settles on the road, no relief is given—the road remains in play.

Brewster Payne and Colin Mackay were now tied for second place; Harry stood two strokes up. Payne and Mackay blasted their drives safely over the sheds. Harry took a long time getting ready to hit. At 150 yards the sheds were standing in the way of Harry's maximum distance off a tee. He knew he couldn't hit over it. To the right was out-of-bounds and a hotel; the left looked to have more hazards than Dante's Inferno. There was nothing for it but to attempt the improbable.

Shaking from head to foot, Harry looked as though overtaken with ague when he addressed the ball. He swung and a low drive bounced off the sheds and landed out of bounds. He was the only player who did not clear the sheds that day. After having done so well the previous two holes his self-esteem took a severe blow. He looked to the sky for help.

"Buck up, Harry," said Fiona. "Take your time. You can do it, I know you can."

Harry teed a new ball. He stiffened himself at address to keep from shaking. Francis Ouimet again merged with Harry. Harry's stiffness relaxed and a picture perfect swing sent the ball high and long over the Black Sheds. That was Ouimet's last bit of assistance for Harry. Harry, left to rely on his own abilities henceforward, directed two fine shots to reach the green, then managed a two-putt for a triple bogey seven. He reeled with delight. Brew, following his caddie's suggestion, saved his par with a daring putt across the road to within three feet of the hole. Brew and Colin parred the Road Hole and were leaders heading to the home hole. Harry fell two strokes behind.

"There is no chance now for Golub to win unless he pulls a miracle out of his bag," announced Ward Diggs. 'I can only assume that an injury or pressure got to him. What is your grasp of the situation, Finn?"

"I think Golub's a scaredy cat. No guts. A Manila folder. An overcooked wiener. He let the pressure get to him, Diggsie," remarked a thoroughly disgusted backer of lines. "He's let the team down. That's unforgivable. And you can quote me on that."

"The British Open is not a team sport," Diggs corrected.

"You sure 'bout that?"

"I'm sure. It's akin to boxing, wrestling, fencing, horse racing wherein the individual faces all comers."

"Wow. Live and learn. They picked the right man for this job when they picked you, ol' bud."

With grim purpose in his bright young eyes, Colin Mackay shed his windbreaker on the 18th tee and handed it over to the care of his caddie, Angus Mackegan. And when Brewster Payne likewise handed his over to Jock Muckross, a momentous murmur spread among the spectators, all of whom were then encircling the home hole, fittingly named the Tom Morris. When each reached for his driver they took on the appearance of unyielding duelists drawing sabres from scabbards held by their seconds. They stood apart flexing, loosening their limbs, brandishing their weapons.

There was a third antagonist on that field of honor—Harrison Golub—albeit Harry did not, as did Colin and Brew, take on the action of a Tiger Woods. No, Harry's aspect remained that of a carefree juvenile unleashed in Disney World.

"Lord luv a duck," commented one observering Harry unphased by the unfolding drama. "'e's cool as a cucumber, 'arry is. 'old on … wot's 'e got up 'is sleeve?"

Truth to tell—nothing. Harry was duly sensible of his own limitations and was now eager to shun the limelight. After he finished the last hole, and once he returned "Old Tom" to Old

Tom, he would get on with his life with Fiona. Fiona, the ultimate source of his good fortune, his happiness. They could play decent games of weekend golf together. He had already possessed everything he could possibly hope for. No more pretense, no more feelings of inadequacy, and, praise God, no more loneliness. His best years were ahead of him, he felt.

Silent expectation absorbed the spectators. All eyes were fastened on Colin Mackay. The resolute Scot swung with added velocity and sent the ball soaring through the still air, over the Swilkan Burn, over Granny Clark's Wynd, and in line with the Royal and Ancient Club House clock. The ball landed and rolled down into the Valley of Sin, a drive of 320 plus yards. The spectators roared with delight for the plucky local lad.

Again the crowd stood silent as Brewster Payne instinctively tugged at his shirt to slacken it while he studied the broad space ahead and considered his options. There was nothing for it but to attempt to duplicate the heroic drive of his opponent. He hit it soundly but it faded slightly and stopped a yard or so from the Links Road fence; leaving him a 60 yard pitch from light rough.

Harry's turn. The little chap was still the sentimental favorite. Enthusiastic supporters yelled encouragements to him: "C'mon, Harry!" "Buck up, Harry!" "Ye can dae it, lad!" "Bravo, Harry!" *"Heinrich ist Ubermensch!"* cheered a Dortmunder. *"Desgleichen!"* answered Sydney. "Whack the hell out of the ball!" called Gunther. The Swilkan Burn was a mere 100 yards in front, aside from it there were no hazards on the par four 18th to give Harry cause for worry. He drove the ball low over the burn, when it landed got a good roll to within a few feet of Granny Clark's Wynd. He was left with a 160 yard shot to the hole. Spectators swarmed onto the fairway to follow these last players in. Since Harry was away he was the next to shoot as a crowd of thousands breathed down his neck. He connected better than he had expected with his three-wood and the ball shot over the green, hit a back-fence post and bounced straight up and dropped onto the back edge of the green. The crowd went wild, for if Harry could sink a twenty-foot downhill putt, and his opponents came in with a bogey, there would be a threeway tie and a playoff. It was a long shot. Stranger things have happened in golf. This was Harry's predicament: sinking a putt from where he was was a near impossibility; if he struck the ball too softly it would stop well short of the hole and he would still be facing a dicey downhill putt; if he struck it well enough to reach the hole it would have to be dead center else the ball would gather speed en route and end up at the foot of the Valley of Sin.

Brew was away. He played a daring pitch-and-run that landed too briskly on the green, slipped past the hole, and rolled down near Colin's drive. An unlucky bit of business that kindled a slight flare-up for a fleeting moment before he regained his newly acquired equanimity.

For his second shot Colin chose to use his putter since the fairway around the green was closely cropped. He was 35 yards from the flag. He pushed his ball up and out of the Valley in line with the hole but it came up short by eight feet.

Brew chose to chip his ball. He struck his third shot with assurance and it settled pin high about two and a half feet away. Brew and Colin marked their balls.

Harry putted his third shot and it rolled past the hole gaining speed as it went. It, too, ended in the Valley. His fourth shot, a chip, rolled weakly up the bank, and then came right back to where it had started. Using a putter for his fifth shot was a wise choice as his ball stopped a foot from the hole. He putted out for a double bogey six. The sustained ovation he received overwhelmed him. He had to keep himself from jumping up and down and hugging everyone in sight. Teary-eyed, he gathered himself and held up his hand for quiet.

Brew opted to go ahead of Colin and sank his par. The ovation he received was the warmest thus far in his career, which he acknowledged with uncommon courtesy.

Colin was left with an eight-foot uphill putt for a birdie and the championship. Tension was rife as Colin, assisted by Angus Mackegan, studied the putt-line from every angle. Accurate speed is the most crucial component for a slightly arcing uphill putt, more so with the Open championship on the line. Colin stood ready. The gallery hushed. His unhurried, long smooth stroke directed the ball up along the chosen line, slowing, it curled to the upper brink of the cup, hesitated, then fell most securely in. A tumultuous uproar split the air.

Colin turned to jelly and fell to his knees. Angus helped him to his feet and they embraced like long-lost brothers. Before Harry or Brew could congratulate him a seething mass of people had scrambled onto the green. Colin, waiving his putter, was hoisted on shoulders and danced round in a circle. A lone Scottish piper in full parade dress stood at attention by the Royal and Ancient Club House above the green playing an upbeat version of Scotland Forever. Never have I witnessed more exuberant rejoicing at the conclusion of match. A glorious win for young Colin Mackay; an heroic challenge by Brewster Payne; and, as it turned out, Harrison Golub's final tournament. That event has become another red letter day in the long illustrious history of St. Andrews and was henceforth hailed as "the year young Colin Mackay took the Jug."

Laying waste to all in his path, the backer of lines got to Colin as he was being jostled and manhandled by ecstatic fans.

"Nice job, Mackay," said McRae and shoved a microphone in his face. "What ... ah ... whaddaya know for sure?"

"Never in my wildest dreams did I expect ... in my whole life ... dinna know what tae say," said the bewildered champion as he scanned faces looking for one in particular.

"You're doing fine, keep talking."

"Fae a lang stretch Mr. Golub was brilliant, masterful. I knew I could never catch him sae I jist tossed cautioned tae the wind and went a' out. And Brewster Payne?—that man would no let up. He's the best I've ever played against." Colin spied Jean Forsyth lost in the crowd and ran to her with arms upraised in victory.

"Over to you, Diggsie."

"Thank you, Finn. We have in tow the fine American golfer and runner-up, Brewster Payne, whose magnificent play provided us with nail-biting drama down to the final putt. Well done, Brewster, sensational finish."

"Glad to have taken part in this best of all tournaments, Ward," he said showing a side of himself unfamiliar to Diggs. "I want to extend my congratulations to Colin Mackay, and to tell you and your vast audience that we will be hearing a lot more of Colin Mackay." His eye was drawn to Harry Golub joking with a group of professional golfers. "I'd like especially to thank Harry Golub for forcing me to do my best—on and off the course. The little guy is a big inspiration to us all."

"What caused Golub's sudden collapse?"

"Don't know. Near the end he seemed to struggle with every shot. Must have hurt himself. Hope it's nothing serious."

"Thank you for your comments, Brewster. Best of luck."

"Thanks."

Brew then joined his old crew for a round of back slapping. Harry and Fiona had found Cam and Sydney and they, too, were in a state of joyful fellowship when Colin and Jean joined them.

"Are you no fit, Harry?" asked Colin, putting an arm round him.

"I've permanently lost my edge, Colin my friend," said Harry with a gleeful twinkle in the eye, "but I'm fit as a fiddle."

"Pardon?"

"The only explanation I can give is that I had a streak of luck that rarely happens to mortal man." Harry curled his arm round Fiona's waist and held fast. "Even though I'm back to my old self—I'm a far better golfer."

"Ye left me in the dark, Harry. But as lang as ye tae air happy, I'm happy. Fiona. Harry. Ta."

Fiona kissed Colin and Jean, and off they went. Brew appeared and offered Harry his hand. Harry hesitated, then examined it. They both laughed uproariously. They shook hands.

"Thanks, for more than you know," Brew said sincerely. "To my mind, Harry, you are far and away the best man here." And to Fiona, "You got yourself a real winner."

Fiona checked with Harry for approval and received a smile and nod. She kissed Brew on the cheek. He smiled warmly, gave Harry the thumbs up, and rejoined his mates.

As the crowd waned into the gloaming, spirits began to appear on the 1st tee.

"Thanks, Tom!" yelled Harry, waving to nobody."

"You see him?" asked Fiona in amazement. "He's here?"

"Let's go, love of my life. I have a rendezvous in a few hours with the grand old man of St. Andrews."

CHAPTER 58

Kindly permit me to interpose a few last remarks. I am obliged to confess to you that my principal motive for narrating this most unusual story was to illustrate how even a nondescript individual can make a difference for good in the world. There are among mortals a rare few whose constitutions are so perfected that they are content to live without hate, without prejudice without covetousness; who look upon each day with a clear, not a jaundiced, eye; sportive, jocular fellows, generous and humane; principled people who are often ignorant of the effect their exemplary lives have had on the consciences of the most intractable cads and, as a consequence, transforms them from selfish ogres to selfless advocates for the common good. It is hardly necessary to state that Mr. Harrison Golub possessed such a capacity to a very large degree.

Near the stroke of midnight Angus Mackegan and his three cronies were on their accustomed bench celebrating the end of another Open. They were deep in their cups. The first crony spoke.

"Angus, wha's the best ye've caddied fae?"

"Noo that wad hae tae be young Colin Mackay hissel'," pronounced the reeling man. "Nixt ... twad be a toss-up atween Dow Finsterwald and Harrison Golub frae New York, Massachusetts."

"Ye caddied Harrison Golub?" asked the first crony with a trace of skepticism.

"Aye, lad, 'twere a few months past. He war no goffer then; he war a daft wee man. Hooiver, lads, I cad see he had the richt stuff in him. He war the best fae followin' my instructeeons tae the letter. And afore we feenished ower roun' his game and his senses improved michtily. Aye."

"And yer stories, tae, improve michtily efter a roun'," said the third crony reaching for the bottle. "Ane guid roun' deserves anither."

"Aye."

"Aye. "

"Aye."

While wetting their whistles, Harry, unnoticed, walked across Granny Clark's Wynd carrying a club.

"Colin Mackay," spoke the first crony, "noo, lads, their's a gentlemon and trew."

"Aye, and a Scot," said the second crony.

"Aye, a trew Scot and a gentlemon," seconded the third.

Mackegan held his bottle aloft

So lang—sweet goffer o' the year!
—Shall bloom that wreath that ye hae won;
While Scotland wi' exultin' cheer
Proclaims Mackay!—ower native son.

"Hear! Hear! Tae Mackay!"

A bank of black clouds shut out the moon just as Harry reached the 5th tee. Harry could see no one, nor could anyone see him. The air was soft, warm, and redolent of the sea. He stood still, not knowing what to expect. In a hoarse whisper he called out, "Hallo, Mr. Morris, are you there … here … somewhere?"

A path of light appeared leading into the thicket. A familiar voice, warm and welcoming, came from within, "Harry, m'lad, come alang in."

Warily, Harry entered, unhindered by thick vegetation. Old Tom was seated on a boulder. He rose to great him.

"Ye air an honorable mon, Mr. Golub." With extreme politeness in his voice he extended his hand, "May I hae the club, Harry?"

"Yes, sir, most certainly." Harry held the club at arm's length so as not to get any closer than need be to the spectre. He turned to go.

"Bide a wee, Harry. Ye need no worry, lad. Please," he motioned Harry to sit on the boulder.

While Harry sat watching, Old Tom moved within a circle of rowan berries with a tiny oak tree in its center. With his pen knife he extracted the meteorite screw from the club head and replaced it with another screw. Bending over he grabbed hold of the little oak, yanked and uprooted it. He dropped the meteorite into the hole and tamped it down with his foot. Then he gently lashed the club three times with the oak. Harry, utterly in the dark, watched the odd ritual. Tom then passed the club over the hidden spring counterclockwise, three times. Solemnly he stepped out of the circle, and in a prepared hole replanted the oak. He held out the club to Harry.

"Harry," he said with the aplomb of a king bestowing knighthood, " ye air the sole possessor o' a goff club fashioned by a nonliving entity. Will that be a burden tae ye?"

"No way. I love this club. Thanks a million, Mr. Morris."

"I've removed the spell—'tis merely a showpiece fae yer collection."

Harry, glanced lovingly at the club and respectfully at Old Tom. He spoke with reverent gratitude, "This marvelous golf club of yours has brought me more happiness and thrills than I have ever known. You have given me ... ."

"Tut-tut, Harry, enough. I'm no a blessed saint, lad. I'm jist a fellow like yersel'. I maun be off, but afore I gae I'd like tae pass on a wee bit o' advice tae ye in the way o' goff."

"Great. Fire away."

"I watched ye taeday, Harry, struggling in the end," his manner was fatherly. "I dinna want ye tae despair. Ye hae the makin's o' a guid goffer."

Harry was highly pleased. "You think so." Unnoticed by Harry, Francis Ouimet materialized.

"Aye, indeed I dae," continued Tom. "Dinna swing sae hard lad, and swing through the ba'. Keep these tae things in mind and yer game will improve considerably."

Ouimet spoke up, "He's absolutely right, Harry. Absolutely right."

"Francis Ouimet!" Harry's joy was immense. "I feel like I've died and gone to heav ... oh, oh."

"Fear not, Harry," said Francis. "We shan't meet again for a long, long while."

Fading, Old Tom and Francis turned away.

Harry called out, "I'm eternally grateful for everything ... Mr. Morris ... Francis. Goodbye."

Ouimet looked back, "We've tee times set aside for you, Harry. Fiona, too." And as rare things must, they vanished.

Harry stood in the pitch black thicket waving goodbye. He was saddened that his relationship with good spirits had come to an end. He began groping his way out. He felt a golf ball under foot and picked it up. Outside the thicket he brushed himself off. The sky was clear and full of stars. The city lights seemed to have halos round them. Tangy wafts from the sea filled his lungs. What a glorious night, what a glorious day. He started walking back to town using his club as a walking stick. He hesitated. He looked at the ball in his hand. It was so old and weather-worn that all of its identity marks were obscured. He dropped it on the ground and lined it up to where he thought the fairway should be. He took too forceful a swing and pushed it back into the thicket—

"Yipes!" a woman screamed.

Harry, bug-eyed, was set to run back into the thicket when out charged Queen Mary with a glowing burnt log in arrears. He fled in the opposite direction like a shot.

"Burn 'm alive!" crackled the log, and stood back to watch the Queen hotfoot it across the darkened fairway.

"Miscreant!" screamed the Queen, running at a full clip holding onto her skirts with one hand and rubbing her royal rump with the other. "Miscreant! Varlet! Abuse our royal person! We'll have your head! Varlet. Villain!" She stopped running but with her hands cupped over her royal mouth continued her lambastes, "Rogue! Scullion! Blackguard! Caitiff! To the gallows with you!"

Angus and his cronies had seen Harry coming toward them with the ghost of Queen Mary in hot pursuit. They rose to flee, but considering the handicap under which they labored, bounced off one another and reeled in circles out of a scene from *Tam O'Shanter*. After sorting themselves they managed to run together down The Links road and up Golf Place. With great presence of mind—or more likely instinct—each had a death-grip on his bottle. Harry passed them as if they were standing still. Unknown to them, Queen Mary had long since given up the chase. She hollered after them one last time. "I'll have your miscreant heads! *Allez-vous-en!*" Then to herself, *"Voila!* That was jolly sport."

She was left with a very short walk to the first tee where she was scheduled to play along with Joe Louis, William Howard Taft, and myself, Ernest Spectre.

And there you have it. The true, illuminating adventures of Harrison Golub. Until we meet again, what.

"Messieurs."

"Your honors, your Majesty."

"Fore!"

The End

LaVergne, TN USA
20 July 2010
190089LV00001B/90/P